MOONRISE

An imprint of Moonrise Publishing
36181 E Lake RD suite 204
Palm Harbor, FL 34685

Library of Congress Cataloging-in-Publication data is available

TXu 2-358-073

Illustrations by Jason Kang

MOONRISE

by M.J. Claiborne

CONTENTS

A MOST BLOODY
CEREMONY

1

The annual Morgan & Green Enterprises retreat was intended as an introductory welcome for new hires. The gathering served as no such orientation to Anthony though, as he had been working for Mr. Morgan for over six years; he was no longer invited to attend such team-building events, but rather, required.

He sighed with restlessness before looking up at the radiant glow of the half-crescent moon, which shone down over the enveloping woodlands as hours of obscurity passed over the raucous gathering. The three-story chalet stood atop rows of towering, snowcapped redwoods, surrounded by dark, uninhabitable wilderness. Anthony adjusted his red-framed glasses while peering out from the balcony. He had always favored the city over the quiet backwoods he now found himself in, but felt it necessary to take time and appreciate nature's wonder. Still, he would have preferred staying at home in his one-bedroom apartment with his girlfriend, Sidney, over social climbing at some frivolous reception. He would have given anything to be in bed with her just then. Sure, the gathering might be exciting for some forlorn soul still looking to forge new relationships, but that was not Anthony.

He removed his frigid palms from the lumber top rail, taking in one last admiring glance at the natural wonders surrounding him before being forced to engage in meaningless social banter. He reluctantly exhaled, knowing he would soon have to put on a fake smile and act interested. He took one last look at the snow-covered woodlands before entering the opulent cabin, rejoining the gathering masses inside.

Anthony paced down the chalet's wooden staircase, bypassing the small crowds of well-dressed colleagues as they chatted. He stealthily weaved through the multitudes adorning the side rails and observed the partygoers' red, spurious expressions, accompanied by random roaring outbursts of fictitious laughter accented by foggy cigar smoke. He jostled through the crowds, making his descent farther down the staircase and coming to the main foyer of the chalet, where he observed the highlight of the evening's festivities: the food.

Generous portions of lamb, sirloin, and pork were sprawled out on an elongated table where servers hurriedly filled their empty trays.

After their platters were stockpiled with mouthwatering morsels, the waitstaff hastily delivered the delectable cuts of meat to the formally dressed patrons. The dining experience was made complete with paired wines from Mr. Morgan's vineyard.

As the evening drummed on into a drunken foggy haze, Mr. Morgan stood in the center of the living room in front of a blazing fireplace. He was a stocky, midsized man, with a full head of gray hair accompanied by a manicured beard. The stout CEO spoke with a Southern drawl and wore a dark suit that snugly fit over his barrel-chested frame.

"May I have your attention, please? Attention, please!" the cantankerous mogul yelled over the conversing patrons. He turned and signaled for an associate to join him in front of the fireplace.

"Brandon, if you would, please join me," he boisterously requested while scanning the assembly.

A hazel-eyed young man with a medium build and short brown hair, wearing a fuchsia suit, enthusiastically pushed his way through the crowd. The overzealous youth joined Mr. Morgan in front of the crackling fire. Anthony crept to the bottom of the stairs and joined the consortium of onlookers leaning against a nearby column. Mr. Morgan paused before proceeding with his address as Brandon stood idly next to him, wide-eyed with excitement.

"I hope you all are enjoying tonight's festivities," the gray-bearded CEO declared.

"I wanted to make a brief announcement. Then you all can get back to that delicious buffet table. First, I want to introduce you all to Brandon, the newest member of our pack." The congregation immediately quieted their chatter.

Mr. Morgan paused and brazenly placed his hand on Brandon's shoulder while simultaneously reaching into his breast pocket. His face turned red as he began to withdraw a large, hollowed-out wolf's paw. The assembly went eerily mute upon seeing the taxidermied limb.

"Now, now, don't be alarmed. For many years we've carried on this age-old tradition. So don't worry, folks. Only one animal was harmed in the manufacturing of this paw!"

The onlookers nervously chuckled in response to their superior's shitty joke while he valiantly held up the sizable wolf's paw, displaying a cup hole in the center of it.

He abruptly turned the appendage palm-side up, and a tuxedoed server poured red wine into the furry mitt. Once the cavern was filled, Mr. Morgan raised the paw to the skylight, illuminated by the half-crescent moon.

"Great spirit Gaia, we ask that you bestow your wisdom and power upon Brandon!" He turned to the crowd, proudly holding up the wine-filled paw. "*Oooowwwwooo!*" The enigmatic businessman let out a bellowing, wolflike howl.

The assembly responded to their leader's wails with nervous laughter.

He turned to the naive young man at his side and handed him the wooly goblet. "Drink up, boy!" he commanded.

Brandon grabbed the paw and took a sip. Red wine trickled down the sides of his pale cheeks and ran down his chin.

What a shitshow, Anthony thought. *Never got a ceremony like this when I was promoted.* The whole wolf-paw thing grossed him out and made him want to leave; his flight instincts were beginning to kick in.

After Brandon was done drinking, he lifted his head to the skylight and let out a howl. The newly indoctrinated admin turned to the crowd and glared at the assembly with a fiendish grin.

The gathering erupted in laughter before howling back at him. Mr. Morgan beamed, waiting for the onlooking mob to silence. After the crowd's hollers quieted, the boisterous alpha ordered the server to refill the paw. Once the hollowed-out metacarpal pad was refilled, Mr. Morgan raised the libation-filled limb, looked into Brandon's eyes, and stated, "Omega."

"Omega," Brandon ignorantly replied.

Jeez, this is too much. Anthony quietly chuckled to himself as the ritual played out.

Mr. Morgan drank from the paw, draining the remainder of

wine from the wooly chalice. After he was finished, he removed a hand-kerchief from his suit pocket and wiped the excess liquid from his chin. He proceeded to clean the interior of the metacarpal pad and stuffed the emptied paw back inside his breast pocket.

"Now, y'all enjoy the rest of your evening, and please partake in the wine. It's from my personal vineyard." He tucked his soiled handkerchief back in his pocket before shaking Brandon's hand with congratulatory fervor.

After observing the bizarre ritual, Anthony gave in to his flight instincts. He sneakily made his exit out of the congested cabin, forging into the piercing-cold wilderness. As he marched farther away from the chalet, his red-framed glasses began to fog. He wiped them with the tail end of his maroon jacket as he looked back at the towering log-wood chalet. The sprawling cabin seemed to shimmer beneath the waning crescent moon.

As he slogged farther away from the shelter's warm, inviting glow, the snow flurries started to increase, and he knew that his tracks would soon be blanketed. He figured as long as he kept a visual on the chalet, he would be able to find his way back. He was particularly concerned with the increased snowfall (his getting lost in the woods was not something that Sidney or his Auntie Glo would be happy with), so rather than venture farther into the thicket, he elected to walk along the dirt road near the backside of the cabin.

The drifting snow lingered in the atmosphere as he ventured along, painting a quixotic scene. He mindlessly hiked, taking in the natural ambience as he made his way along the icy road. In the distance, he heard the slow crunch of tires rolling. Two glowing headlights suddenly beamed down the narrow path. A jet-black limo with a chrome-plated tristar emblem approached from the darkness.

The overly stretched vehicle stopped beside his feet, plowing flurries onto his almond loafers. He immediately recognized the vehicle. Seated in the back was Ben Damien. Ben was one of the younger executives at the company, arrogant and chauvinistic to his core. The limo stopped, and a large bald man suddenly exited from the driver's side.

The bulky, black-suited chauffeur stomped his way through the snowfall toward Anthony, giving him a half grin as he walked by. He was a hefty man, six-foot-four and girthy. His face was worn and semifurrowed with hardship. The large, dagger-like scar just under his right eye added to his mystique.

Anthony warily observed the knife-shaped wound as the driver opened the passenger-side door.

Dude must work out. He was impressed with the sizable chauffeur's muscular physique.

The driver boldly stood amid the flurries and confidently held the door ajar. In an instant, the tall, slender Mr. Damien emerged.

His jet-black hair was slicked back with slippery wet gel, and he wore a gray peacoat that draped over his $5,000 navy-blue suit, which complemented his artificial tanning-bed complexion. The driver produced an umbrella from the passenger-side door, concealed within the doorframe's compartment. He sharply opened it, holding it above Ben as he got out of his chariot.

"Anthony, why are you out here all alone? The party's inside," he questioned with a perplexed look on his face.

"I, uh, needed some air. It's getting kind of crowded in there. Way too much cigar smoking going on." Anthony's unshaven facial stubble bristled with the steadily rising wind chill as he spoke.

He thought of how successful Ben was within the company. Making senior partner under Mr. Morgan was something he admired. In a way, Ben was his competition. Although he was an asshole, Anthony respected his crass, nonchalant attitude; he wished he could be more like him sometimes. He figured he was just too honest of a man to ever be able to reach the upper echelons of Morgan & Green Enterprises, and he was okay with that. Ben was the man Anthony had always aspired to be, but wasn't evil enough to become.

"You sure you don't want a lift back? It looks like the snow's going to pick up soon." Ben placed his hand on his shoulder, encouraging him to get inside the limo. His lean, six-foot-two frame towered over Anthony's five-foot-ten, 180-pound body.

"Ah, I'm good, thanks. I'll see you inside."

Anthony redirected his gaze from the statuesque driver holding the umbrella over Ben to a nearby stump.

"You need a coat or something? You look like you're going to freeze to death." Anthony knew Ben was pretending to be concerned.

He removed his hands from his pockets to reveal black leather gloves snugly placed over them.

"Thanks, Ben, but I'll be all right. I'll catch you inside."

"Okay, I'll see you in there. I'm curious to see what Mr. Morgan has in store for us this year. I have my eye on some new prospects myself!"

He gave Anthony a hard, playful pat, accompanied by a slight wink, before hopping back inside the limo.

Anthony observed the driver close the umbrella before sliding it back inside the door's compartment. He violently swung the passenger-side door shut and begrudgingly stomped to the front of the limo, giving Anthony a piercing look. The hulking motorist plopped into the driver's seat. Anthony watched the dark limo slowly pull away as Ben rolled down the window. He lurched out, his dark hair shimmering under the moonlight.

"Anthony, maybe you should relax a little bit. Show Mr. Morgan you're one of the boys. Look around you. We couldn't be farther from the office, and you still need space… Just a tip,"

he asserted with a deviant grin.

Since when did you ever give a fuck about me? Anthony peered into his eyes and smiled. "Good advice, thanks."

Ben rolled up the window, and Anthony watched as the red tail-lights began to disappear under the falling snow. He couldn't help but imagine what Ben would say about him to Mr. Morgan, knowing that he had seen him outside alone, mindlessly wandering.

"Sir, Mr. Montgomery is not MGE material! He's just not a team player. Saw him outside by himself in the cold, with all these good people and tasty food in here. It's just plain disrespectful, sir." Anthony played out the fictitious conversation in his mind before he turned away from the icy road and brushed the snow off the stump he had scouted while talking with Ben.

He took a seat atop the coarse stump, allowing the scent of pine and cedar to drift through his nostrils. There was something special about the rough country air, rarely touched by the pollutants of humanity. It was a treasured, comforting smell that filled his soul. He took in the natural ambience, cherishing the calming silence of the surrounding forest.

After some time had passed, the temperature began to drop, and the snowfall started to increase. He knew his forlorn outing would no doubt be short-lived.

"Hey, hot stuff," an enchanting voice called out from the forestry behind him.

Anthony jolted in surprise. He crooked his head around to see Luna. She was wearing a black suit that revealed her cleavage as her long red hair swayed in the night wind. Her beauty was accented by her manila skin accompanied by her serpentine frame. She enthralled him.

God, she looks good, he thought, hoping not to accidentally say those words out loud. "Jeez, Luna! You scared me!"

Anthony's chest heaved with excitement as he adjusted his glasses.

Luna had been working at the firm just as long as him. She had started as an admin and worked her way up to become a member of the board.

"Easy there, cowboy. You look like you could use some company… I saw you sneak out the back porch," she explained with a calming tone while approaching him. "You know, the snow's starting to come down pretty hard… Here, I brought this for you."

She affixed her penetrating brown eyes on his and tossed him an overcoat, which he caught in midair.

"Nice snag! We should get back inside," she suggested.

"Thanks, Luna. I'm just going to stay out here a little bit longer. Things are getting a little too weird inside for my taste." He blushed as he ran his arms through the coat.

She brushed back her flowing ginger locks and tilted her head toward him.

"I know what you mean… I'm bored as fuck too. Sometimes I

feel more at home out here in the wilderness than back in the city."

She reeled in closer, keeping her enchanting eyes gridlocked on his as she bent down, positioning her bosom just above his stubbled chin.

"Tony, why haven't you made a move on me?" she questioned while puckering her lips.

Luna had made several advances toward him over the years, and while he was flattered that an attractive woman such as she would have interest, he was spoken for, and that was the end of that.

Oh God, give me the strength! Anthony restrained his animalistic desires and did his best to reject her advances in a respectful manner. "You know I'm very happy with Sidney. You've met her a few times."

"Yes, we've met." Luna condescendingly crossed her arms and backed away. "I see the way you look at me, Tony."

Well, there's no harm in looking, is there? He was becoming frustrated; he just wanted to be alone.

"Look but don't touch—isn't that how the saying goes?" He jokingly shrugged with a smile.

Her full lips and supple voice captivated him as she pressed her red-painted fingernail tightly over his mouth. Her lavender, earthy scent further enticed his urges. She was right: he was attracted to her, and her unwarranted advances made it harder for him to resist.

Can't believe she followed me out here. She must really want it bad. He imagined what it would be like to have sex with her. Immediately after, he thought of Sidney and felt overwhelming guilt.

"I'll see you inside. Thanks for the coat," he dismissed her, his heart pounding.

She advanced over him one last time and crouched down, pecking him on the cheek with a departing kiss that sent chills up the nape of his neck.

"Don't get lost out here, hon. I'd hate to lose someone as qualified as you." Her russet eyes slowly undressed him before her departure.

She strutted down the snowy back road for the cabin. Anthony watched as her curvaceous frame angelically floated away, dissipating into the shadowy, enveloping wilderness. He sat for a while, taking in the stillness of the forest. A calm chilling breeze rushed over him.

I should be getting back. They'll be asking where I am now that both Luna and Ben have seen me out here. Anthony dreaded going back to that cabin, but he knew he had to. He got up from the stump, brushed the moss off his brown slacks, and began making his way back to the chalet.

As he trekked along the back road, he turned to the lodge, relying on Luna's footprints to guide him across the snowy thicket. With each crunching step, his shiny loafers became impacted with frost. While shielding his eyes with his gloved hand, he glared off into the distance through the increasing flurries.

"*Owwwooooooo!*"

A thunderous howl suddenly broke the silence of the surrounding forest, shattering the quiet and causing his eyes to water.

His immediate reaction was to run, but he had always been an observer of habits.

The cries of a wounded animal echoed from deep within the darkness. The shrill hollers were coming from twenty or so paces north of him. Anthony debated whether to go back to the safety of the cabin or investigate.

Someone's dog must have gotten loose, he reasoned. *Wouldn't want my dog to freeze out here—if I had a dog, that is.* He ultimately veered away from the welcoming lights of the overlooking chalet and cautiously marched through the snow-covered brush, foolishly giving in to his voyeuristic tendencies and heading deeper into the woodlands.

As he peered across the dark thicket, he could distinctly hear an animal wincing in pain. His lips, ears, and nose went numb with coldness, becoming brittle amid the mounting snowfall. He trudged deeper into the brush with an unwavering determination as the rapacious winds coursed through him.

He came to a clearing, where he saw in the distance what appeared to be a bear-like creature.

What the fuck is that thing? His thoughts swirled in a mix of wonder and fear. The beast was hunched over its prey, voraciously swaying its head in an attempt to disjoint its kill.

Anthony's immediate reaction was to bolt. However, he knew that if he were to flee, the feasting monster would surely hear him. He rubbed his snow-covered glasses and skulked closer to the scene, hiding behind the trunk of a redwood tree. As he put his specs back on, he observed the slaughter in front of him, mindful not to disturb the interaction between the predator and its prey.

I need to get a pic of this. He was enthralled with thoughts of fame and fortune while reaching into his pocket, slowly pulling out his cell phone. With his heart racing, he grabbed onto a branch and peeked around the massive trunk to get a better view. A loud crack sounded as he inadvertently snapped a weakened branch, breaking the silence of the surrounding forest. The sound alerted the looming beast, and the goliath stood upright on its hind legs. The snowy-haired monster was well over six feet and jetted its pointed ears toward him. As the hoary creature scoured, Anthony could tell that this was not a bear. Its facial structure was that of a wolf. Its long snout was splattered with blood. Its faded-ashen muzzle bore lacerated scars from years of hunting. The beast's paws were massive, with sharp talons on the ends of its fingertips, dripping with the fresh blood of its kill.

Anthony shook with paralyzing fear as he raised his phone and snapped a picture. The flash illuminated over the brute. The monster's red eyes transfixed on him amid the sporadic flicker.

Shit! That was stupid! Anthony's fear-driven regrets mired in his mind as he began to ponder a possible escape route.

The wolf-like being snarled, baring its black gums and revealing jagged teeth stained with chunks of dangling flesh. Anthony shakingly dropped his phone into his pocket. He was stunned with dread as he nervously viewed the mountainous creature, which was both magnificent and terrifying. It had a Cro-Magnon posture and was slightly hunched over; its pearl-white fur was doused with splatters of blood.

The lifeless carcass of a wolverine crunched inside the beast's vise-like jaws.

Anthony and the brooding Lycan suddenly locked eyes. The monster's undaunting gaze pierced his fortitude while also captivating him. The brute opened its maw and let the half-dead wolverine dribble down its corpulent sternum, leaving a trail of darkened blood in its wake. Anthony's heart raced as adrenaline coursed through him.

Just one more pic. He again imagined the fame and fortune that his discovery in the backwoods might bring, stupidly ignoring the imminent danger.

The monster's fatally wounded prey landed on the ground with a faint thud. The juvenile skunk bear lay limp on the forest floor as it took its last breath, encircled by its own frayed and puréed tissue. It was a scene painted by an unadulterated massacre. After releasing its prey, the bloodied Lycan advanced for Anthony.

Shit! Petrified, Anthony frantically climbed up the coarse trunk of the redwood tree, tearing his gloves and exposing his palms to the elements. As he desperately scrambled, the brute smelled the fresh blood from his torn hands and lunged for him. The gigantic creature unexpectedly stopped from its advance, giving him time to climb farther up. The Lycan lifted its snout, sniffing the air, before turning away from him. The creature proceeded to drop down on all fours and began to snarl. The beast's belly rumbled as it wrinkled its snout, exposing its flesh-tearing fangs.

Anthony had managed to climb midway up the tree, affixing himself to a branch. He desperately held onto the limb while fearfully glaring down at the monster below.

Maybe he'll leave me alone. I'll be safe in this tree. Wolves don't climb, do they? He did his best to console himself with false hope as he gazed down from the thin branches. Looking over the scene, he could distinguish a myriad of yellow glowing eyes in the distance.

Suddenly, from the darkness of the thicket, a black-coated timber wolf lunged at the Lycan's neckline. The bloodstained beast turned and snatched the vaulting wolf, suspending the woodland predator's assault. The abrupt impediment of momentum snapped the wolf's spine with a crack. All the while, the beast kept its foreboding gaze on Anthony, who trembled as he released his footing from a branch. He urgently scampered farther up the trunk.

Just keep climbing, he told himself amid his frenzied state.

The dark-furred timber wolf cried in pain as the brute squeezed tighter. The wolf desperately whimpered as the Lycan constricted its talons over its throat. The faint and desperate whining soon washed out, and the timber wolf's spastic attempts to break free from the monster's overpowering grasp were useless. The wolf's skull bulged as its eyes extended from its cranium. Soon nature took its inevitable course, and the animal of the forest was no more. Feces and urine sprayed the already-defiled ground as the bloodthirsty Lycan released its latest victim. The timber wolf's body hit the snowy ground with a hollow thump. The woodland predator's corpse laid beside the mutilated carcass of the massacred wolverine. The monster lowered itself to the blood-soaked earth, sniffing at its kill. The onlooking pack's shimmering eyes quickly disappeared from deep within the thicket as the Lycan turned its attention back to Anthony.

Turn around! Please, God, turn around! he internally pleaded while looming over the scene with fright

The brooding Lycan stood upright, tucking its ears behind its head before rushing toward him. Anthony had managed to make his way approximately ten feet up from the base of the tree. He knew that the creature could easily snag him, and he had to make a choice: drop down and try to run for it, or continue to climb higher. His hands were ablaze with splinters and bark chunks.

Fuck it! He released his grip and dropped to the ground. He heard a crack followed by sharp pain. His landing had been flawed. He had rolled his ankle, and as he scrambled to his feet, his glasses rolled off his face.

Fuck! Get up! he encouraged himself before quickly shooting up on his good leg. He hurriedly drudged across the chalky landscape, blindly hobbling through the snowy wilderness. He felt the monster's blistering breath on the back of his neck and heard a deflating crunch as the brute stepped on his red-framed glasses. His heart raced with panic as he knew the creature was not far behind.

The stalking Lycan raised its talons and struck him, knocking him to the ground with a thunderous smack. He hit the cold mucky earth with a bang. The creature's dark nostrils expanded and contracted, making abrupt sniffing sounds as it studied over its fallen prey.

Just play dead! He agonizingly held his breath, hoping the beast would turn away. Lying face down, frigid and paralyzed with fear, he realized that playing possum was his only chance of surviving. He was thankful that he had at least landed on his stomach, hoping to avoid the inevitable slaughter of his vital organs. As he laid still atop the frozen earth, he could feel the beast's acidy breath leaking farther down the back of his neck. He felt a sharp, agonizing puncture over his calf as the beast's talons sliced through his flesh with ease. The pain was unbearable. He chomped down on his forearm in an attempt not to scream, but the agony was insufferable.

"*Aaaahhh!*" He let out a desperate cry.

Upon his shriek, the bloodthirsty Lycan realized that he was live meat. He immediately felt the freezing winds enter the inside cavity of his flesh-torn leg. He only prayed that the foreseeable carnage would be fast while he buried his head in the glacial snow, waiting in thoughtless terror to be ripped apart.

Please, God, I don't want to die, not like this, Anthony pleaded to his Creator, desperately bargaining for a chance at life.

Quiet stillness unexpectedly ensued. He was baffled as he heard the creature sluggishly stomp away. After a few minutes had passed, he realized that this was his opportunity for salvation; his prayers had been answered. His vision was blurred without the aid of his glasses, and with no knowledge of what was behind him, he briefly debated the peril of his choice before deciding to crawl.

The trauma from his injury was now setting in. Bit by bit he slithered on his belly to a nearby brush, where he took cover. He looked down at his right leg, tattered with blood-strewn flesh. The horror of the carnage began to sink in. His limb was reduced to nothing more than useless, exposed bone surrounded by shredded fatty tissue and murky chunks of gelatinous torn muscle. He started to cry.

With a pounding heart, he rallied enough strength to roll onto his back. His whole body started convulsing. He shuttered as he took notice of the veinlike trail of blood behind him.

Fuck, that's a lot. He shivered as his blood pressure dropped. He nervously gauged the area around him with half closed eyes and realized that his injury had left a bloody trail to his location, but to his astonishment, the creature had disappeared. He was relieved, but he now faced new life-threatening challenges.

While the frozen earth helped soothe his wound, he knew that he would surely bleed to death. He frantically reached into his jacket and pulled out his cell phone.

"Shit!" He was disheartened after realizing he had no reception.

He felt a chilling weakness overtake him as blood drained from his body. He knew that death was not far away as irreconcilable shivers overtook his already trembling frame. The paralyzing cold engulfed him, and he dropped his phone. His trembling hand draped over the icy ground and was quickly buried under the relentless snowfall. He was certain that this was his fate. He only had the strength to stay conscious as he lay in a mire of his own blood.

Come on! Stay awake! Don't close your eyes! After just a few minutes, an overpowering numbness overcame him. Despite his efforts, Anthony gradually closed his eyes, allowing the snow-laden flurries to cover his face before he lost consciousness.

Hours passed before he regained his senses; still unable to open his eyes, he could feel himself being dragged by his unwounded leg. Snow collected under his overcoat as he helplessly plowed over the earth. His face was covered in a thick, icy slush, and his arms lay spread out in a crucifix. He was beyond relieved that the paramedics had found him.

Thank you, God! I'm not going to die! He thought of Sidney and his aunt, how upset they would be at him, but he didn't care; he was just happy to be alive, with or without a leg.

Still, to open his eyes took great effort. After a few minutes, he suddenly came to the horrid realization that a paramedic would not tend to him in such a crude manner.

Wait a minute. This doesn't seem right. Come on, Anthony. Open your fucking eyes! He had to conjure the strength to unlock his frosted eyelids. The grip around his left ankle began to tighten, followed by a penetrating stab that sent daggering shards of pain down his leg.

Shit! That thing came back for me! Now I'm being dragged to its den! He pictured the beast devouring him alive as he lay helpless inside a dark cave.

Anthony tried to lift his hand to uncover the frost from his face, but he was too weak. His meek arms were no contest for the collecting snow which had accumulated under him. In a frenzied quaver, he shook his head, enabling him to flake off just enough frostiness to get a blurry-eyed visual out of his right eye.

He could distinguish a slim, charcoal-haired creature. Unlike the monster that had wounded him, this wolf-like being was thinner and more agile. It appeared to have a docile and calculating demeanor. As Anthony was aimlessly dragged across the snow-covered forest, he managed to sound out a desperate cry.

"Stop… Helllppp!" he mercifully gargled.

The mongrel's ears propped up as it loosened its grip, releasing him. Anthony's leg dropped to the ground as the slender Lycan dropped on all fours and inquisitively stalked toward his midsection. He could feel the creature's damp snout rubbing against his exposed rib cage. The slender being scuttled its crawl over to his shoulder.

With blurry vision, Anthony could make out the creature's brindle-patterned face. He glared deep into the monster's yellow eyes as its dark, diamond-shaped pupils sharpened. The Lycan studied him, cocking its head with enduring curiosity.

He faded in and out of consciousness just before the creature sank its fangs deep into his shoulder. He felt a stabbing pain as the Lycan's incisors cut through the thick overcoat Luna had given him. The beast's flesh-tearing teeth dug deep into his collarbone with a nerve-shattering sting. He glared into the Lycan's ungodly eyes as his body started to tremor. He knew death was at hand. He succumbed to the overwhelming pain accompanied by the tremendous blood loss and lost consciousness.

After hours of impenetrable darkness, Anthony began to feel a warmness over his face and could sense a bright light illuminating over him. He started to faintly perceive voices, beeps, and metallic clamors. The commotion became more distinctive as his hearing returned to its normal faculties.

He was alive; they had found him. He creaked his eyelids open and could distinguish the hazy, blurred outline of doctors attending to him, accompanied by a distinct synthetic smell.

"This one's an odd case," one of the doctors proclaimed.

"Yes. He's lucky we were able to salvage the leg. You see here, the calf was only hanging by tendons, fatty tissue, and ligaments. The freezing snow is what saved the limb. Because of that, the skin graft was a success."

Thank God. I still have my leg. Anthony was more confused than relieved.

The combination of the drugs and events leading to his stay in the hospital were overwhelming and disorienting. As his thoughts mired in a tailspin, the surgeons manically inspected his thrashed leg.

"This patient is healing faster than any other case I've seen," the surgeon announced with shock.

The doctors shrugged at each other, their identities concealed under their N-95 masks.

"I don't know what to make of the shoulder though. The bite looks canine, but much too large to be from a wolf. But hey, I'm no vet."

It was a fucking monster! Not a dog! Anthony wished he

could speak.

"Well, he's lost a lot of blood, but he's stable now. Good work, Doctor."

"Thank you, Doctor."

"How's he doing?" Anthony heard the prideful Southern accent of Mr. Morgan as his half-closed eyes struggled to focus.

"He's doing remarkably well," the doctor answered.

"Good! We need this man... He's essential to our firm's future!"

Mr. Morgan? Now all of a sudden I'm important? Must be an insurance thing—he doesn't want to get sued, he contemplated before drifting off into a drug-induced slumber.

Anthony made another attempt at opening his eyes, arduously straining his face. The hazy radiance of the hospital room's lights blurred his vision. As he struggled through the pain, he slowly creaked open his eyelids. He felt a soft, tender palm grasp his wrist.

He turned, and with blurred vision could distinguish the blurred outline of his girlfriend, Sidney, hunkered by his bedside. She was wearing a hoodie with matching purple sweatpants. Her midnight flowing hair and soft touch calmed him as he observed tears flowing from her watery blue eyes.

"I thought I lost you, baby." She was choked up as she wiped away tiny droplets from her cheek.

Anthony tried to talk, but his words wouldn't come out.

I'm so lucky to have her. Will she even want me after all this? I mean, I'm alive, but there's probably not much left of me. I probably look like a sideshow freak! He squeezed her hand, thinking of all the good times they'd had together, hoping that she would still want him.

They had met in college, when Anthony's parents were still alive. She had been there for him after they had unexpectedly died, and although he was often hesitant to admit it, he loved her. His displays of affection would often fall short, leaving Sidney yearning for his attention. He felt that openly confessing love was a sign of weakness, and it took a great emotional toll on him just to profess his feelings for her. Perhaps his stern upbringing had something to do with it.

Sidney had met his parents a few times before their untimely death. He held a special place in his heart for the people who had known them. They had been strict disciplinarians, both having served in the military. His mother, Dorris, was a fighter pilot, and his father, Henry, was a mechanical engineer for the navy. Both his parents were disappointed when he elected to go to college in lieu of joining the service, but over time their liking of Sidney and Anthony's dedication to his pursuit of an MBA warmed them up to the idea that their son would not be a military man.

"Auntie Glo's over there too." Sidney pointed to his Aunt Gloria, curled in a ball on the recliner, pressed against the far corner of the room.

The elderly woman was in a fetal position, snoring in an unwavering slumber. Her green nightgown overlapped her midsection, with one of her pearl-blue knitted sweaters draped over her feet. Her curly brown hair was disheveled from sleeping in an awkward position.

"She's been on that couch since you got out of surgery. What happened to you out there?" Sidney questioned while zipping up her hoodie.

She wouldn't believe me if I told her. Plus, she's already scared. I mean, look at her. I haven't seen her cry since... I don't think I've ever seen her cry. God, why can't I talk? He struggled to sound out words while his girlfriend mulled over him.

She wiped away more tears as she bent over and kissed his forehead. She laid her head on his chest; the scent of her flowery hair comforted him in his bewildered, drug-induced state.

She smells so good! He turned to see his aunt still in her fetal slumber. After scanning over the room, he took notice of his right leg, heavily bandaged and suspended by a sling.

"My leg!" he uttered.

"Anthony!" His aunt sprang from the lounger upon hearing

his voice. She ran to his side and gripped her wrinkled hands over the bed rail.

"For God's sake, child… That bear could have cremated you!" she shouted while tearing up.

Gloria had taken legal guardianship of him after his parents died in a plane crash. After her service, Dorris still enjoyed flying, and Anthony's father would accompany her on trips. On one routine flight, things had gone wrong, and they both met their demise in a fiery crash. Anthony was devastated, but Gloria was there for him. She was the only family he had left; they had a special bond forged through the finality of death and the grief of loss.

"I made a promise to your mother that I would never let anything happen to you, and here you lay butchered half to death!"

She abruptly stopped crying and her complexion flushed with anger; she raised her open palm and delivered a swift slap across his face. Her unassuming strike was surprisingly powerful and left Anthony's ears ringing.

"Jeez, Auntie!" he hollered as his cheek throbbed.

I could've used her in the woods back there. She'd slap the shit out of that…whatever that thing was that bit me.

"Anthony, I swear to the Virgin Mary herself, if you ever pull a stunt like this again, I'll be in the bed next to you, because I'll have a heart attack. I made a promise to my sister that I would make sure nothing would happen to you if she passed, and I don't break promises! Anthony Ramone Montgomery! Don't make me out to be a liar!"

She draped her flabby arms around his neck and gave him a tight embrace. She was a strong woman, regardless of her small stature. Anthony could still feel the vibrations from her thunderous slap.

"The doctors say you'll be out of here in a few weeks. They say you're healing fast." Sidney draped her hand over his shoulder, gently coursing her fingers over his knotted sutures.

After their displays of affection, Anthony knew that, at the very least, he was loved.

All I need is right here. He was at peace.

The door suddenly flung open, and in marched Rey. His gangly, six-foot-tall frame shot through the doorway holding a pink teddy bear.

"Oh… Sorry to interrupt, ladies. Shall I come back later?" He grinned.

Rey was Anthony's oldest and best friend. They understood each other. They had a bond and kinship that had been shaped from childhood. Both Sidney and Gloria couldn't help but giggle at him. After all, Rey was a humorous-looking person. Not only was he skinny, but his eyes seemed to outsize his square head. He often changed his hair color; today it was bleached white. Rey was the type of person who lit up the room no matter how grim the situation might be.

Anthony chuckled, then coughed. *What a clown—ever since middle school.* He shifted his weight in an attempt to sit up, but he was too drowsy.

"Easy there, turbo. Just lie back. I bought this for you, my dear."

Rey propped the teddy bear next to his shoulder. "Damn, dude, you survived a fucking bear, man!" Anthony could feel his aunt's infuriating gaze lock in on Rey. "Sorry, I mean you survived a motherfucking, shit-kicking, goddamn, son-of-a-bitching bear. *Fuck!*"

Gloria couldn't help but laugh at his raunchy sense of humor.

"W-w-water…please." Anthony's voice cracked as he reached for the pitcher atop the swing table in front of him.

Sidney grabbed the jug and poured some water into a paper cup. He shifted beneath the bedsheets and managed to sit up. He took four long sips; the ice-cold water soothed his dry throat.

"That's better. Now I can talk."

He was so elated to be alive with his loved ones that he briefly forgot about the beastly attack. He just wanted to be in the moment. Their uneasy and joyous laughter was abruptly halted by a knock at the door. Mr. Morgan, fully clad in a dark designer suit, boldly stomped into the room with a doctor by his side.

Oh, shit, he's going to be pissed. Shouldn't have wandered off like that—probably going to lose my fucking job. Anthony glared at his boss with worried anticipation.

The doctor beside him was a short, skinny man with frizzy hair; he wore bifocals and had a calm demeanor. Anthony was nervous, hoping that his diagnosis would be a favorable one. Mr. Morgan stepped aside, holding the door open for his loved ones to exit.

"Ladies and sir, would y'all mind stepping outside for just a bit? The doctor and I have to speak to Mr. Montgomery in private."

Rey clenched his fists and raised his voice. "Listen here, hoss. Anything you have to say to Tony, you can say to us!"

Mr. Morgan possessed an unexplainable dominance and said nothing. A simple glare deep into Rey's inflamed eyes sent him into a state of submission.

"We'll be right outside, dear. Come on, Sid… Rey!"

Gloria had to firm up her voice to unlock Rey's stare from Mr. Morgan.

"Yeah, we'll be right outside, buddy."

He looked at Anthony with a reassuring nod before sidestepping out of the room, with Sidney and Gloria succeeding, bypassing Mr. Morgan, who seemed to growl at them under his breath. His boss abruptly closed the door and loomed over his bedside.

The doctor withdrew a tablet from his lab coat and vigorously scanned the screen. Mr. Morgan stood with his arms crossed as he spoke.

"Mr. Montgomery, I am Dr. Geani. You suffered severe blood loss due to your leg and shoulder injuries. However, we were able to skin graft your leg, and hopefully you will regain most of your motor functions with time. We will need to keep you under observation for at least two weeks or so to see how your leg heals. During your time here, we will have you start on a physical therapy regimen to help you regain some of your leg's basic functions. I should warn you that physical therapy will be painful at first. That is why you must push yourself."

Okay, Doc, give it to me straight: Am I going to walk again? Or am I going to be a crippled mess for the rest of my life?! Anthony perspired with nervousness as he thought of the pain and suffering that laid ahead.

"You will no doubt walk again, but it will not be easy. The ligament damage in your leg is quite severe."

26

Thank God! He let out a sigh of relief after hearing the doctor's less-than-encouraging prognosis.

"And as for your shoulder, there are fifty stitches, which should also heal in about two weeks' time. I expect that you will have some scarring, but your recovery rate has been extraordinarily fast. My only concern is for the ligaments and tendons in your leg. While your flesh wounds seem to be healing unusually fast, I'm afraid the damage to your leg will take longer than expected, hence the rehab."

"Thank God Luna found you when she did," Mr. Morgan interjected as he studied Anthony's bandaged limb. "That woman is a godsend."

She's a lot more than that. Anthony chose to remain silent as Dr. Geani resumed with his diagnosis.

"Mr. Montgomery, you are a very lucky man. Most bear attacks are not of this nature. Believe me, I've been a doctor in this hospital for a long time, and at least one out of every three cases either die or lose limbs." He slipped the tablet back inside his coat and addressed his drug-induced patient. "As I mentioned before, your body is recovering at an unprecedented rate. It seems that your vision has also improved, as I am sure you've noticed by now that you can see perfectly without your glasses."

Holy shit, I guess there is a silver lining in all this. He rubbed his eyes in astonishment.

"I would like to draw some more blood samples, once every three days, to analyze exactly what factors are allowing your body to make such remarkable recoveries...with your permission, of course."

"Sure, Doctor, do what you have to." Anthony deflatingly beheld his bandaged leg, held up with metallic pins and thin cables. He was worried and scared. Although he was grateful to still be alive, he knew there was a long and hard road ahead of him.

Dr. Geani lowered his spectacles to the tip of his nose and began examining his suspended leg when Mr. Morgan suddenly grabbed him by his forearm.

"I'll take it from here, Doc. Thanks."

Dr. Geani looked down at Anthony with a sympathetic smile.

"Mr. Montgomery, you're a lucky man. Most people don't get a second chance at life. I'll be seeing you. Best try and get some rest."

After his examination was complete, the doctor gave him a saluting nod and departed. Upon exiting, Anthony could immediately hear his family berating him with questions just outside the door. He could tell that they were anxious and worried by the tones of their voices. Mr. Morgan remained stationary in his stance, stoically lurching over him with a domineering presence.

"Montgomery, what the hell were you thinking?! Those woods are no place for anyone to be, especially at night! Why did you go out there?" he deposed with an infuriated scowl.

Shit, he's pissed. I knew it. Anthony turned away, hoping Mr. Morgan would have mercy on him for his stupid mistake.

"I...I just needed some fresh air, sir. I enjoy being alone sometimes. I, uh, wanted to take advantage of the scenery before we had to go back to the city," he nervously rambled, hoping his boss would take pity on him.

"Montgomery, you've been one of the best associates I've ever had, and believe me, I've had a lot of 'em. You don't buckle under pressure, and you always perform. Once you were stabilized in that hillbilly hospital, I had you airlifted to St. Josephine here in the city. I made sure you had a private room. I spared no expense."

It's about time he took notice. He was thankful that Mr. Morgan had finally started to appreciate him. He reflected over the years that he had spent sitting at that same old desk in the lower cubicles next to the mail room, where nobody paid him any mind; now he was finally getting the attention he deserved. Mr. Morgan rested his hands over the bedrail with an aggressive posture.

"I...I don't know what to say, sir." He was overtaken with gratitude.

"It's no problem, Montgomery. I want to make sure you have everything you need to get back on your feet—or foot, rather."

"Ha, good one, sir." He insincerely chuckled, in hopes of alleviating the tense mood.

"Because once you recover, I want to make you a member of the board!"

Holy shit! I don't believe it! Finally! After hearing his proposal, Anthony was reinvigorated with a sense of accomplishment. His whole life was about to change.

"I...I..." he enthusiastically stammered, trying to think of the right words to say.

"Say yes, Montgomery. I believe you're ready for it, son."

"Yes! I won't let you down, sir!" He cheerfully accepted, realizing that his future was finally starting to take shape into the life he deserved.

"Let's hope not." Mr. Morgan smirked while stroking his beard in a calculating manner.

"Well, son, you just relax and focus on healing up so we can grab the bull by the horns together. I'm going to need you at a hundred and ten percent when you get out of here. No bullshit. We have some mergers and acquisitions I need you to look over. When you feel up to it, of course."

He pointed his index finger and cocked his thumb back, making a pistol-shooting motion before he headed for the door.

"Sir," Anthony whimpered.

"Yes, son?" He adjusted his suit and faced him; Anthony knew he could sense the fear in his voice.

Should I tell him the truth? That a monster attacked me? No, I can't tell him the truth. He'll think I'm crazy. He mulled over the pros and cons of confessing, before asking, "Sir, have you ever seen anything unusual in those backwoods around your cabin?" Upon hearing his statement, Mr. Morgan haggardly plodded back to his bedside.

"Actually, I have." He adjusted his tie and cleared his throat.

I knew it! Anthony felt a sense of relief as Mr. Morgan placed his hands on his hips, inquisitively inspecting his bandaged shoulder.

"I saw bigfoot last week!"

Shit! No one's going to believe me. He was distraught after hearing his flippant response.

"Best you get some rest, son." He gently patted him on the top of his head with a hardened callousness as if he were a child before trudging out of the room. After his departure, Rey, Sidney, and Gloria rushed back in, collectively crowding around the bedside. Anthony was so thankful to have them in his life; the energy in the room had shifted, and he felt as if he were home.

"Sidney?"

"Yes, babe?" She admired him with doting eyes.

"Kiss me again."

"I love you." She lowered her head, and their lips met.

While kissing her, he briefly forgot about himself, as if his body and soul had elevated to another state of consciousness. After their lip-locked embrace, he sarcastically announced, "I know you do," and they both smiled.

"Ahhh, my leg!" he screamed, as searing pain shot through his wounds, like a vise grip had tightened around his flesh. *Fuck, this hurts!* He feverishly pressed the trigger on his morphine drip. "Does this shit even work?!" Anthony yelled in agony just before a wave of drug-induced drowsiness overtook him. He knew that soon he would be in a deep slumber. *Oh, wow, this stuff kicks. I don't feel anything.* His once pain-stricken leg now felt light as a feather. "You guys should go home… I'm going to be just fine," he lethargically ordered while glaring up at the pink teddy bear perched by his bandaged shoulder. He subtly beamed at the notion of his new employment status in conjunction with his eyes growing heavy.

Gloria lifted his hand and kissed it. "Okay, my little ant. I'll see you tomorrow."

His worried aunt scurried along, collecting her belongings from the recliner. As she shuffled her way to the door, she took one last admiring glance at her surrogate son. Anthony noticed her eyes welling up as she left.

"Okay, homeboy. I better go let you and the lady tie up some loose ends." Rey made the hole-and-index-finger gesture with a foolhardy smirk.

"No, actually, Sidney, baby, if you don't mind, I need to talk to Rey alone. Guy thing, you know," he slurred, with a drowsy, morphine-induced sneer.

"Okay, babe. I'm glad you're still with us. I don't want to lose you.

Don't ever scare me like that again, or I'll kill you myself." Her tone was worrisome as she grabbed his hand, interlocking their fingers. "I'll see you tomorrow." She slipped away, and she gave Rey a nudge before leaving.

"What's up?" Rey's frosted hair seemed to glow under the fluorescent lights as he reeled over him, grinning like a Cheshire cat.

Anthony listened for the sound of Sidney's footsteps to dissipate down the hall before he spoke.

"Rey, I need you to be at a two… Right now you're at a ten. These drugs are going to start kicking in. And I need to tell you something… You're the only one who will believe me."

Rey pulled up the reclining chair, still warm from Gloria's body heat, and scooted next to his bedside.

"Shoot. I'm all ears." He plopped down and hunched over him with curiosity.

"Rey… What attacked me wasn't a bear," he clarified as the medication started to take hold of him. He knew he only had a few seconds to explain what he could.

Shit, I'm fading out! His eyes grew heavy, he was struggling to stay awake.

"It…was…a…wolf." The cocktail took over, and Anthony nodded off into an intoxicated slumber. Everything spun and went black. He heard Rey get up and leave, quietly closing the door behind him. Anthony fell into a dark void. His slumber was dreamless, uninterrupted, and long.

The next day, he open his eyes to see a large nurse with short blonde hair standing over him.

"Good morning, Mr. Montgomery. Time for your rehab. My name's Ramona." She had a stern Eastern European accent.

He rubbed his eyes, still a bit drowsy from the morphine.

Oh, man, she's big. She looks like she could play linebacker for the Myrin City Knights. This is going to hurt. He smiled and nodded. "Nice to meet you. Take it easy on me, okay?" he nervously pleaded.

"There's nothing easy about rehab, my darling. Come. Let's get you out of bed." She unfolded a wheelchair and pushed it to his bedside, lowering the guardrail. Next, she unbound the cables that suspended his leg.

He screamed as his damaged limb suddenly dropped. The pain was insufferable.

They should've just cut the damn thing off! He thought about the suffering that lay ahead; he was on the verge of a breakdown but managed to keep his emotions together as he slipped on the navy robe his aunt had left for him.

"I know it hurts, but the more it hurts now, the less it will hurt later," Ramona revealed, consoling him as best she could.

"I bet you say that to all your patients." Anthony writhed as he shifted his frame.

"Come. Give me your hands." She reached out with her big arms, he grabbed her palms, and she pulled him to the edge of the bed.

With every move, he experienced sharp, daggering pain; everything hurt, but he knew he had to push through. With Ramona's help, he hopped into the rubbery confines of the wheelchair. She shrugged her broad shoulders and eagerly wheeled him down the hall.

"Off to rehab we go!" she announced with excitement.

She's a real wacko, I can already tell. He was not in the mood.

He had already broken out in a cold sweat and was exhausted from the pain. His leg was throbbing and tight; just bending his knee hurt like hell. As Ramona enthusiastically rolled him down the corridor, he could hear bloodcurdling screams, beeps, chimes, and faint, muffled conversations. It was obvious that his hearing was becoming more acute. Sounds from far away were as distinct as if they were next to him. However, the intensity of his hearing faculties quickly became chaotic. His head throbbed with overwhelming strain. As Ramona propelled him farther down the hall, the chaotic clamoring in his head started to subside.

Thank God it stopped. Now I can think. He was relieved that the incessant chattering and background noise clouding his mind had unexpectedly muted.

Ramona ushered him through the automatic doors, bypassing the reception desk, and wheeled him across the rehab facility. He scanned the large room scattered with recovering patients. Some were missing limbs; some were burn victims; others were cancer patients recovering from their chemotherapy. He immediately felt lucky upon witnessing the sickly patients working with their therapists. Some threw squishy rubber balls, tossing them back and forth, while others held onto flimsy tensioned rubber bands. A few patients were stationed along the rows of cardio machines, gingerly walking on treadmills.

I'll never complain about my leg again. He knew he had a lot to be thankful for, and in that moment he stopped feeling sorry for himself. The throbbing in his head had subsided to a dull, manageable hum, and he felt he owed it to himself to at least try and push through the pain.

"Let's try walking." Ramona wheeled him over to a treadmill with handrails attached to the sides.

"How about we try standing first?" he nervously responded, doused in sweat underneath his robe.

His hands were clammy as he pushed himself up. The sharp pain in his calf radiated throughout his mauled leg and traveled up to his inner thigh. He shifted his weight onto his good leg, hobbling over to the treadmill in a pain-filled slog. He grabbed the guardrails, steadying himself while standing atop the rubbery treads, hunched over and out of breath.

"Very good!" Ramona encouraged. "Now time to walk. The treadmill will only go as fast as you do, so take your time."

He glared down at his furry hospital slippers, too small for his feet, and began to shuffle. The tracks started to roll, and though it was painful, he was walking on his own. He shakingly grasped the side rails and warily marched, each step filled with radiating agony. His gait was flawed, swaying from left to right, favoring his left leg over his bandaged limb.

"Try and put some weight on your right leg. It won't get any better unless you use it," Ramona raised her voice, distinguishing her stern accent above the background chatter.

He obliged her request and put weight on his right leg. The pain was insufferable. His slaughtered and misshapen calf tightened and cramped with a debilitating tension.

Fuck, this hurts! He took a deep breath and continued at a snail's pace. The stench of his rank hospital bed, which he had laid in for over three days, permeated from under his skin. After twenty minutes of throbbing, pain-filled steps, Ramona disengaged the treadmill.

"Very good, my darling! You'll be walking out of here in no time," she congratulated while lowering his sweat-riddled frame back into the wheelchair.

God, I can't wait to get the fuck out of here! So fucking depressing. He struggled to catch his breath as he looked around the rehab floor, again noticing the suffering patients glaring back at him with their gaunt expressions.

And to think, I'm one of the luckier ones. He could feel their stares as Ramona wheeled him out.

She ushered him back to his private room and stopped next to his bedside.

"Aren't you going to help me?" He gleamed at her with puppy dog eyes.

"I am helping you by not helping you." She smiled.

What a fucking masochist—she likes this shit. He begrudgingly pushed himself up.

Exhausted, he mustered enough strength to hoist himself onto the bed. He grabbed hold of his throbbing limb, which felt as if it were going to explode from tightness. He painstakingly maneuvered himself, negotiating his sweat-soaked body under the covers to a comfortable position.

"See, that wasn't so hard, now, was it?" she encouraged as he shook in anguish.

Morphine time! His thoughts were suddenly filled with excitement, accompanied by angst and desperation. He reached for the drip but couldn't find the button.

"Where's my morphine?" He frantically shuffled under the covers in hopes that the trigger was nearby.

"No morphine for you. Doctor's orders."

"What?! You can't do this to me. I'm in pain here!" He panicked, shaking uncontrollably. "So much for the Hippocratic oath!"

"Don't worry, darling. We have these for your pain." She reached into her scrubs' pocket and pulled out a bottle of OxyContin.

She positioned the vial on the swing table and poured him a cup of water before administering the pill.

Okay, now we're talkin'! He opened his mouth, and she administered the small green pill.

He gulped it down, taking a swig from the flimsy paper cup, and waited. After a few minutes had passed, she grabbed the pills and said nothing before her departure.

Jeez, so much for bedside manner. He was too tired to give a shit.

Exhausted from his rehab, he lay in his bed and waited for the pain to go away. A few moments later, he felt as if his body was levitating, and he fell into a deep, comforting sleep.

"Hey, babe, how are you feeling?" He suddenly heard Sidney's soft voice as he groaned and opened his eyes; his slumber seemed to have been only seconds in time. He looked into her crystal-blue eyes, half-conscious.

"Okay, I guess. They gave me some Oxy." He examined the room with intoxicated drowsiness. It was just the two of them; they were alone. He didn't feel any pain for the first time in a long time. The drugs were working, and he felt good.

"Be careful with those pills. I heard they're really addictive." She grasped his pale knuckles.

"Yeah, I know. Don't worry. I'm no junkie, babe. Besides, the nurse administers the pills. Ah, what time is it?"

"Four thirty."

Anthony rubbed his eyes; although his slumber had been brief, he felt rested and well.

"Sid, can you help me to the bathroom? I need to rinse off. I smell like shit," he embarrassedly asked.

"Sure thing, babe." She lowered the handrail, and he slipped out of bed, draping his arm over her shoulder. This time he felt no pain as he limped to the bathroom.

35

"Pew, sheesh, you smell!" she exclaimed with watering eyes as she got a whiff of his rank body odor.

With her aid, Anthony hobbled over to the bathroom and closed the door; they both stood looking at each other in a time-bending stare. He disrobed and limped over to the shower and sat on the bench, when he noticed her face flush with desire.

She must have a thing for cripples. God, she looks good. She had just gotten off work and was wearing a white blazer with black pants.

There was something about a woman in a suit that activated his primal sexual desires. She turned on the shower as he propped his bandaged limb on the bench, clear of the sprinkling water.

I must look ridiculous. I don't know what she sees in me. Honestly, I don't. He closed his eyes and sat for a while before he lathered himself with a small bar of soap.

"Remember that time in college when you snuck into my dorm after hours?" She beamed.

"Yeah, your roommate was sound asleep. I thought for sure she was going to wake up." Anthony thought of that night. How he wished he could go back in time to before all this had happened.

"Yeah, and we were loud too!" She giggled.

Their college years were filled with sex and parties—in between their studies, of course.

She majored in political science, and he had been working toward his MBA. They had met in their undergrad English class. Anthony had asked her to help him study for an upcoming exam, and the rest was history. In a way, their college years were like their honeymoon, as their now hectic work schedules would often leave their passions lacking. After he washed and rinsed off, he noticed Sidney removing her blazer.

Oh, it's about to go down. Good thing I washed my Johnson! He felt the blood rush to his genitals as he observed his girlfriend unbutton her shirt.

His heart raced as she removed her lace bra, exposing her breasts. He adjusted himself on the bench with excitement.

Finally! he thought.

Sidney reached over and shut off the shower. He just hoped he could perform in his injured, drug-induced state. She lowered her head over his crotch, placing her tongue and mouth over his nether regions. He felt a hint of a tingle on the tip of his dick, but couldn't manage to get hard. He closed his eyes in frustration while she slowly bobbed.

Shit! Come on! Don't do this to me now! he pleaded with himself.

He precipitously began to think about Luna. Her slender, athletic frame and flowing red hair sent his mind into a rush of passionate desire, but it was not enough. After some time had passed, it was clear that he could not perform. He felt bad for Sidney and placed his hand on her head. They suddenly heard a stern knock.

"Hello? Anthony? Are you in there?" his aunt called out.

Fuck! Can't even get my rocks off! He was enraged with frustration.

"Yes, Auntie. Sidney was just helping me, uh, use the bathroom." He blushed with embarrassment.

"Sorry, Sid, it's the drugs. I'm sure of it."

"Don't worry, babe. We'll make up for it later." She encouraged him with a wink before wiping her lips. She rinsed her mouth over the sink and got dressed before helping him up from the bench. Embarrassed, he slipped on his robe.

"Thanks, Sid." He was upset, but happy to still have her in his life. He was nervous though. He knew that if he did not get better and perform his sexual duties, eventually she would leave him.

She tramped out of the bathroom with his arm over her shoulder. Gloria was standing in front of them, wearing a bulky peach shirt with flower-patterned pants. She exuberantly displayed a new cell phone, along with some envelopes.

"I got your mail, and your company shipped this to you," she announced. They both had embarrassed looks on their faces as she handed Anthony the phone and his mail.

"What happened to my old phone?" he asked, remembering the picture he had taken of the dreaded beast. He desperately wanted to show them the evidence—after all, he was in this mess over that picture.

"When the paramedics found you, they said your phone was gone.

37

Only your wallet and half of your pants were left. You're lucky to be alive," she uneasily explained.

"The courier said it's ready to use. MGE downloaded all your contacts. Same number and everything."

Well, wasn't that nice of them! He was infuriated that his phone was lost in those backwoods and felt an almost unmanageable rage consume him.

"Boy oh boy, technology sure has changed since I was young. I remember when all we had was a radio—no TV, no internet, no nothing!" Gloria shook her head.

Yeah, and I bet you had to walk ten miles to school in the snow! Save the lecture for someone who gives a shit! He was upset; he just wanted everyone to leave.

Gloria stepped aside and allowed Sidney to help him back onto the bed. He sprang over the sweat-stained sheets and draped his robe around himself.

"Thanks." He slipped the phone into his pocket when a searing pain cursorily shot up his calf, followed by a pounding migraine.

My head! There's that ringing again! God, make it stop! He pressed the call button for the nurse as the throbbing increased. He did his best to conceal his agony from his overbearing aunt and girlfriend.

"Well, I can see you're tired and that you've had a long day. I'd best be going, or I'll be late for bingo. That bitch Ethel wins every time. I swear she's cheating!" Gloria boisterously declared. She kissed his forehead before saying goodbye to Sidney. Just as she exited, a nurse came rushing in.

"You called, sir?" A young man with an athletic build and short dark hair wearing scrubs casually strode over to him.

"Yes, I need some Oxy. I'm in a lot of pain here!" he asserted as Sidney stood by, gripping his trembling hand with concern.

"Okay, we have you scheduled for one more pill tonight, but I'll check with Dr. Geani and see if we can up your dosage."

"Please, I'm in pain!" He was disheartened with the nurse's response and knew that complaining would only lead to him not getting what he wanted. So, he shut his mouth and endured the pain, realizing he had no choice. The nurse hastily left as Sidney pulled up a chair, still holding his hand.

"Sid, you don't need to stay here. I have a phone now. Why don't you just go home? I know you must be tired." He wanted to be alone; he felt vulnerable and embarrassed, especially after his failed attempt in the bathroom.

"You sure, babe?" She examined him with a worried glare.

"Yeah, Sid, no use in both of us sitting here in this godforsaken place," he reasoned with a pain-filled grin.

"I'll stop by tomorrow after work," she assured.

They kissed and Anthony watched as she headed for the door. "Sidney," he called.

She glanced back, standing halfway between the hallway and the open door.

"I love you."

"I know you do," she sneered and left.

She gave me a taste of my own medicine with that one. He had expected her to say that she loved him and was disappointed, although he knew she was joking.

For the rest of the afternoon, Anthony checked his emails and watched videos on his phone, enduring the episodic pain and torturous headaches that would come and go at random. He suffered through the tightness in his leg and the pounding migraines for hours. As midday turned into evening, the night nurse entered the room. Anthony laid in anguish. He noticed a short, portly woman who reminded him of a stuffed pig shuffle to his bedside.

"I have your pill," she said as if talking to a toddler.

Thank God! His anxiety was alleviated. *I don't know what's worse, the pain or the anticipation of the pain. Either way, she showed up just in time!*

She gave him the Oxy and he gulped down the smooth green pill with haste.

"Did the doctor up my dosage?" he asked after swallowing.

"I haven't heard anything," she noted with fake smile.

Fucking nurses, they don't do shit! He was infuriated that his request had not been received by the doctor, but happy that he had at least gotten his pill. "Okay, thank you, ma'am." He politely nodded, concealing his frustration.

After she left, Anthony viewed the radiant gleam of the half-moon shining through the flimsy window blinds. As he glared down at the moonlight cast onto the floor, he thought of that fateful night in the woods. His PTSD was triggered as he imagined the beast's devilish eyes fixated upon him. The OxyContin soon took effect, and he felt no more pain. His thoughts drifted as he viewed the darkened room. Everything slowly cascaded into an enveloping haze as he drifted off into a deep slumber.

He opened his eyes and found himself in a vast field of tall grass. He mindlessly trudged through the brittle grasslands, standing over seven feet tall. He tramped across the overbearing stalks for some time, becoming disoriented. He came to a clearing, where he saw his aunt. She was seated in a rocking chair, vigorously twiddling her knitting needle along with a spool of yarn.

"Auntie, what are you doing out here?" He approached her, pushing aside the overreaching grass.

"You kids today, all it takes is some blinking lights and symbols with some music, and you all become stupider than a lemming! Follow, follow, follow, follow, like, like, like, dance, dance, dance, you fools! Follow the dancing lights and symbols on your phone, and you'll feel better!" She started to knit and rock faster amid her furious tirades.

He stared at her, trying to discern what was happening.

His aunt suddenly screamed.

"Look, the plane, the plane!" She pointed to the skies.

He looked up to see a small bush plane soaring overhead. He recognized his mother and father in the pilot and copilot seats.

"Mom! Dad!" He was so happy to see them.

Suddenly, they took a dive. He watched in horror as the small plane dipped into the grasslands, disappearing from view. Instantly, there was a loud boom, followed by a horrific explosion. Raging fires and billowing smoke rapidly surrounded him. He turned from his aunt and ran. The smoggy fields were disorienting; nonetheless, he followed the rising smoke ascending into the picturesque skyline, guiding his path to the crash site.

As he came to the charred clearing, he saw the contorted, mangled parts of the plane scattered about. He overlooked the site in a frenzied panic, when he saw his mother and father, burning. They were screaming in torturous agony. Their skin melted off their faces as they writhed on the scorched earth. Their bodies were nothing more than a bloody, dismembered splatter. Anthony turned from the fiery carnage, sobbing uncontrollably as the flames spread around him.

"Mom, Dad, why?!" He broke down with a heavy heart.

The brittle grass served as fuel for the fire, and soon the flames skipped around him in a deadly tango. He gagged as he felt the heat and smog intrude over him. He took off running, sprinting through the smoldering fields. As he fearfully raced, he heard the indistinct battle cries of a native tribe. He ran farther and faster across the growing pyre. He glanced back and saw the tribesmen chasing him. They wore wooden masks and had chalky white paint pasted over their bodies. They shot litanies of arrows in his direction. Anthony ran as fast as he could, hoping to escape from the flames and the battle-hungry tribesmen. Without warning, an arrow struck his calf. The wood-carved projectile shot through his leg, and he fell to the ground.

He looked up in horror as day quickly transitioned into night. With the flames rapidly growing around him, he loomed up at the shimmering full moon, waiting for death. He stared up at the dark skies as the fire encircled him. Ominous howls suddenly rang out in the distance. He scrambled to his feet with the arrow protruding from his calf. It hurt like hell as he hobbled away from the threatening wails. He looked back to see a brooding pack of black-haired Lycans on his trail.

The beasts were brooding monsters, with sharp teeth and red eyes.

They howled and barked like jackals as they chased him. He frantically rushed past the smoldering grasslands and came to a clearing. There, he saw Sidney standing before him naked. She opened her arms amid the inferno. He collapsed into her embrace. He laid his head on her breasts and hugged her tightly. As he held his lover, he noticed the hairs on her chest and arms starting to grow into a wooly brindled pattern. He apprehensively looked up, terrified at what he saw.

Her face was that of a Lycan, with daggering pupils and equally piercing fangs. She opened her wolf-like maw and sank her teeth deep into his neck. Blood violently spurted as she devoured him. After she had her fill, the trailing pack descended upon him.

Anthony screamed as the beasts tore him apart, gulping down his organs with delectable fervor amid the rising flames.

He suddenly awoke from his beastly nightmare, doused in sweat. He opened his eyes, confused. The light of morning peaked through the cheap shades, casting a barred radiance on the linoleum floor. He was out of breath, still writhing with fear from his horrible nightmare. He glanced down at his bandaged leg and noticed it was soaking with blood. He started to panic when he heard a light knock at the door. He turned his fear-filled attention over to the doorway and noticed Dr. Geani entering with a smile.

"Good morning, Mr. Montgomery. How are we feeling today?" he greeted as he crept to the bedside before noticing Anthony's hemorrhaging leg.

"Nurse! Come quickly!" he shouted down the hall.

"What happened? Why am I bleeding?" Anthony was scared, wondering if his leg would ever be the same again.

The young nurse with the athletic build rushed in and stood next to Dr. Geani, bewildered.

"You must have hit your leg in your sleep. Let's remove the bandage and take a look at the wound," he ordered.

The nurse carefully undid the wrapping. What Anthony saw next shocked him. His mangled calf was covered in brown hair, matted with darkened blood.

"What the fuck is that?!" he screamed in horror.

"Um, I've never seen this before, but don't be alarmed. Nurse, shave the hair from his leg and clean his wounds." Anthony locked eyes with the doctor.

Real reassuring, Doc! God, I need to get the fuck out of this place already! Anthony just wanted to go home. He was tired, frustrated, and terrified.

"I'll come back and check on you a little bit later to draw some more blood. Don't worry, Mr. Montgomery, you're in good hands." Dr. Geani lightly patted his shoulder in an attempt to console him.

"Can I get some more Oxys, please, Doc?" he asked with hopeful desperation.

Geani reluctantly nodded. "I'll up your dosage."

"Thanks, Doc." Anthony could feel the doctor's pity over him and was pleased with his response.

He exited the room, leaving Anthony alone with the nurse. The young orderly opened a fresh razor and started shaving the bushy, wolf-like hairs from his leg. Anthony was disgusted as his gloved hands methodically stroked his mangled calf, mired with dried blood and hair. The young orderly delicately shaved around his gnarled flesh, mindful of the stitches. As he did, the matted fur was cut back to unveil the twisted bruises underneath.

This was the first time Anthony had seen his leg unbandaged. Discolored lacerations ran across his shin and down the lower half of his leg. His calf was bulbous and misshapen, like an overstuffed turkey. He did his best to conceal his tears from the nurse, who was almost done shaving. After he finished, he cleaned the excess blood from the wound and dressed the limb. The nurse hesitated with disgust before collecting the blood-soaked hairs, placing them in a biohazard bag.

"What are you saving my hair for?" he asked with a depressed tone.

"The doctor wants to do some tests."

"Can I get another Oxy, please?" he pleaded.

"I'll see what I can do." The nurse threw his gloves in the trash bin

43

beside the door, along with the razor and the bloody bandages.

See what you can do then, you stupid fuck! Anthony was enraged; he just wanted all this to be over.

The nurse marched down the hall, clutching the bag containing the bloody hairs as Anthony viewed his bandaged leg with apprehension. He turned on the small wall-hung TV, hoping for a distraction.

"Good morning, Myrin City. I'm Tom Fillmore, and here are today's headlines," a dapper news anchor wearing a dark-gray suit announced from his desk.

"*Macbeth* opens today at the Muse Theater in the heart of the Entertainment District. Check your local listings for show times and dates. In other news, protests continue in the Tenderloin Point District. The residents there are still angry over the proposed redevelopment site of the Dockside Port. Morgan & Green Enterprises purchased the apartment buildings, and their plans for redevelopment have some residents concerned. Here's Linda Haskins, live from the protests taking place directly in front of the entrance to the port. Linda?"

Anthony knew about the project; he had worked on several purchase agreements for the acquisition of the surrounding properties.

"Thanks, Tom. I'm here in front of the Dockside Port with some concerned residents." Linda was a thin, attractive woman with long blonde hair; she wore a dark-blue suit and stood amid the circling protestors.

She held the mic tightly as she witnessed the protestors holding signs, aimlessly patrolling and chanting, "Hell no! We won't go!"

Linda approached a man carrying a sign that read, "No gentrification! Homes over business!"

"Sir, would you mind saying a few words about the protests and why you are marching here today?" She held the mic up to a skinny, angry man; he was wearing a brown Dickies outfit stained with construction debris.

"We are out here today to let MGE know that the people of Tenderloin Point are not going anywhere! They can't just force us out of our homes without any compensation. We want fair, affordable housing for our people! And we're not leaving until we get what we want!" he shouted with fury before rejoining his cohorts marching in a circle.

Well, you can't stop progress, dude! What are we supposed to do, keep that place a slum forever? They had a chance to change their neighborhood for years—all those tax incentives and programs—and they did nothing. The place is a fucking shithole! So now it's time for a change. Anthony had no compassion for the people of Tenderloin Point; in fact, he had developed a disdain for them. He saw them as a hindrance to his company's progress and ultimately the city's future development.

"Well, there you have it. The people of Tenderloin Point will not go quietly."

The camera switched from Linda back to Tom, still seated at his desk.

"Thanks, Linda. In other news, an ancient artifact was stolen from the Natural History Museum last night. The piece was a stone amulet said to be from the nomadic Neuri tribe. The talisman was discovered in the early 1920s during an excavation of the Temple of Anubis. If you have any information regarding the stolen amulet, please contact the Myrin City Police Department. There is a sizable cash reward for anyone with information regarding the artifact's whereabouts. In sports news, the Myrin City Knights started training camp today. Hopefully this season will be better than the last." He nodded while sarcastically smiling into the camera.

Anthony shut off the TV. He lay in bed for a while, going over everything that had happened to him over the past week. His thoughts commingled in a swirl of anxiety intertwined with confusion and uncertainty.

He thought about Sidney, wondering if their bond was strong enough for them to stay together through all this chaos. He was concerned about his job; although being on the board came with a significant pay increase, he knew that his already-intense workload would be doubled given his new position, which in turn would put more strain on their relationship. He was concerned about his thrashed leg and what types of physical limitations would be in his future. The fear of the Lycan that had attacked him in those backwoods seemed minuscule compared to the harsh realities that he would soon face. It was overwhelming and almost too much to bear, but the pills helped, and he was thankful for that.

Damn it, where is the nurse with my Oxy?! He scanned the whiteboard schedule and was glad that his rehab had been moved to tomorrow. *Thank God. There's only so much one man can take.* He heard an assertive knock, and Dr. Geani marched in, making his way to his bedside.

"Mr. Montgomery, I'm going to draw some blood now. The nurse did a nice job on your bandage," he noted before producing a syringe from his coat pocket.

He abruptly jammed the needle into his arm. After the syringe was filled, he produced a vial of OxyContin.

"Take these as needed for pain." He placed the pills on the bedside table with a jingle.

Yes! Finally! Anthony was overjoyed and scrambled to pour himself a cup of water. He swallowed two pills with haste.

"Thanks, Doc."

"Take them sparingly, Mr. Montgomery. Now, I know you have been experiencing some headaches, is that correct?"

"Yes, I have this ringing in my head that comes and goes, and I've noticed that I can hear things from far away. I can hear people's conversations as if they were in the room with me, but then I get really bad migraines and I can't concentrate. Everything becomes muffled and chaotic." He described his symptoms as best he could; he was starting to feel the levity and euphoria of the Oxys. He grinned aimlessly, awaiting the doctor's response.

"I see. Well, I have something for your headaches." He withdrew another vial, this one filled with white triangular pills.

"Take these as needed. It is my special blend. I engineered the formula myself." He confidently slammed the bottle atop the table.

"Got it, Doc. White for headaches, green for pain." Anthony leered with reprieve, admiring his medications.

"I'll be back later this evening to check up on you. Rest up, Mr. Montgomery. You will have rehab tomorrow, and next week I will be removing your stitches. You are actually healing up rather nicely," he explained while scrupulously inspecting his shoulder.

"Good to hear." He was pleased that his time in the hospital was coming to an end.

Dr. Geani gave him a reassuring nod before leaving. Anthony focused his newly acquired hearing abilities, tuning in to the sounds of his footsteps as he paced down the hall. He was able to block out the background noises, but his head still throbbed. He listened for a while and unexpectedly heard Mr. Morgan's booming voice.

"Well, Doctor, how's our boy doing?"

What's he doing here? Must be here to visit me, he reasoned while eavesdropped on their conversation.

"His blood is that of a hybrid, sir. I've never seen this type before. This is very exciting. The genetic potential is limitless. I just took a fresh sample."

"I'm glad to hear that. We'd best keep our eyes on him then."

"Yes, sir, he's been healing at an unprecedented rate. I'll be removing the stitches next week, and he will be released."

"Excellent. Keep up the good work, Doctor. I'm glad my patronage to this hospital has not gone unnoticed. How's the construction of your new office coming along?"

"Very well, sir. Thank you."

"Good. I'll leave you to it then." Anthony listened intently as Mr. Morgan's hard-toed shoes clamored away from his room.

What the fuck? The doctor's on Mr. Morgan's payroll? He was concerned and uneasy. *What the hell is a hybrid?* He pondered whether to ask the doctor next time he saw him. *And why didn't Mr. Morgan come visit me? Strange. Best to keep that conversation to myself. Don't want them to think I'm eavesdropping. The last thing I want is more tests and more time in this godforsaken place!* As the effects of the OxyContin overtook him, his enhanced hearing muffled to a low, manageable hum, and he was at peace.

In the afternoon, Sidney came to visit him; she was wearing her work attire, which he had taken a particular liking to.

"How are you feeling, babe?" she asked, standing by his bedside.

"Better now. They gave me these, and the doctor says I'll be out of here next week."

"That's good. I'm glad you're feeling better." She had a solemn tone, and Anthony could tell something was troubling her.

"What's wrong, Sid?"

"Well, Anthony, I've been thinking."

"Don't do too much of that. Your head might start hurting," he joked in hopes of lightening the mood, but he knew where this conversation was going.

"All jokes aside, my lease is up next month, and I need to know if we're going to move in together."

"Sid, I don't know. Why are you bringing this up on me now? I mean, I'm in the hospital, I almost died, and now you want to put more pressure on me?! Have some consideration, please!"

He knew that it was not easy for her to see him like this. He was tired and didn't want to have this debate; in fact, he had been avoiding it altogether. He hoped that his time in the hospital would dissuade her from bringing it up, but she had insisted, and he was growing irritated with her demands of him.

He enjoyed his space, and his one-bedroom apartment was not big enough for the both of them. He had a small bathroom and an even smaller closet. He knew if she moved in, she would not be happy, and they would ultimately have to find a bigger place, which would cost more money and put even more of a strain on their relationship.

"Have some consideration for me!" she shouted.

Oh shit, here we go. He had experienced her temper many times, and he knew she was going to make him feel her wrath.

Her face turned beat red before she let him have it.

"Look, Anthony, we've been dating since college, over six years now! We don't live together. I have to pack a fucking bag like I'm going to some slumber party to stay at your place. I put up with all your bullshit,

48

and this is what I get! I need more from you. I need a real commitment!"

"I'm committed to you, Sid. Now's just not the time, babe," he responded in a soft voice, in hopes of calming her.

"It's never the right time for you! I'm a good woman, Anthony, and I deserve to have a man that appreciates me and wants to move in and start a family. I'm not going to wait around forever. You need to decide: Do you want a future with me or not? I'm done being the girlfriend who sleeps over sometimes!" Tears of fury rolled down her pallid face as her chest heaved and her nostrils flared.

Shit! The last thing I want is a kid! Some mindless half-wit running around calling me "Daddy"? What a nightmare! Plus, her body will go to shit, and all our money will go toward the kid. I'm still paying off my student loans, for fuck's sake! We'll have no time for ourselves. Then she will complain and file for divorce and take half my shit. I can see it now. Got to convince her to see things my way. He contemplated his future in conjunction with his physical limitations. It was all too overwhelming.

"Sid, I want a future with you, but now's not the time. I mean, I haven't even been able to walk straight." He hoped that mentioning his injuries would sway her, but she was aware of his tactics and gave him an ultimatum.

"Anthony, if we don't move in together by the end of the month, we're done!" After her proposition she stomped out of the room.

His heart sank. He knew she would leave him, and he wanted to make her happy, just not at the expense of his own happiness.

HOMECOMING

The rest of the week droned on in an OxyContin-mired haze. Anthony lost track of the days, going to rehab in between taking his pills. It all became routine for him. Sidney did not come to visit him, nor did she call. He was upset, but he understood. His leg had managed to heal to the point where he could walk with a limp using a cane.

After his last exhausting physical therapy session, Ramona escorted him back to his room, where he sat on the recliner facing her while perspiring and out of breath.

"You are doing so good, my darling," she encouraged him. "I told you that you would walk out of this hospital."

"That you did, Ramona. Thank you for pushing me." He felt a bond with her and was slightly disappointed that their time was coming to an end.

As he glanced up at the broad-shouldered woman, his head began to throb, and his ears rang with a high-pitched screech. He struggled to focus amid the chaotic resonances.

"Ah, my head! Ramona, can you hand me those white pills on my table there?" he pleaded.

"No, you must fukus!"

"What did you say?" He was confused; her accent made it sound like she was cursing at him.

"Fukus. You know, concentrate!"

"Oh, you mean 'focus,'" he corrected while enduring the incessant pounding.

"Yes. Close your eyes and concentrate," she instructed with a calm tone.

Worth a shot. He closed his eyes.

"Now breathe slowly in and out. Fukus on your heartbeat."

Anthony slowly drew breath, listening to his heart. The low methodic rhythm calmed him. His mind quieted, and the frenzied noises radiating through his skull became clear and concise. He realized he could control his enhanced hearing just by focusing on specific sounds, which he could hone in on at will.

Oh my God, she's not as crazy as I thought. He was relieved he had found a way to control his heightened senses without pills, but decided to keep his meds handy just in case. "Wow, that actually worked!" He was shocked as he opened his eyes.

"Good. I'm glad. The doctor will be in shortly to remove your stitches, and tomorrow you will be released from the hospital." Ramona beamed with accomplishment before leaving.

Yes! I'm finally getting out of here! He was beyond excited; he felt like he had been there for months.

He gingerly shuffled to his bed, resting his cane on the guard rail. He tucked himself under the covers and reached for his pills, popping two Oxys. His tolerance had gone up during his stay; he now needed to take at least two pills to feel the euphoria.

He lay in bed for some time with a smile on his face, overjoyed that he was leaving tomorrow. He folded his hands over his stomach and stared at the ceiling. He didn't even care that Sidney had not called him. He was going home, and that was all that mattered. His eyes grew heavy with jubilatory intoxication before he nodded off.

When he awoke it was late. He knew it was late from the hands on the clock, which he could see perfectly: 3:30 a.m. An auburn hew radiated around the numbers as he rubbed his eyes.

What's this? I'm not dreaming—no clocks in dreams—plus I can smell the nurse's jelly doughnuts from down the hall. Anthony was confused as he examined his surroundings.

He held up his hand in the dark and could distinguish the details of his knuckles and fingernails perfectly. There was a radiating aura cast over the areas he focused on. Numerical patterns and lines exuded with an orange halo, and the rest of his surroundings were illuminated by a dark green afterglow.

Holy shit! I have night vision! He was excited as he came to the realization.

He grabbed his cane, limped over to the restroom, and peered into the bathroom mirror at his dark reflection that seemed to leer back at him with shimmering yellow eyes.

What the fuck am I? His thoughts were a mix of amazement and uneasiness. He crept closer to his reflection, glaring deeper into his sharp pupils. *I'm a hybrid.*

Anthony was filled with gratitude and relief. He was thankful for the care he had received and was reinvigorated by the anticipation of finally going home. No more stale hospital food, no more agonizing physical therapy sessions, and no more chatty nurses to make small talk with. It was finally time for him to go.

After two pain-filled weeks in the hospital, he was going to be released, and he couldn't be happier. Dr. Geani removed the stitches from his shoulder, along with the sutures and bandages around the skin grafts on his leg. The scars were gnarled and misshapen, but he had regained most of his motor function, with some episodic pain. His gait was reduced to a limp, and he needed a cane for support. Anthony had come to accept the fact that he might never be able to run again, let alone walk without a cane, but he was thankful just to be alive and getting out of the hospital.

"Mr. Montgomery, I wish you well. Your recovery went as good as can be expected. You are a very lucky man. Ramona will be in shortly now that you have signed all your discharge paperwork. I want you to check in with me should you have any questions or problems," Dr. Geani confidently assured.

Anthony zipped up his white tracksuit that his aunt had left for him a few days earlier. He felt good wearing some normal clothes for a change, instead of that open-back hospital gown and robe, which didn't leave much to the imagination.

"Thanks, Doc." He scuffled to his bedside and plopped his pink teddy bear atop his duffle bag.

"Ready to go?" Ramona entered the room pushing a wheelchair as Dr. Geani exited. They briefly acknowledged each other as they passed. Anthony eagerly hopped into the chair, and she wheeled him down the insipid corridor to the exit. Although he was capable of walking with a slight limp and with the aid of his cane, the hospital's policy would not allow him to leave unless ushered in a wheelchair.

Ramona stopped and ordered, "Get up, my darling. Remember I said you will walk out of this hospital. Don't make me a liar."

"That you did, Ramona." He grasped his cane.

As he hoisted himself up, the pill bottles jingled in his tracksuit pockets. He grabbed his belongings and hobbled to the doors.

"Take care of yourself," she whispered with a tearful smile as she clutched the empty wheelchair. "And remember to fukus!" she exclaimed before departing down the hall.

"I will, thank you." He looked back at her with gratitude.

She's a character. Thank God for that woman. I'm actually going to miss her.

The automatic doors zipped open, and a bitter chill brushed his face. Waiting for him outside was Mr. Morgan, outfitted in a gray designer suit and shiny dark shoes. He was standing in front of the familiar jet-black limo that Ben Damien had used the night of the ceremony. The overwhelming sounds of the city quickly penetrated his skull. He shuddered, clutching his head while seizing his pink teddy bear. As he endured the auditory onslaught, he slumped farther down, grasping his cane in desperate hope for some relief.

That ringing again! Why can't it just stop! Don't do this in front of Mr. Morgan, not now! He clenched his forehead while shutting his eyes, forcefully trying to compensate for his sensory overload, using all his faculties just to try and not throw up.

His head pulsated amid the uproars of the overpowering horns and ambulatory sirens, coupled with the indistinguishable racket from the surrounding buildings. Mr. Morgan rushed to his aid.

"Easy, son. I gotcha." He swathed his bulbous hand over

Anthony's shoulder and helped him to the limo.

This is worse than any hangover! Now your boss is going to think you're weak. He nearly fell over.

"Montgomery, come on! I know your head hurts. Just try to block out the noise."

He could barely hear him over the deafening resonances as a fiery sting inflamed his temples. He crouched down and felt the ominous presence of the driver close by.

Come on, Anthony, focus! You're embarrassing yourself! He was in a defeated state as he tried to make the overwhelming throbbing subside.

"Marcellus, don't just stand there!" Mr. Morgan shouted.

The black-suited driver snatched him up and laid him in the back seat. As Anthony was being manhandled, he peered through his semi-closed eyelids and caught a glimpse of the burly man handling him. He was the bald-headed driver with the notable scar under his eye who had driven Ben the night of his attack. Marcellus jammed his cane and possessions next to him before closing the door.

Mr. Morgan sat beside him as he clenched his teddy bear, providing some comfort against the ear-splitting ruckus.

As they sped away from the hospital, Marcellus studied his passengers through the rearview mirror with a pensive stare. Anthony found little relief from the debilitating racket as he sat up against the posh leather seats.

Come on, Anthony. Focus! You're making a fool of yourself! He tucked his head between his legs as if preparing for a crash landing.

The limo picked up speed as he reached into his pocket and withdrew the vial of Dr. Geani's pills.

"What are those?" Mr. Morgan asked while still grasping his shoulder.

With little effort, his boss had forced him upright.

He's pretty strong for an old dude. He was impressed as he shakingly popped the bottle open. "They help with migraines. Dr. Geani prescribed them," he explained before downing two triangular tablets, quickly chewing them into chalky bits before swallowing.

"That Dr. Geani is really something, isn't he?" Mr. Morgan asserted.

Probably because he's on your payroll. Anthony wisely elected not to mention overhearing their conversation as he stuffed the vial back in his pocket.

"He took good care of me, sir. Thank you." The ringing in his head had started to subside, delivering some relief.

"Don't mention it, son. All the expenses are already paid for. MGE takes care of its own. Remember that." He winked.

"Thank you, sir. I really appreciate everything." He was taken aback at Mr. Morgan's generosity, but he figured he was being nice to him in order to avoid a lawsuit.

Nonetheless, it was nice to be cared for, even if the reasons were financially motivated. As the limo journeyed across the snow-laden streets, the chaotic clatters dissipated. With his ears humming, Anthony managed to sit up on his own.

"Sir, my apologies. I'm trying my best to not upchuck in your limo."

"No apology needed, son. Don't worry. You just focus on getting healed up." The stout mogul grinned and playfully patted him on the knee.

Anthony was confused by the almost fatherly approach Mr. Morgan had recently adopted toward him. He remembered when he had first started working for MGE. His office was a windowless cubicle by the mail room. He was as insignificant as a fly, but as a fly he heard everything, especially what went on in the mail room. Anthony had learned to keep his mouth shut when needed and to speak only when it was appropriate. He also came to realize that information was the most powerful thing in the modern world. After a year or so, he understood how to cleverly navigate the corporate landscape and had inevitably drawn the attention of his superiors.

Ben took notice of him one day, dropping off some packages in the mail room. He realized that Anthony had redlined a merger with some key notes that had saved the firm from taxation penalties. That's when Ben mentioned him to Mr. Morgan. He hadn't even formally met his boss until last year, when Ben introduced them at one of the company's fundraisers for genetic research.

"Sir, I don't mean any disrespect, but why am I suddenly getting the red-carpet treatment? I mean, for years I've worked for MGE, and within a period of only a few weeks we've engaged in more conversation than we ever had… I'm just a little baffled, sir. That's all. Are you making me a board member because you feel responsible for what happened?"

I'm not a charity case, and I don't need any fucking handouts! Anthony felt emboldened by asking his boss these tough questions. He had a renewed sense of confidence. Perhaps it was the pills or his enhanced abilities; either way, he liked the person he was becoming.

"No! Is that what you think, Montgomery? The attorneys drafted up a substantial operating agreement for you to review. It's your decision, not mine. I can only bring the offer to the table. Now, if you don't want to take advantage of this opportunity… Well, that's entirely up to you."

They accelerated onto the Pioneer Bridge. The impressive red iron structure sprawled atop the vast, frozen-over Nicolo River.

Shit, now you pissed him off. He wisely changed his tone.

"Thank you for the opportunity, sir, and I appreciate it. I'll start looking over the contract tonight. When do you need an answer from me?"

"Don't worry, Montgomery. Whenever you get around to it. No rush." He reassuringly sneered.

After an hour of awkward silence, they arrived at his seven-story redbrick building. He let himself out on his own volition, tucking his duffle bag under his arm. The snowy gusts ripped through his tracksuit, sending an icy chill throughout his body. As he leaned back into the car for warmth, he shivered while extending his hand to his boss. They shook and made eye contact.

"I appreciate everything, sir." He trembled, grasping his cane for balance amid the rapacious gusts.

"Don't mention it, son." Mr. Morgan leered with a fatherly gleam. "I had Luna email you the contract and also sent a courier with a sealed copy. Review at your convenience."

"Thank you, sir." He closed the door and limped up the steps.

"Montgomery! Aren't you forgetting something?" Mr. Morgan hollered from the rolled-down window, waving the teddy bear.

"Ha… Thanks, sir." He turned from the doorway, and Mr. Morgan tossed the stuffed animal to him.

He caught it before hobbling into his building. The limousine sped away, careening down the snow-powdered streets as Anthony limped across the lobby and into the elevator. He pressed the seventh-floor button. The pungent, acidy smell of urine tinged his nostrils as the cab ascended to his floor.

Home sweet home, he thought as the indicating lights flickered in conjunction with his ascent.

An abundance of odors flooded his nasal passages as he exited the lift and made his way down the hall. It appeared that along with his hearing enhancements, Anthony's sense of smell had also heightened. He was thankful that his newfound sniffing abilities did not obstruct him like his hearing did, which he fortunately had under control, thanks to the pills. However, his odiferous sense did not only detect recent aromas; smells from the past also enflamed his nose.

He limped to his unit, drawing labored breaths as he inhaled the sticky, sap-riddled odor of spilled cola, along with various perfuming fragrances and fabrics, accompanied by individuals' distinct body odors. The amalgamation of scents swirled his subconscious, providing a subliminal image in his mind of the various scents as he tramped to his door. While staggering farther down the hall, he distinguished the divergent odors of Sidney, his aunt, and Rey.

He staggered to the door and withdrew the keys from his pocket. While wedging his teddy bear and duffle bag under his armpit, he briefly paused and inhaled the aroma of burning candles, melted wax, and soft sugary cream.

He stood there for a moment and inhaled, allowing the atmosphere to penetrate his nostrils. The diverse odors rushed his nasal cavity and instantly sent an image into his mind. He subliminally envisioned his loved ones, along with pastries and balloons.

He swung open the door, and just as his senses had foretold, he saw Auntie Glo standing under a "Welcome Home" banner wearing an off-white blouse with large pockets. She stood at the head of his dining room table, with Sidney and Rey seated on either side of her. Placed on the tabletop was a frosted ice cream cake shaped like a grizzly bear, with candles blazing. Anthony chuckled as he viewed his family amid the streamers and balloons.

Wasn't expecting this. Glad she's here though. He was happy to see them all in one place again, especially Sidney, given their last conversation. He cherished these moments.

"*Surprise!*" all three of them shouted.

He pretended to act stunned as he dropped his belongings on the dining room table.

"Thanks for everything, guys." He blushed with gratitude.

"Anything for you, buddy. Come sit down and have some bear-maul cake!"

Rey announced with a wide-eyed grin as he rolled up the sleeves of his neon-green shirt, motioning for Anthony to sit next to him. His hair was dyed orange and styled in a mohawk. Before Anthony took his seat, he gave his aunt a welcoming embrace. After, he kissed Sidney while lustfully wrapping his hands around her hips and tightly pressing her pelvis into his. The soft fabric of her joggers and Myrin City College sweatshirt reminded him of their college years.

"I missed you," she confessed, peering into his eyes.

Well, you should have come and visited me then! He elected not to mention their argument; he was just happy to be kissing her.

He withdrew from her grip and pulled out a chair, sitting next to Rey. After glancing at his friend's overexaggerated smile, he laughed.

"Pretty clever, huh, Ant? I tried to get some red frosting around the claws, but, you know, extra shit like that can get a little pricey." He motioned his lanky fingers over the top of the cake, excitedly pointing out the details.

"Thanks, Rey, it's great."

"Well, don't just stare at it… Make a wish!" his aunt shouted.

It wasn't his birthday, but nonetheless, Anthony obliged and blew out the candles. After their applause, he grabbed the knife, slicing the first piece. The inside of the cake was red velvet and had a rubicund caramelized filling that mimicked bloody entrails.

"Yeah, the blood batter was extra but worth it!" Rey announced while witnessing Anthony's delight.

"This one's mine!" he exclaimed with childlike exuberance. "All I've had is stale hospital food for the past two weeks!" His eyes dilated with hunger as he slid the frosted cake onto his plate.

Rey nudged him and asked, "How does it feel to take a bite out of that bear?"

"Well, Rey, I guess it's true what they say… Revenge is a dish best served cold!"

They all giggled before serving themselves. Anthony was elated to be home with the people he loved.

"Anthony, I want you to have this. It was your grandmother's. She gave it to me before she passed, and now I'm giving it to you." Gloria pulled out a black-beaded rosary from her pocket. The tiny cross dangled as she grasped the beads in her wrinkled hand.

"Thanks, Auntie." He accepted her gift, gently laying the prayer beads on the table.

"It's a shame that Anthony had to get hurt for all of us to get together like this," Sidney chimed in before taking a bite.

"Yeah, I'm with Sid. We should get together more often," Rey noted.

"Amen to that," Gloria concurred with her mouth full.

After they finished, she scuttled to the kitchen and shoved the rest of the cake into the freezer.

"Well, kids, I'm taking off. I want to catch the train before it gets too dark." She snatched her purse from the counter and headed for the door.

"Wait a sec. I'll drive you." Rey grabbed her by the wrist, halting her stride.

She slapped his hand. "Thanks, Rey, but don't you worry, kiddo. I can handle myself. I've been living in Myrin City since before you were a glimmer in your father's eye."

"Yeah, Rey, I've never owned a car or had a license. Myrin City has one of the safest public transportation systems in the country," Anthony declared with pride, as if he had something to do with it.

"All right, well, excuse me for trying to carpool!"

"No one wants to sit in your grooming van, dude," Anthony cajoled.

Gloria cackled before blowing them a kiss. They waved goodbye as she put on her coat and left.

"I guess that's my cue then. I'll leave you two lovies to yourselves." Rey shot up and rubbed his stomach.

"That was some good fucking cake, man!" He rolled down the sleeves of his neon shirt and lunged at Anthony.

He wrapped his arms around his neck and put him in a head-lock. "Let's see you get out of this one, bear hunter!"

Anthony answered with a swift punch to his gut, almost causing him to regurgitate.

"Enough said," Rey winced while swallowing his vomit.

"Welcome home, buddy," he managed to squeak.

"Thanks for everything." Anthony gave him a hug.

Rey took one last look back at them before jovially striding down the hall. After he was gone, Sidney strolled to the door. She locked the top lock and faced him.

God, she looks good, he thought.

She tore off her sweatshirt and strutted to him. She undid her bra, and an overwhelming sense of anxiety overcame him as he thought of his sexual failure in the bathroom. He had taken three Oxys and two of Dr. Geani's pills earlier in the day.

Come on, Anthony. You can do this. Just like riding a bike. He was unsure as he watched his girlfriend approach him with lust in her eyes.

Her elegant movements and graceful mannerisms, accompanied by her sensual voice, immediately stimulated him. He felt the blood rush down to his genitals as she gazed at him with desire. She gyrated her athletic frame over him, straddling his lap while giving him a forceful, lust-filled kiss. As Anthony caressed her, he picked her up and tottered to the bedroom. She wrapped her legs around him and he felt no pain as they stumbled to the bed. His erection was not as hard as he would've liked, but he was able to perform. He was just thankful to have finally gotten his rocks off and to be with her again.

Thank God. He was relieved as she rested her head on his sweaty chest. He transitioned his gaze to his leg and was immediately disgusted. The bulging, distorted musculature made him insecure and upset.

I'm fucking disgusting. I don't know what she sees in me, especially now. I guess she really does love me. He wrapped his arms around her, holding her tight until they both fell asleep.

Anthony woke to find that Sidney was gone. She always got up earlier than him. Most nights they stayed at her apartment on the other side of the city, across from the Nicolo River. Her equally modest unit was near her office, where she had just started as a social worker.

He rubbed his blurred eyes and outstretched his arms. After a long, refreshing yawn, he glanced at the clock on his nightstand. Underneath it was the sealed envelope (Mr. Morgan had mailed a hard copy to his residence during his stay in the hospital) containing the Morgan & Green Enterprises agreement. Sidney had propped the pink bear against the base of the clock and draped his aunt's rosary over its neck.

She made a fucking shrine. He smiled as he admired the arrangement she had curated for him.

She had wedged a note between the teddy's arms:

I'll be staying at my place tonight, so if you feel up to it, come over.

PS: My landlord wants to know if I'll be renewing my lease. We need to have a serious discussion about our future.

Have a good day. I love you!

Jeez, she's really putting on the pressure. He felt tense as he tore open the envelope. After thumbing through the terms and conditions, he sighed. *This is all boilerplate stuff.* He knew what to expect from Mr. Morgan because he had drafted similar contracts himself. This was not unchartered territory.

After delving in a few pages, he rolled out of bed and limped to the bathroom, hobbling in pain while grasping his cane. He brushed his teeth and took a long, hot shower.

God, this feels so good! He relished the streams raining down on him as he lathered. It had been a long time since he had taken a shower standing up. His leg throbbed as blood circulated throughout his body. The gripping pain inflamed his calf as he trampled out of the shower. He stared deep into the medicine cabinet mirror, observing his worn reflection. He saw the effects the pills had on him; he looked old and sullen. He sighed before opening the cabinet and dumping three pills into his hand.

"Fuck it." He gulped them down, shoveling water into his mouth from the sink.

He shut off the faucet and put the bottle back inside the cabinet before draping his robe over his shoulders. He flopped on his living room sofa and immediately started to feel the effects of the Oxy. He was happy and uplifted as he reached for the remote and turned on the local news. Coverage consisted of the usual weather forecast and traffic reports, but then a story gripped his attention. A senior news anchor sat at his desk and addressed the camera in a serious tone.

"A deeply upsetting scene taking place at the Sky-Blue Apartments south of Pioneer Bridge. This morning, two homeless men were found literally torn to pieces. Here's Linda Haskins with the latest developments. Linda?"

Holy shit! He was captivated.

The coverage transitioned to a live shot of Linda, donning a bright green suit. She stood in front of a dilapidated building, surrounded by a crowd held back by caution tape.

"Thanks, Henry. Two homeless men, one Caucasian and the other gentleman African American, were found murdered under the Pioneer Bridge, just a few feet away from where I'm standing. They were discovered earlier this morning after a jogger reported the grisly scene to authorities. Police Chief Benjamin Ramsey released this statement."

A picture of the uniformed commander appeared on the screen. He was a tall man with salt-and-pepper hair styled in a crew cut.

"The remains of the victims were dismembered, with most of the trauma caused postmortem, meaning the victims were deceased prior to the mutilation. We have reason to believe that we are dealing with a copycat serial killer of the full moon murders that took place in the eighties. We encourage all residents to stay in groups and report any suspicious behavior to the Myrin City Homicide Unit."The shot quickly transitioned back to Linda.

Great! Another psycho on the loose. Anthony hunched closer to the TV, inebriated with excitement accompanied by a tinge of fear.

"Yes, truly a horrific scene here this morning. As you can see behind me, police and homicide units are searching under the bridge for any possible leads in this case. The names of the deceased have yet to be confirmed. If you have any information related to these murders, please call the Myrin City Police Department at the number appearing on the bottom of your screen. Once again, two homeless men butchered, their remains found scattered under the Pioneer Bridge. This is Linda Haskins, Channel 9 News."

Anthony shut off the TV, making a pistol-recoil motion with the remote. He limped over to his bedroom window and staggered to his telescope. He was excited that he could finally indulge in his voyeurism now that Sidney was gone. Viewing people was a hobby for him. Sidney had always assumed the telescope was for astronomic endeavors.

He was thrilled as he peered into the eyepiece. He viewed the neighboring units, scanning the apartments adjacent to him. One woman in particular had caught his eye. She lived in the crimson-bricked co-op across from him, just one floor above. He focused the lens on the beauty, draped in a sheep-white robe, preparing eggs on her stove top.

Good morning, beautiful. How's my girl doing today? His heart fluttered with exhilaration as he observed the woman with carnal desire.

Her hair was light and curly; she had a healthy, tanned complexion, accompanied by almond-brown eyes. He couldn't help but be infatuated with her, even though his love for Sidney was absolute. After his muse was done cooking, she absconded from his view.

See you next time, hon. His voyeuristic tendencies were satisfied, but his ears started to ring in pain.

He scrambled to the bedroom and snatched Dr. Geani's pills from his tracksuit pocket, which he had thrown on the floor during last night's lustful ravage.

He hurriedly popped open the vial and swallowed a handful of the triangular pills. The buzzing in his ears gradually subsided and was dulled against the overwhelming street noise. Comforted, he laid on his sofa, propping his feet up on the armrest.

There, that's much better. After several minutes he closed his eyes and fell asleep.

His slumber was long and dark. After hours of uninterrupted rest, he awoke and reached for his cell phone atop the glass dinette table in front of him. He checked his home screen; it was midnight.

Damn, those Oxys are stronger than I thought. Never took three before. He rose and extended his arms.

Suddenly, the joints in his elbows and extremities cracked and broke with insufferable agony. Searing pain encapsulated him. He collapsed while tremoring uncontrollably. It felt as if his veins were on fire.

Oh my God! What's happening? I'm having a fucking seizure! Anthony couldn't get up; the pain was insufferable.

He desperately tried to scream, but the harshness coursing through him wouldn't allow him to emit sound. He began to spasm violently, twisting and turning in inhuman ways. The intense torture burned, jolting him off the floor and sending him crashing through the dinette table with a shattering impact. As he writhed in torturous agony atop crushed glass, the uncontrollable tremors became joltingly stronger.

He helplessly laid amid the fragments of thick shards stabbing through his neck. His bones and tendons grew with insufferable anguish. He started to slip out of consciousness while desperately trying to crawl for the bathroom. His despairing attempt to retrieve more Oxys from the medicine cabinet was futile as he was too incapacitated to even move.

He thrashed on the floor like a dying fish for what seemed to be hours, semiconscious and debilitated by an intense radiating sting. Without warning, the overwhelming agony and tremors abruptly stopped. Paralyzed in anguish, Anthony laid over crushed glass, bleeding and helpless as his body metamorphosized into something unhuman. He suddenly felt an overpowering warmth drape over him; it was a comforting embrace amid the intense torment. After his momentary relief, he lost consciousness.

Hours passed before he cracked open his eyes. The world was different. The blackness of the witching hour had no bearing on his sight. He could smell and taste his surroundings past and present. He looked down at his hands to view enlarged furry mitts with elongated talons protruding from his fingertips.

His body was that of a lycanthropic brute, covered in brown fur accented with thin swirls of black fuzz. He felt immense physical power as he stomped to the bathroom. His injured leg had no pain, and his consciousness was that of a ravaging beast, reacting to instincts rather than cognitive thoughts.

As he stalked to the medicine cabinet, he noticed his reflection was that of a canid, with a long protruding snout. He snarled, inquisitively ridging his dark lips to reveal daggering fangs underneath his blood-red gums. His eyes shimmered in the darkened reflection as he studied his new form.

He was now a Lycan, consumed with the desire to hunt, kill, and devour flesh over all else. He raised his clawed hand and plucked the glass shards from his thick neck. Blood rivered over his collar, blemishing his flawless bronze coat. He sneered again, further admiring his hulking physique. His belly rumbled with hunger as he howled a shattering, ill-omened wail from his gullet.

The ungodly holler echoed against the walls of his small bathroom and resonated throughout the building.

Overwhelmed by the lascivious craving to hunt, Anthony turned and jumped out the window. Shattered glass danced around him as he landed on the fire escape with an echoing clang. He crouched low while grasping the iron top rail, allowing his senses to take in the atmosphere of the bitter night.

While he surveyed his snow-white hunting grounds, he twitched his furred ears, scanning the jumbling auditory cluster that emanated from the city beneath him. He swiftly locked in on the gentle sound of ruffling bedsheets. His ear canals detected that the soft crunching noise was coming from the apartment he had viewed earlier with his telescope.

He squatted, using the rail for support before launching himself toward the neighboring building. He crashed onto the fire escape. The wrought stairs trembled as he slammed atop the platform. He clawed his way up to the maiden's ninth-floor window and smashed the glass with the top of his skull. He broke through the shattered opening, scampering into the apartment.

His nostrils stung upon detecting a vulgar odor. His snout guided him through the small apartment, where he discovered a black cat crouched on the floor. The feline's back was arched as it let out a sharp hiss. With one broad step, Anthony snatched the cat in his monstrous forepaw. His prey was paralyzed, trapped within the grasp of his piercing talons. Blood gushed over them as he creaked opened his jaws. The cat's mangy hair brushed his tongue, leaving a nauseating tinge. He brusquely loosened his grip, releasing his catch in revulsion. His wounded prey lay helpless on the living room floor as the aroma of human flesh enticed him.

He salivated while creeping through the slightly ajar bedroom door, nudging it open with his snout. As he entered, the scent of a woman altered into taste, bringing into view the beauty he had viewed earlier with his telescope. She was sound asleep. He could hear her heart slowly beating as the ivory sheets ebbed in conjunction with her breaths. He stealthily snuck closer, hovering his wet snout above her neckline.

He clamped down. The flow of blood was a sweet, euphoric dew that lined his gums. She awoke and desperately struggled. Her attempt to scream was muffled by cascading spouts that sprayed across her headboard.

His helpless victim hysterically scratched and tore at his muzzle. As she desperately squirmed, Anthony violently shook, stunning her. He rose from the bed with the side of her neck clenched within his jaws. His prey flailed aimlessly amid his forceful jerks, desperately attempting to break free. Her efforts were useless. In an instant, her neck snapped, and she went limp. He could hear the fluttering of her heart come to a stop before he released her from his deadly jowls. She dropped to the floor with a hollow thud. He victoriously admired his kill before he crouched down and devoured her.

Tearing and ingesting her flesh appeased his emptiness. He did not pause on any part of her anatomy; her organs were especially delicious to him. He chomped on her tender innards, swallowing the gelatinous chunks of oily entrails with a mouthwatering zeal. He felt a satisfying fullness as the fleshy insides of his kill ran down his throat and into his stomach.

After his hunger was satiated, he turned from his victim's hollowed-out cavity and exultantly stood over the bed, splattered with scarlet-red blood. His gorging was complete, and he was content. Only a gut-torn carcass of the curly haired woman remained. Anthony felt an unadulterated power course through him as his kill's soft tissue stewed in his belly. He licked his lips in satisfaction before turning from his flesh-filled feast.

An overwhelming instinct to flee suddenly arose within him. He departed from the gore-painted bedroom, proceeding across the living room and over to the shattered window. As he climbed onto the fire escape, he glanced back at the paralyzed cat, laying on the floor helplessly watching as he jumped onto the landing.

The callous winds stroked his blood-soaked snout as he scaled to the roof. He wrapped his claws around the parapet and leaned over the edge. As he veered down at the empty snowplowed streets, he could hear a long, ominous howl in the distance. The shattering cry disrupted the calm night. He instinctually responded with an equally long wail.

The resounding howls rolled over the thoroughfares as powdery flurries tinted the midnight skyline. He peered through the snowfall and could distinguish a dark figure in the distance, leaping from the adjoining rooftops. Anthony watched as the looming creature hurdled toward him. The beast's form was that of a Lycan, similar in shape to him. The large, shadowy figure landed on the rooftop and came into view.

The villainous brute stepped down from the parapet, and the two colossal beasts glared at each other with a soul-piercing ferocity. The warring Lycans' snouts flickered in the icy wind as they circled each other, only an arm's length between them.

As they postured, Anthony smelled a distinct odor emanating from the dark-haired beast. It was a wet, earthy scent. The opposing Lycan reached down. Anthony watched with tense aggression as the brute broke off a cinder block from the parapet and swiftly hurled the brick at him. He had no time to react. The projectile somersaulted and cracked over his head, crumbling into bits as it struck his wolf-like skull. The brick's smashing impact fractured his eye socket, knocking him back. Disoriented, he stumbled over the roof's ledge and flipped over the side.

As he rapidly fell, gusty winds ripped through his fur-covered body. He crashed onto the snowy boulevard with a thunderous, earth-shattering bang. As he lay stunned on the cold pavement, he looked up to see the creature looming over the roof's ledge. It raised its snout and let out a victorious howl. The dark-haired Lycan wailed in victory as it leapt between the neighboring rooftops, disappearing into the night.

Anthony lay paralyzed on the street. His body was broken. Blood flooded his muzzle and rolled over his gums, streaming into a nearby drain. He helplessly viewed the ruddy flow leaking from his jaws as it trickled into the murky inlet. His body turned cold when he noticed a pair of menacing red eyes appear from deep within the cavernous gutter. Moments after, he passed out.

Faint light gently crept in through Anthony's tightly closed eyelids. He slowly opened his left eye to find himself back in his bed, naked. Confusion over the previous night's ordeal sent his thoughts into a spiral.

Thank God, just a bad dream.

He sat up and felt as if his entire body had been pumped with a euphoric invincibility. His physical vigor was accompanied by an acute mental clarity. The thoughts and sounds that had once clouded his senses were now fine-tuned and concentrated.

He sprung from his bed and looked out his window to see flashing blue and red lights. Police cars had blocked off the street with flapping caution tape. He came to the horrid realization that the previous night's endeavors had not been a dream. He perspired with fear as he examined the commotion below through his telescope. His heart raced in a panic, when he unexpectedly heard a three-tap knock at his door. He scampered across the living room, frightened.

Holy shit, I'm walking with no pain! His flustered state was briefly met with joy as his leg was no longer debilitated with soreness. He looked down and noticed that the scars on his misshapen calf had completely healed.

He grabbed his robe and brushed off the broken glass from the shattered dinette table. He noticed fluffy brown fur sheddings scattered about his living room as he tied his robe and rushed to the door. Fear and anxiety overtook him as he peered through the peephole.

THE
PUREBLOODS

Anthony cautiously peered through the peephole to see a bald man in his late fifties wearing a black suit with a red tie draped in a dark leather trench coat. His face was tan, and he had olive-green eyes.

What the fuck is going on! He's a cop! Fuck! He was uneasy; his heart was pounding as the terrifying notion of going to jail entered his mind.

"Mr. Montgomery, I suggest you open the door. We haven't much time." The man spoke sternly with an English accent while glaring at his wrist, which bore a gold Rolex watch accompanied by a silver wolf's-head ring on his index finger.

How does he know my name? His mind was racing as he pondered whether to let him in.

After observing the mysterious Englishman for a few moments, he reluctantly decided to open the door.

He's definitely not a cop with a ring and watch like that. "Can I help you?" Anthony shakingly asked while standing in his doorway, doing his best to act natural.

"My name is Mr. Shepard," the man revealed.

Anthony extended his clammy palm, riddled with sweat, and they shook.

"Mr. Montgomery, I was sent here by Mr. Morgan. Please clean yourself up and get dressed. We have to get moving," he calmly ordered as he entered, closing the door behind him.

Anthony peered at his waist; dried streams of blood were splattered over his midsection and chest.

Fuck, I'm screwed! Mr. Morgan sent this guy. What choice do I have? Either go with him or deal with the police. This seems like a trap, but what choice do I have? Fuck! He stared at his uninvited guest uncertain of his intentions.

"And I strongly encourage you to do so expeditiously. The authorities outside will be coming for you shortly, and it would be best if we were elsewhere," he instructed while surveying the modest apartment.

Upon the Englishman's directives, Anthony hastily ran to his bathroom and jumped in the shower. He feverishly scrubbed as best he could. Trickles of stale blood flowed off him and oozed down the drain as he lathered. He quickly dried off with a damp towel before racing to his closet, where he impulsively threw on a white button-down shirt and blue jeans, accompanied by a gray sport coat.

As he threw the wrinkled blazer over himself, he grabbed his cell phone and keys from the nightstand. Anthony was so frantic that he didn't even realize he was doing all this with no pain and without his cane. He slipped his arms through his coat while noticing his mysterious guest's mannerisms.

Why is he so calm? He was taken aback by his even demeanor as he slipped on his sneakers.

Mr. Shepard steadily adjusted his blood-red tie as Anthony tramped over the shattered glass from the broken table, delicately stepping to the door. He swiftly grabbed his pea coat off the hanger, and they both departed. Mr. Shepard slammed the door behind them as Anthony jumbled his keys and shakily locked the door. They both jogged across the hall, bypassing the elevators and continuing through the stairwell.

They bolted down the stairs and came to the ground-level exit. Anthony thought about how he could possibly explain this to his loved ones as they filed into the alleyway behind his building. He raced past Mr. Shepard. The brisk morning wind ran through him as he rushed ahead. He secured his coat tightly around his chest, shielding him from the penetrating windchill.

Holy shit! I'm running! His angst-driven sprint was briefly interrupted by joy as he came to the realization that his leg was fully healed.

Mr. Shepard lagged behind, out of breath. They both hurried down the alley to the intersection, where a black Lincoln Town Car was waiting.

"That's our car!" Mr. Shepard huffed while pointing.

They both jumped into the back seat. Anthony saw the driver's reflection in the dashboard mirror as the car slowly pulled out from the alleyway. He was shocked. It was Ramona. The burly, square-shouldered woman looked back at him with a smile. She was wearing a black suit, indicative of a chauffeur.

"Ramona! What the fuck are you doing here?" He was relieved but also worried.

"All will be explained, my darling. Don't worry." She turned the wheel, and Anthony spotted that she, too, was wearing a silver wolf's-head ring on her index finger.

This whole situation is fucked! His world was turned upside down. *You've really gone and done it this time!* The fact that he had shape-shifted into a Lycan and murdered a woman last night seemed to be the least of his concerns. He felt safe with Ramona though; he was happy to see her again, even if the circumstances were less than ideal. Anthony didn't fully trust Mr. Shepard, and because of that, he remained quiet.

As the Town Car ventured past his building, Anthony fearfully ducked while they slowly drove past the crime scene. He peeked from his scowling posture to view a roped-off boundary of caution tape, accented by dancing red and blue lights. Mr. Shepard laughed, sitting beside him while boldly glaring out the window. "Don't worry, the tints are too dark for anyone to see."

"Where are we going?" Anthony asked with his heart racing.

He was inundated with thoughts of the previous night's slaying, the repercussions of his murderous actions swirling in his mind as Mr. Shepard studied him.

"I suggest you let me talk. We haven't much time. Mr. Morgan feels that you are of great importance to the success of his firm's future, or else he would not have sent me here to remedy your current predicament. But to answer your question, we are going to see Dr. Geani," he asserted as Anthony gazed back at the roped-off murder scene.

Why are we going to see the doctor? You'll never be able to get out of this one on your own. Better listen to what he has to say. Just stay calm and listen. Don't worry. Mr. Morgan sent him. MGE takes care of its own. He was doing his best to convince himself that everything was going to be okay.

They accelerated across the bustling crime scene, and Anthony watched as the detectives carefully examined the street corner for evidence. Peering out from behind the concealment of the tinted window, he was confused and fearful at what lay ahead. Police cars and barricades were redirecting traffic as Ramona sped away. He leered back with apprehension, noticing two homicide detectives enter his building.

We got out of there just in time. He was grateful that, at least for the time being, he wasn't going to jail.

He inquisitively leaned forward and examined himself in the dashboard mirror, discovering a large bruise on his forehead. Ramona nodded with a sympathetic glare, acknowledging his battered reflection.

What the hell was that beast that hit me with the brick? What the hell am I, for that matter? This is fucked! The reality of his situation had started to sink in. His anxieties grew into unfathomable worry. *God, I wish I had some Oxys right now.* He just wanted all this to be over, to go back to his normal life, the way things were before he had transformed into a Lycan.

"Mr. Montgomery, what happened last night was no delusion. You have been blessed to have evolved into something much greater and more ancient than any type of being on this planet. As such, you must follow the rules and govern yourself accordingly. Unfortunately, you failed to accomplish this during last night's rampage. However, your ignorance to the Purebloods' code of conduct may have salvaged your life."

What the fuck is a Pureblood? He was overwhelmed and confused.

Mr. Shepard reached between his legs and produced a leather suitcase; he opened it and handed him a contract.

"Mr. Montgomery, it behooves you to sign this for your own protection."

"I already have an operating agreement. Mr. Morgan gave it to me when I got out of the hospital," he corrected.

"This is not the same contract. This agreement will supersede that one," Mr. Shepard retorted with a blunt smirk.

"What the fuck is going on here?!" Anthony shouted with coursing, fiery rage. His heart pounded with a hummingbird-like flurry as his anxieties started to take hold of him.

God, I need an Oxy right now! Although his pain was gone, he longed for his pills, especially in the middle of all this chaos.

Mr. Shepard calmly placed the document, along with a black-tipped pen, on his lap and addressed him with a stern tone.

"Make no mistake, you are a murderer. You brutally mauled an innocent woman last night for your own lascivious desires. You are in direct violation of the laws by which the Pureblood pack governs themselves. I'm afraid if you do not sign this contract, I cannot help you in resolving your current predicament. You will be left to fend for yourself as a lone wolf. Best of luck to you, sir."

Mr. Shepard snatched the document along with his pen and signaled for Ramona to pull over. The car slowed.

Anthony knew that he had to sign. His hand was being forced. There was no way Mr. Shepard would give him enough time to read through the extensive pages. Besides, he was right. He was a murderer. They had him dead to rights.

Fuck it. It's either sign or go to jail. I need MGE's protection right now. Anthony felt no remorse for his actions; he only cared for his own self-preservation.

The car gradually came to a stop alongside the pedestrian-riddled sidewalk.

"Wait, goddamn it! I'll sign the damn thing. Give it here!" he commanded in frustration.

His head began to throb. He rubbed his bruised forehead in an attempt to relieve some of the pounding. Mr. Shepard delicately handed the document back to him as if handling an ancient parchment while the Town Car journeyed for the hospital. Anthony sprawled the document over his knee and begrudgingly grabbed the pen from him.

Fuck it! What do I have to lose? Only everything. He abruptly turned to the last page of the agreement and signed without reading. He knew he had no other choice; contesting anything would only lead him to jail, or worse. He needed MGE's protection, or so he thought.

He was disgruntled as he handed the executed contract back to Mr. Shepard, who responded with a satisfactory sneer.

"Very well, Mr. Montgomery. You will not regret your decision,

I assure you." He beamed with confidence after tucking his pen inside his coat pocket.

The tanned Englishman delicately slid the document back inside the suitcase, tucking it under his seat. They remained silent for the remainder of their trip. Once they reached their destination, Mr. Shepard glared at him with a stern, penetrating look.

"Didn't think we'd be back here so soon, huh, Ramona?" Anthony noted with a nervous cadence, attempting to lighten the tense mood.

He glanced in the dashboard mirror to see her wink back at him. Anthony assumed her reserved mannerisms were due to the presence of Mr. Shepard. He didn't know who the players were in all this madness, but he realized that a lot of people deemed him valuable enough to protect him, despite him being a murderer. He and Mr. Shepard exited the vehicle and climbed the snow-covered steps. They entered the hospital and zig zagged down the clinic's corridors into the west wing. As they trekked, they passed an under-construction entrance with a large sign hanging above the remodeling site. It read, "Funded by MGE. Building the future."

Amid the commotion of clamoring workers and hospital patrons stood a blank door, the signage not yet completed. Mr. Shepard proceeded through the unmarked doorway into Dr. Geani's private office. Anthony observed the waiting room's decor, made up of bronze chairs and leather sofas. He and Mr. Shepard hung their coats and sat across from each other in awkward silence, anxiously awaiting Geani's arrival.

"What kind of doctor is this guy, anyway? Some kind of witch doctor or something?" Anthony broke the uncomfortable silence.

Mr. Shepard tapped his wolf's-head ring on his knee before snickering.

"Humor must serve you well in times like these. I implore you to be patient. Dr. Geani is the best in his field. I'm sure he will be with us shortly. But to answer your question, he is an expert in lycanthropic studies." He paused, studying Anthony's confused reaction to his revelation.

"Mr. Montgomery, Dr. Geani and I are part of a secret society, known as the Keepers of the Bloodline."

"So, you guys are Lycans too?" he sharply questioned.

"No, we are human. We're direct descendants of the Knights Templar, tasked with keeping the Lycan bloodlines genetically pure. In exchange for our servitude, we are granted extended life by drinking the blood of Lycans. Thanks to Dr. Geani's groundbreaking studies, we've been able to keep their lineages genetically pure for over two hundred years."

"Well, congratulations!" Anthony shrugged, more confused than ever.

After his flippant response, the door flung open, and the doctor approached holding a clipboard, donning his lab coat. Mr. Shepard and Anthony stood to greet him.

"Follow me, gentlemen." He adjusted his bifocals and led them down a partially painted hallway.

They followed him to his office, cluttered with various degrees and awards sprawled along the walls. Mr. Shepard and Anthony sat on the leather chairs across from his desk as Dr. Geani swiveled in his chair, inching up to his computer.

"Well, Mr. Montgomery, I hear you had quite the endeavor last night." He turned from his monitor and removed his glasses, leaning toward him to get a closer look at the pronounced bump on his forehead.

"How did that bruise occur?" he inquisitively inspected, looming over his desk.

Anthony rubbed his brow timidly. "I got hit with a cinder block and fell off a roof."

"Astonishing!" Dr. Geani exclaimed while examining him. "Mr. Montgomery, can you show me your shoulder?"

Anthony unbuttoned his shirt and propped his shoulder out through his wrinkled blazer.

"Remarkable!" The scarring from his stitches had completely healed, with no evidence of any blemishes.

"Your regeneration process is unparalleled compared to any of my other patients. Your blood samples reveal a unique hybridized quality I have never seen."

Anthony turned to Mr. Shepard, bewildered. The Englishman looked down at his Rolex before slowly nodding in the doctor's direction, encouraging him to carry on. Anthony tucked his shoulder back under his sport coat and buttoned his shirt in disbelief.

"Please, Doctor, continue." Mr. Shepard tapped his wolf's-head ring on his knee.

"Well, your symptoms are indicative of what I like to call the lunar effect condition, in which the magnetism of a full moon creates a tidal force on the earth, similar to what you see in the ocean, whereby the moon can affect the tides and in turn can affect your brain wave patterns. But in your case, your physical form as well. Many scholars use the term *lycanthropy*, or 'shape-shifting.' Extremely elementary. The fact is you have the ability to slow your cellular degeneration by consuming flesh. Your head wound, for example. In any other case, you would have been in a coma or dead. However, because you consumed flesh, your cells have created reproductive antimicrobial chondriosomes, which enabled you to heal at an expeditious rate. I mean, look, you're walking without a cane only a day or so after being discharged."

So, I'm just some fucking lab rat for these assholes to experiment on. He sat awestruck as the doctor continued with his prognosis.

"In other words, for you to sustain your new metamorphic abilities, you must consume flesh. Otherwise, your body will metabolize itself. I would like to draw some more blood if that's okay," he requested.

Of course you would. Anthony was dumbfounded and had second thoughts about letting the doctor take his blood.

"You don't need consent, Doctor. Mr. Montgomery has signed a revised board member contract. He has an appointment with Mr. Morgan after we are done here. So please make it fast, as I do not like to keep him waiting."

"Absolutely. Anthony, if you don't mind, please help yourself to one of the examination rooms just outside my office, and a nurse will be in shortly."

So much for 'my body, my choice'! I shouldn't have signed that fucking contract, but what choice did I have? He was upset and confused; everything was happening so fast, a whirlwind of emotions raged through him, but he knew arguing would not get him anywhere, so he conceded and marched down the half-painted hallway.

"I'll be waiting for you outside, Mr. Montgomery. Please do not waste any time!" Mr. Shepard yelled, just before he entered the examination room. He gave the pensive Englishman a sarcastic thumbs-up and shut the door.

Back inside the Town Car, Anthony rolled up his sleeve to reveal a Garfield Band-Aid where the nurse had drawn blood. He smirked at Mr. Shepard as they ventured off, plowing over the snow-covered streets for the Financial District.

Ramona careened across the bustling metropolis and came to a stop. They had arrived. Anthony viewed the gigantic bronze-and-silver tower standing sixty-six stories high.

The Morgan & Green Enterprise building was a staple in Myrin City. With expansive floor-to-ceiling windows, the tower was an homage to the business boom of the early 1980s. The shimmering structure was an old building, simple in style, with subtle ornamental features. Positioned beside the rooftop's circular helipad was an imposing antenna, making the structure a recognizable landmark among the Financial District's looming cityscape. Anthony opened the door, looked back over his shoulder, and asked, "Are you coming?"

"I'm afraid not. This is where I leave you. My services are needed elsewhere at the moment. Mr. Morgan is expecting you. Good luck," Mr. Shepard informed before slamming the door.

Anthony watched as the Town Car's tires sputtered flurries onto nearby pedestrians as it skirted off. He marched through the gilded turnstile, past the uniformed security guard, and into the sea of people migrating across the atrium. As he weaved through the crowd, he felt someone grip his shoulder. He immediately recognized the scent; it was Ben Damien. He turned and confirmed what his senses had already detected.

"Come with me," Ben commanded as he adjusted his dark suit while condescendingly gazing down at Anthony's blue jeans and sneakers.

They both paraded past the concierge desk to the board members' private elevator on the east side of the white-stoned foyer. Ben stuck his hand under a palm reader positioned on the side of the metallic lift. A green indicator light on the scanner illuminated, and the shiny doors spread open. They entered and Ben pressed the PH button. As they ascended, Ben casually leaned his tall frame against the handrail and asked, "Well, Anthony, how does it feel to be a delta?"

"What the hell are you talking about?" he replied with angst.

"Ha!" Ben cackled as the doors opened to reveal Mr. Morgan's penthouse office.

The expansive chamber had mahogany hardwood floors leading to his grandiose desk. The white-bearded mogul sat at his throne, which stood atop a three-step platform. Positioned behind him were massive floor-to-ceiling windows, which provided a mesmerizing view of the entire city. It was an awe-inspiring vantage point. Located in the center of the space was a seating area adorned with leather couches and armchairs that were divided by a circular glass table. The stuffed heads of taxidermied animals were sprawled along the walls. Deer, elk, buffalo, and even a lion lifelessly glared down at them as they marched. A towering grizzly bear hovered next to a blazing fireplace near the seating area.

Mr. Morgan tugged on his dark-brown suit as he leaned back in his chair. They noticed Police Chief Benjamin Ramsey seated across from him, donning his uniform and white captain's hat. As they approached, he stood and took off his cap, exposing his salt-and-pepper crew cut.

"Hello, gentlemen... Remember, Ben, tonight there will be a seven o'clock citywide curfew." His voice was low and baritone; Anthony recognized him from the evening news.

"Yes, Chief. This is our newest board member, Anthony

Montgomery," he announced.

"Pleasure, Mr. Montgomery." He quickly shook their hands before heading to the elevator.

"Thank you, Chief. Our city is in good hands with you at the helm." Mr. Morgan waved.

Chief Ramsey saluted from inside the cab before the doors closed. Mr. Morgan sat pensively at his desk and grabbed a cigar from a glass-topped humidor.

"So, I'm sure you have plenty of questions, Montgomery." He proceeded to clip the end of his stogie and light it, sending grand puffs into the atmosphere.

"W-w-well…" Anthony timidly stuttered while surveying the imposing office space, mesmerized by the slain animals' hollow stares.

"Killed every last one of those critters with my bare claws. Hunting with a rifle is so primitive." Mr. Morgan defiantly scoffed.

So he's a Lycan too. I guess this is my pack then. Better than being a lone wolf or going to jail, I suppose, he reasoned with unsureness.

"Why don't we all take a seat?" Ben interjected.

He tramped to the seating area, making himself comfortable atop the sofa. He unbuttoned his jacket, allowing the warm, crackling fire to heat his chilled frame. He crossed his legs and stared at the stuffed grizzly bear ominously towering over him.

"Why don't you have a seat, son?" Mr. Morgan commanded as he lumbered to his chair, holding his lit cigar.

Upon his command, Anthony sat next to Ben. His boss blew billowing puffs of smoke while examining them.

"You are a delta Pureblood, Montgomery. Delta is your rank within our pack, and Pureblood is our pack affiliation. We are descendants of an ancient lycanthropic bloodline that reproduces by transdermal exchange of fluids—i.e., a bite."

I guess all that was in the contract. Anthony was shocked as he realized he was being indoctrinated into the Pureblood pack.

Mr. Morgan took another puff and leered at Ben for confirmation.

"Welcome to our pack!" He gave Anthony a warmhearted jolt,

squeezing his shoulder.

"So, you guys are, like, werewolves too?" He was stunned.

"Sort of. I think of *Teen Wolf* or something like that when I hear the term *werewolf*." Ben stalked over to the rear bar and asked, "Sir, may I partake?"

He eagerly pointed to the rows of illuminated liquor bottles stacked behind the granite serving station. Mr. Morgan nodded in approval. As he tended to his cocktail, their alpha addressed Anthony.

"I'll give you the abridged version, son. Legend has it that all lycanthropic packs are descendants of the Neuri tribe, an ancient nomadic race who partook in Gypsy magic and who could shape-shift into wolf-like creatures during a full moon. As time went on, the gene pool split, and there became two rival packs. Those that could continue their bloodline by sexual reproduction, known as Half-Breeds, and those that could reproduce their bloodline with a bite, known as Purebloods."

Anthony couldn't believe what he was hearing. *This is crazy. Just go with it. Listen and observe. Say nothing until you figure things out.* He was restless and did his best to hide his fears. "Better make me one of those as well, Ben!" he nervously shouted while keenly eyeing the stacked bottles.

"Sure thing, Delta," he replied with a sheepish grin.

"Fix one for me too, Beta. Scotch, no ice," Mr. Morgan bellowed as he rested his cigar on top of a marble ashtray.

"As I was saying. The Half-Breeds are foul beasts that mate with human women. Once impregnated, the women merely become a host for the abominations growing inside them. Not quite human, not quite wolf. All the women who bear Half-Breed offspring die during childbirth. This is why they have to be stopped and our pack must defend our city from these deplorable beasts!"

Yeah, I saw one of them last night. Would've been nice to know all this before I changed into a Lycan! He was upset at the lack of knowledge he had concerning his condition. He felt as if they were hiding something from him, but he couldn't figure out why. He took everything that was said to him as a half-truth.

Ben approached clutching a tray with three half-filled tumblers of whiskey. They took their drinks. Anthony clenched his libation with a shaky hand as Ben laid the tray on the table. They stood for a toast.

"To our newest delta, and to the end of the Half-Breed scourge plaguing our city!" They chimed their glasses.

Mr. Morgan grinned after his proclamation and took a long sip. Anthony peered into his boss' bloodshot eyes before drinking.

Here's to the Purebloods—my new pack, I guess. He knew he had to accept their narrative in order to survive; besides, he had signed a contract.

He made a slight hiss as the liquor tinged his esophagus. After their toast, Anthony removed his coat before retaking his seat.

"That's some good scotch, kid!" exclaimed Ben, noticing Anthony's eyes inflamed with inebriation.

"Now, gentlemen, there's a legend of a hybrid Lycan, which is said to have both sexual and transdermal reproductive abilities."

There's that word again: hybrid. *That's what Dr. Geani and him were talking about in the hallway.* He took another sip and intently listened, trying to discern exactly what all this was about.

"But a hybrid has not walked the earth in over a thousand years. Their bloodline was wiped out long ago."

"Yeah, like the Ultima Lycans. Never seen one of those either!" Ben asserted.

"What's an Ultima?" Anthony delved, hoping for some clarification.

"Ultima Lycans are rumored to be able to shape-shift at will with no pain. But no such pack has ever been documented. It's an urban legend."

Anthony came to realization that all this talk of packs was centered around him somehow.

"I say the only way we will have peace is once the Half-Breeds are exterminated!" Mr. Morgan slammed his drink on the table with a vibrating clang.

Ben's eyes were ablaze with intoxication as he spoke. "So, we as

Purebloods have a few laws by which we govern ourselves. We don't kill women or children. Which you are in direct violation of, given your escapades last night."

Shit! I'm going to jail! Anthony was flushed with fear; his instinct was to run, and it took everything he had just to remain seated. His nerves were starting to take hold of him.

Ben observed his rattled mannerism as he took another gulp. To which Mr. Morgan assuredly retorted, "Yes, Ben, that's right. We don't bite women or children, but don't worry, son. It's not your fault. I should've had this talk with you before you turned. Dr. Geani didn't expect you to begin your transition until the next full moon. But what's done is done, and we have to move on. No use in crying over spilt blood." He plucked his cigar from the ashtray and took another puff.

Anthony was overwhelmed and relieved; he felt protected, somewhat.

"So, as a Pureblood, you cannot bite someone unless that individual is approved by myself and Mr. Morgan. Only men can join our ranks. Violation of this law is punishable by decapitation. So don't bite anyone unless they are sanctioned by us. This is our way. These are our rules, and this is how we keep our bloodline pure," Ben concluded.

Say whatever they want to hear. They're the only ones keeping you out of jail right now. He knew he had to play along. "Don't bite anyone without your approval. Got it," Anthony concurred before taking another swig. "Yes, thank you, Ben. And as for hunting and killing, the same rules apply. No women or children, and all killings must be sanctioned by us."

"So, who bit me then, sir?" he probed.

"We, uh, don't disclose who bites who. It's confidential, for safety purposes. But I assure you, you're a Pureblood," Mr. Morgan stammered.

They're lying. He could sense the uneasiness and deceit in his alpha's tone but decided not to protest.

He looked at Ben, hoping for some assurance that this was all a hoax, but he sat stone-faced, sipping his cocktail.

"You will also live fifteen times longer than any of your human counterparts. You will outlive any of your loved ones—that is, if you manage to not get yourself killed!" Mr. Morgan sneered.

"However, you can only have this longevity if you hunt and consume flesh. We don't hunt humans unless resources are scarce. Only in times of lean game do we sanction humans as prey. We must have balance and order within our ranks. Therefore, we hunt the Half-Breeds. This discipline allows us to grow strong while their numbers decline."

They leaned back, scrutinizing Anthony's reaction.

"So what about silver bullets?" he drunkenly asked.

"We'll get to that," Ben dismissed.

"Yes." Mr. Morgan relit his cigar before persisting. "We'll get to that later. But regarding the Half-Breeds, they kill at will whenever they turn. The full moon murders of the 1980s and the recent killings that have been ravaging our city are their doing. They are a chaotic, ravenous plague that preys on our city's most vulnerable. You can detect a Half-Breed from their foul, earthy scent."

So that's what that smell was. Anthony realized that the intonation of his superiors was more like a call to arms than an indoctrination.

"The Half-Breeds smell like wet dogs in the summer heat. They outnumber us, and their numbers are growing. Their young are starting to become of turning age." Ben rested his drink on a coaster along the table's edge.

"Never mind that now, Ben!" Mr. Morgan sternly interjected as he puffed more clouds from his stogie.

He glared at Anthony through the thick smog. "You asked about silver. Well, if silver enters your bloodstream while you're a Lycan, it will turn you back into a human. Conversely, if you come in contact with silver while you're in your human form, it will burn you. That being said, any bullet can kill you. Just because you're in Lycan form doesn't mean you're bulletproof," he confidently explained. "A shot to the heart is still a shot to the heart, Lycan or not!"

"Silver or no silver," Ben added.

"Yes, Mr. Damien is correct. However, your regenerative abilities will allow you to recover from most wounds. As you've experienced recently. So, you will most likely be able to recover from bullet wounds as long as you consume flesh."

"But if a large enough slug should enter your hide or damage your organs, there is no coming back from that," Ben concluded.

"I think I understand." Anthony laid into the soft confines of the sofa and placed his drink on the coaster in front of him. He felt the jubilant warmth of inebriation course through him as he pondered. *I need to find out who bit me. It wasn't Ben or Mr. Morgan because they were inside the cabin.* He knew if he could figure out who bit him, he would find the answers he needed.

"Good. Well, let's not burden you with too much too soon. Ben, show Mr. Montgomery to his new office and get him situated. I'll see you both later, at this afternoon's board meeting."

Upon his instruction, Ben stood and finished his drink, as did Anthony.

"Oh, and son?" Mr. Morgan called as they headed for the elevator.

"Yes, sir?" Anthony turned to face him.

"Don't ever wear jeans or sneakers to work. It's not befitting of our pack. You're a board member now," he scolded before downing the remainder of his whiskey.

"Agreed," Ben concluded, while Anthony grabbed his coat from the armrest and embarrassingly gawked at his jeans.

They spryly treaded to the elevator and the doors suddenly opened. Standing stoically inside the cab was Luna, wearing a charcoal suit with slacks and red high heels. Her presence was enchanting. She strutted for Mr. Morgan while clutching a stack of folders tucked under her arm. Her red locks swayed wildly as her heels clacked with a pensive melodic rhythm.

"Glad to see you're doing well, Anthony. The last time I saw you, you were bleeding and covered in snow." Her russet eyes penetrated his.

Her lavender, crude scent wafted his nose hairs as she strolled past him.

"Thanks for saving me." He reached out and grabbed her wrist, briefly halting her stride.

"It was my pleasure." She cracked a half-smile and leered at Ben as he withdrew his hand.

"Luna," Ben acknowledged.

"Ben," she coyly responded before taking a seat across from Mr. Morgan.

"Well, gentlemen, it seems like I missed quite the party," she announced while admiring the empty tumblers scattered about the table.

"Indeed you did, my dear." Mr. Morgan dismissingly waved as they entered the elevator.

Just as the doors closed, Luna stared back at Anthony with a lustful gaze.

"That was some pretty good whiskey, huh?" Ben asked as he pushed the fifty-fifth-floor button.

"Yeah, I definitely needed that… So, Ben, how old are you?" He leaned against the handrail; his drunkenness fueled his curiosity.

"In human years or dog years?" Ben jokingly shrugged.

"Very funny."

"After you." The doors abruptly opened, and Ben stuck out his arm to allow Anthony passage in front of him.

They paraded across the endless rows of flimsy cubicles. Encased inside the cross-stitched workspaces were the firm's over-worked employees. The entrapped minions were either soullessly glaring at their computers or on their phones. Anthony couldn't help but think of his time working by the mail room as he snaked through the sea of partitions. He felt pity for his fellow employees, for he knew what it was like to glower at a screen for hours on end inside a plastic box. As they marched past the workspace floor, they came to the foyer. Suddenly, Brandon hopped out from behind the tall concierge desk, halting their stride.

"Good morning, Mr. Damien, Mr. Montgomery. Nice jeans, Mr. Montgomery!" Brandon spoke fast and wore an oversized coffee-brown suit, accompanied by an avocado tie.

He eagerly clutched a stack of folders containing a litany of extensive contracts. Ben let out an annoyed sigh before addressing him.

"Hmmm, good morning, Omega." He pulled away and winked

at the blonde receptionist seated behind her desk.

"Good morning, Brandon," Anthony greeted, turning sideways to allow him passage between them.

"I was just going to show Mr. Montgomery to his new office." Ben placed his hands on his waist, revealing a shiny Ferragamo belt buckle.

The secretary blushed as she observed the interaction between the pack leaders.

"Perfect! These contracts are for your review and approval, Mr. Montgomery," Brandon exclaimed while eagerly patting the folders.

"C'mon, Delta. I can show you the way!" He enthusiastically raced ahead and turned at the end of the hall.

They followed Brandon down the side windowed corridor. He waited for them in front of a rosewood door with a Greek delta symbol embossed in fresh gold leaf.

"After you, sir." Brandon fervently swung open the door to reveal a 1980s-style office with wood-paneled walls and floor-to-ceiling windows.

A magnificent view of Myrin City served as the backdrop behind a baroque desk. To the right of the doorway sat a banquette booth with hoary stitched cushions.

"Well, what do you think?" Ben slithered onto the couch as Brandon dropped the documents on his desk.

"It's definitely retro, but I like it." Anthony removed his coat and hung the weatherworn garment on the hanger next to the door.

He paced past Ben and took a seat behind his desk.

"This is nice! Better than my old cubicle in front of the mail room." He was overcome with joy; finally being recognized for his work gave him a sense of accomplishment.

"It suits you, Mr. Montgomery. Your new Notebook is in the drawer," Brandon informed him while stepping back.

He opened the cabinet to reveal a brand-new laptop. He unfolded it before positioning the computer on his desk.

"Will you gentlemen be needing anything else?" Brandon queried.

"No, I think we're good. thanks," Anthony acknowledged while swiveling in his chair.

"Very well then." Brandon stood midway between the half-closed door. He leaned in and asked, "Sir, what's it like? You know...changing?"

"Painful, in more ways than one," he informed.

"That'll be all, Omega!" Ben glared at him with a vehement stare.

The unnerved underling shook with fear before swiftly closing the door, leaving the higher-ranking pack leaders to themselves. Ben adjusted his tall frame atop the manila booth and starkly addressed him. "My suggestion, Delta, is that you cut off any ties with your peers and lovers. It's very difficult to explain to humans why you don't age. You'd be sparing yourself a lot of hardship and pain. Lord knows we will have plenty of that in our extended lifetime... Oh, I almost forgot. Open your drawer," he excitedly directed while inching himself to the edge of booth.

Anthony cautiously pulled open the cabinet to discover a silver-wrapped box. He placed it atop his desk, glaring at it, wondering what could possibly be inside.

"Well, that thing isn't going to open itself, Delta!" Ben anxiously hollered with an encouraging smile.

As he tore through the wrapping, a green Rolex box revealed itself underneath. He excitedly opened the case to view a white-gold watch. Next to the extravagant timepiece was a small handwritten note that read:

Welcome to our pack, Delta.

F. Morgan & S. Green

He slipped the shimmering gift over his wrist, clasping the crowned latch.

"It suits you, Delta," Ben complimented.

Wow, I can't believe this. You're in the big leagues now! He was enthralled.

"Well, I'll let you get to it then. I see you have a lot of contracts to review. Mergers, acquisitions, and whatnot."

Ben stood and buttoned his suit.

"Think about what I said, Delta—you know, cutting off

relationships. Things can get pretty messy, trust me. I've been there."

Anthony turned from admiring his watch and called out to him as he exited. "Ben."

"Yes?" He ran his hand through his slick black hair while leaning in through the doorway.

"Don't ever tell me what to do in regard to my personal life," he snarled with rage.

"Okay…sorry! I'm just trying to help. I'll come get you before the board meeting in a few hours." He retracted and slammed the door.

Anthony took time to admire the view behind him. He observed the hustle of cars slogging along in conjunction with the flocks of ant-sized people.

Clueless sheep, he thought. *Ready for the slaughter.* He licked his lips while contemplating, then adjusted the knob on his gleaming Rolex.

From his vantage point, he could see the entire city. South of the bustling Financial District was the expansive Nicolo River, frozen under the sprawling, red-ironed Pioneer Bridge. The oblivious populaces twirled about the expansive tributary, ice-skating in their colorful winter coats, unphased by the killings that had taken place near there just a few hours ago. A stark contrast to Tenderloin Point's decaying tenement buildings farther south. Just beyond the decrepit housing complexes was Myrin City's port, comprised of warehouses and boat slips. West of the dock was the Midcity Entertainment District, adorned with neon signs.

His cell phone chimed with an interrupting ring. He turned from his awe-inspiring view and reached into his pocket, pulling out his phone to see Sid's selfie.

"Hi, babe," he answered.

"How's it going?" she asked.

"I'm not sure. These past few weeks have been a whirlwind, to say the least. My new office is nice. You should see this view. I can see your apartment from here," he described while scanning the snowcapped cityscape.

"Wow, that's great, baby. You're already back at work! I heard there was a murder last night near your place. I was worried about you when I didn't hear from you this morning."

"I'm fine, Sid. Sorry, I forgot to call… I had a, uh, really busy morning." He did his best to sound normal while nervously pacing.

He pondered Ben's relationship suggestion; his conversations with her had become mundane and tiresome, but he loved her and wanted her in his life. He just didn't want her to get hurt.

"It's okay. I'm surprised you went back to work so soon though. I thought you were going to take some time off." Her voice altered to a more serious intonation.

"Well, Sid, I was feeling a lot better this morning, and they needed me to come in, so I couldn't say no," he anxiously lied.

"That's great, babe. I'm so proud of you for stepping up." Her response was coy and flat.

"Thanks. I have to get back to work, hon." He wanted to get off the phone before she could depose him any further.

"Did you have any time to think about what we talked about? You know, moving in together?"

Shit, there she goes again. She's not going to give up. He knew he had to decide whether to continue with his relationship or not; he couldn't elude this conversation forever, and Sidney was not one to concede. "Yeah, let's talk it over later, alright?"

"Alright, but we need to talk sooner rather than later," she warned.

"Sure thing, babe. I have to get back to work."

"Okay. I love you," she professed.

"I know you do. Gotta go." He hung up and tucked his phone back inside his pocket before laying atop the booth.

He folded his hands over his chest and reflected. He thought about his parents and how proud they would've been of him. He was finally a member of the board. Immediately after, he thought about how disappointed they would be if they knew he had killed an innocent woman. He was still intoxicated as he contemplated his future and what the Purebloods' true intentions were with him. It was nice to be part of a family again, even if it was a bunch of Lycans. After his parents' untimely deaths, Anthony had always been in search of a family. Perhaps now he had finally found a group to belong to. He mulled over the hybrid legend and wondered if maybe he was the Lycan they were referring to. He didn't exactly know what a hybrid was or what that meant, but he knew if he found out who had bitten him, they would have the answers. It was all too much for him to comprehend. A lot was happening, and it was happening all too fast. Drowning in his own thoughts, he eventually dozed off.

"Wake up!" he suddenly heard Ben scream, breaking his brief slumber.

He jolted from his minute nap with a quaking fright.

"Jeez, Ben, you almost gave me a heart attack!"

"Time for our board meeting. I see you haven't made much progress on those contracts, sleepy."

"Yeah, sorry, that whiskey hit me hard." He got up and tugged on his wrinkled blazer.

"Okay, well, get yourself together. I'll see you in the conference room. It's just around the corner to the right." Ben hurried down the hall, leaving his door ajar.

Anthony rubbed his eyes and followed suit, shutting the door behind him.

THE HUNT
FOR KANE

Inside the windowless conference room convened Chief Ramsey, Mr. Morgan, Ben, and Brandon. Their alpha sat at the head of the long table, while they were seated alongside him. Anthony entered and sat as Chief Ramsey approached a canvased screen hanging from the ceiling. He hit the lights and the room went dark. The projector illuminated over the awning as he pulled out his phone, syncing the device. Cast onto the canopy was an image of a young man with a beard and long dreadlocks. He plopped his captain's hat on the table and cleared his throat before addressing the board.

"Gentlemen, this is Kane. Our intelligence tells us that he is a high-ranking member of the Half-Breeds, possibly a beta or a delta rank. We have reason to believe that he is responsible for the resurgence of the full moon murders currently plaguing our city."

He slid his finger across his phone's screen. Shone onto the canopy was an image of a large, black-furred Lycan. Anthony immediately recognized the beast as the creature he had encountered on the rooftop.

"I've faced him!" he blurted.

Chief Ramsey squinted through the shimmering hue of the projector's light path.

"Then you know of his strength?" he questioned.

"Yeah, he hit me with a fucking brick!" Anthony exclaimed while rubbing his brow, coursing his fingertips over his bulbous contusion.

The chief turned on the lights, collected his hat, and sat beside Mr. Morgan.

"That's why I've called you all here," he announced. "The next full moon is in two days. It will be Brandon's first time transitioning and Mr. Montgomery's first time changing with the pack. I want you, Ben, to lead these two on a hunt for Kane. Kill him on sight. The three of you should be able to handle him."

As Ben brooded, Brandon cuffed his hands, attentively listening with ignorant delight.

"Well then, Anthony, do you think you can finish the job this time? Or will you be hunting innocent women and cats?" Ben asked.

How did he know about the cat? He was annoyed at Ben's belittling of him in front of the board but elected to stay quiet.

"Yes, Mr. Montgomery, you created quite a mess last night. My homicide unit has been very busy canvasing the neighborhood for potential witnesses and/or suspects," Chief Ramsey condescendingly interjected.

Fuck, the jig's up! You're going to jail. He felt their stares fixate on him as he awaited their verdict.

The room went eerily mute. Chief Ramsey put his hat back on and vindicated, "Well, we all know Kane is the culprit. And he must be stopped. I've issued a citywide curfew starting at seven p.m., effective tonight. All pedestrian traffic will be off the roadways, and all subway cars will be shut down, along with any and all public transportation."

Thank God they're protecting me. This is my family now. Like it or not, for better or worse. At that moment, he let out a sigh of relief and accepted them as his pack.

"Thank you, Chief," Mr. Morgan acknowledged.

Their enigmatic alpha glared at his underlings before delivering his orders.

"On the night of the full moon, y'all take the subway line to Tenderloin Point, where our intelligence believes the Half-Breeds' den is located. Chief Ramsey's officers have obtained some of Kane's fur as evidence to use against him."

He produced a clear bag containing clumps of black fuzz and threw it on the table. Ben opened the pouch and stuck his nose inside. He inhaled the pungent, earthy scent before passing it to Brandon, who did the same. After, he tossed it to Anthony. Immediately upon inhaling the overpowering aroma, he was transported back to that fateful night when he had encountered Kane on the rooftop.

"Thank you, Chief," Mr. Morgan again recognized, before stating, "In two days' time, upon the next full moon, I want you three to go down to Tenderloin Point. Find Kane and kill him!" He pounded a clenched fist on the table.

"Understood, Alpha," Ben sharply replied.

"Understood, Alpha," Brandon agreed.

"Understood," Anthony concluded.

"Looks like our pack is getting stronger by the day," Chief Ramsey boasted before grabbing the evidence bag from Anthony. He excused himself as Mr. Morgan rose and shook his hand.

"Only time will tell, Chief, and your assistance in this matter will not go unnoticed."

"I should hope not. I'll see you gentlemen at tomorrow night's gala." He gave them a departing salute before exiting with his hat tucked under his arm, concealing the evidence.

"Gala?" Brandon inquired.

"Yes, gentlemen." Mr. Morgan adjusted his suit and condescendingly addressed them.

"Tomorrow night is our annual gala. I will be announcing our firm's redevelopment plans for Tenderloin Point as well as the dockside revamp." He unbuttoned his jacket and crossed his arms while scowling at them. "Well, you three must have some work to do!"

After his angered tirade, they rose in unison and departed with haste. Anthony headed back to his office, while Ben and Brandon dispersed to their workspaces. Once he was settled at his desk, Anthony delved into the pile of contracts.

As the hours passed, he leaned back in his chair and rubbed his eyes in reprieve. One contract in particular stuck out to him. It was a merger with a foreign genetics lab called Gene-Con. The document outlined Morgan & Green Enterprises' strategy to acquire Gene-Con's genetics testing and research laboratories, whereby Gene-Con would perform genomics, proteomics, genetics experimentation, and analysis within Myrin City's district. As he studied the agreement further, his phone's text alert sounded. He diverted from his work to see Sidney's selfie displayed on the screen.

"Dinner tonight?" the message read.

"Sure, let's do Timmy's Diner. 5:30pm?" he typed.

"That works, this curfew has us all eating before sundown. Lol."

"Ok, see you soon." He slid his phone back into his pocket.

As 4:20 approached, Anthony closed his laptop and left his office, snatching his coat on his way out. As he strode past the front desk, the receptionist smiled at him.

"Have a good night, Mr. Montgomery," she announced.

"You too, uh… Sorry, I didn't get your name," he embarrassingly stammered while waiting for the elevator.

"I'm Camden."

"Nice to meet you, Camden. Have a good night," he uttered before shuffling into the overcrowded lift.

As he stood among the jam-packed amalgamation of admins, a rush of scents flooded his nostrils, causing his eyes to water. The lift made its snail-like descent, finally stopping at the lobby. The doors retracted and the masses filed across the congested foyer. Anthony intertwined amid the migration, spilling out into the streets.

A chilling breeze ran through him like a possessed apparition. He shuddered while pulling his overcoat tightly around his chest as he headed for the subway.

After braving the freeze for a few blocks, he transitioned from the snowy streets to the city's warm, bustling underbelly. As he crept down the urine-stained steps, he observed the crowds standing idly about the platform. He could distinctly hear their conversations as he witnessed humanity mingling in an unorganized, zigzagging horde. Some people chatted on their phones while others wandered about the platform, waiting for their trains.

As he approached the rusted turnstile, he swiped his card and strode through. He ventured to the platform, taking in the sounds and smells. Upon reaching the landing, he cut across the crowd and made his way to a nearby bench. He took a seat next to an elderly, balding man. While he waited, he watched the station's darkened tunnelways. He felt the rushing windchill of a passing train caress his cheek as it violently roared past him. The cab's railway pulsations burned his ears. He unnervingly reached into his pocket and unscrewed the cap on Dr. Geani's pills, thankful he had left the bottle in his coat. He emptied two capsules into his hand and swallowed them. After, he dropped the vial

101

inside his pocket. He reticently watched the fleeting train and caught a glimmer of a man wearing an olive field jacket standing on the balcony of the bolting caboose.

The figure stood within the open doorway of the rushing car just above its unconnected gangway with his arms crossed in front of him. Anthony hunched forward to get a better view. While peering through the multitudes, he was able to gain a vantage point of the man standing on the back of the rushing train.

It was Kane! His dreadlocks aimlessly fluttered in the tailwind of the speeding caboose's inertia. Anthony stood and watched as the train disappeared down an intersecting tunnel. As he picked up on the Half-Breed's wet, earthy scent, his heart raced with thoughts of confronting him.

Several bystanders noticed his unusual behavior. Once he perceived their onlooking stares, he bashfully smirked and sat back down. His ears were no longer ringing, thanks to the ingestion of the pills; however, he caught a whiff of an unusual synthetic odor coming from deep within the cavernous underpass.

His instincts drew him to the strange sent. He tracked the smell to the edge of the platform and cautiously leaned over the threshold, glaring into the gloomy tunnel. He noticed a pair of fierce red eyes staring back at him from deep within the darkness. As he studied the shadowy figure, he could distinguish an ethereal silhouette of what appeared to be a massive ten-foot-tall Lycan.

The mountainous brute beamed back at him as it stealthily lurched across the tracks. The looming figure suddenly vanished, scampering into the obscurity of an intersecting burrow, and the peculiar scent was gone.

In an instant, Anthony felt someone grabbing him from behind, pulling him from the platform's edge. As he fell, he viewed the elderly man who was sitting next to him. They stumbled, avoiding a speeding train that whizzed by, almost grazing the tip of his nose.

"Hey there, sonny, you better watch it. These trains move fast. Stay away from the edge." The thin-haired man had a weathered voice as he reached up and assuredly patted his shoulders. They regained their footing as the train gradually came to a stop.

"Did you see that?" Anthony questioned.

"See what, sonny?" The old man seemed confused.

"Never mind, sir. My apologies. It's been a long day. Thank you."

"Sure thing. Be careful out there, young feller. Sometimes my medications make me see things that aren't there too," the old man acknowledged after observing his pill bottle poking out of his pocket.

The train sluggishly came to a stop, and the doors abruptly opened with a hydraulic hiss. A rushing crowd exited, flooding the landing. This was his train. Anthony tangled between the exiting passengers and boarded. He grasped a nearby leaden pole, sandwiched amid the cramped commuters. Once the passengers were settled, the conductor came onto the audio system and announced, "Next stop, Midcity Entertainment District."

The doors shut, and the train launched down the tracks with a rattle. Anthony gently swayed along with the speeding turns, thinking about what to say to Sidney. He pondered more about what Ben had mentioned; living fifteen times longer than her, he would eventually see her die, and he would live on for what might as well be an eternity without her. He couldn't imagine putting her through the horrors that he would soon face.

So, should I tell her I'm a Lycan and hope she buys it? If she doesn't have me committed, then I'm going to have to keep her safe from all these damn Half-Breeds, which may want both of us dead. Not to mention the fact that I killed someone last night. She's not safe with me. What if one night I transform and kill her? The hunger is uncontrollable! Although it would be difficult, he knew what he had to do, if for no other reason than for her safety.

He figured she had gone through enough torment already, and breaking up with her would spare her from a future filled with chaos. At this point, there was no going back.

The ride was not long, and soon the train slowed.

"Now arriving, Midcity Entertainment District. Next stop:

Tenderloin Point and Dockside Port," the conductor announced.

The doors opened, and Anthony joined the masses exiting the station. He trailed the rushing mob, hurrying up the stairs and onto the streets of the Entertainment District. Neon billboards shone over the roadways as he ventured through the snow-laced sidewalks, passing the Muse Theater, with *Macbeth* featured on the marquee. After a short trek, he reached Timmy's Diner and Creamery.

The establishment's bright florescent sign reflected against the icy ground. He took a deep breath and grasped the door handle, entering the warm, lively joint. He kicked the snow off his shoes and stomped against the checkerboard floor, draping his coat on the stick hanger next to the entrance. Classic rock blared from a rainbow-colored jukebox as patrons sat in bright-red booths, chatting and eating while Betty Boop–uniformed waitresses frantically crisscrossed carrying stockpiled trays. Anthony glanced into the open kitchen; his mouth watered at the sight of the short-order cooks tending to the sizzling grill. A daunting fear began to arise inside him as he overlooked the diner.

He spotted Sidney sitting with her back to him in the far booth next to a window facing the street. She was wearing a navy-blue suit; her midnight hair glistened amid the hanging lampshades.

Here goes nothing. His heart tremored, stricken with dread.

Afflicted with anxiety, he ambled past the young hostess, fearing the conversation that would soon be taking place. He slid into the booth across from his girlfriend and unbuttoned his wrinkled jacket.

"Hey, babe. Cold out there, huh?" She leaned across the table for a kiss.

"Yep." They locked lips. He savored that kiss, for he knew it was going to be their last.

"Wow, you're already walking without a cane!" she exclaimed in shock.

"Yeah, can you believe it? I guess I just needed a good night's sleep."

"And some loving from me." She winked.

"Yeah, that too." He grinned, recalling making love to her.

A fat, middle-aged waitress interruptingly plopped two hot mugs onto the table.

"A hot cocoa for the lady and a warm tea for the gentleman... Now, have you both decided on anything to eat yet?" she asked while readying her notepad.

"Not yet, thanks." Sidney studied the plastic menu while the server swiftly departed.

"There's so much to choose from, jeez." She looked beautiful as she blew on her hot cocoa. "It's nice to finally eat out."

Anthony took in her mannerisms, savoring them as he nervously sat across from her, viewing the steam rise from his tea.

"Yeah, hard to choose. Not really that hungry though. I had a lot for dinner last night." He nervously chuckled.

She took a sip and noticed his Rolex gleaming under the sleeve-end of his rumpled jacket.

"Wow, nice watch, babe!" she announced in awe.

"Thanks. Part of my promotion," he uneasily stated, as he hid his hands under the table, concealing the opulent gift from her prying eyes.

"Well, maybe with your new promotion, you can finally get a car," she cynically suggested.

"Yeah, I was thinking about it," he deflatingly countered with a sullen shrug.

"What's wrong, babe? You seem anxious."

"You know, Sid, I've been through a lot these past few weeks."

"Yeah, I know. So have I." She lowered her steaming mug. "So, are we moving in together?" She loomed at him with a serious gaze, her chest heaving with agitation.

"Sid, you know I appreciate everything you've done for me. I truly do. But I was thinking. Now's not a good time." He analyzed her expression as her complexion flushed from pallid to a beet red.

"What do you mean?" Her knuckles inflamed as she angrily grasped her mug.

"I mean, things are really complicated. I'm just trying to process everything, and I don't want us to move in together right now. It's too much for me." He watched her tear up with sadness before her eyes dilated with rage.

"It's because you're on the board now, isn't it? More money, new watch, now you want a new woman or something? Am I not up to your standards, Anthony? God, after everything I put up with!"

"So, have we decided?" interrupted the hefty waitress, appearing at their table with beads of sweat dripping off her chubby face.

Anthony tensely sipped his tea, "Not yet, ma'am. Thank you."

She frustratingly sighed and huffed back to the kitchen.

"Sid… It's just that a lot of things have been happening. I can't really explain it right now because the truth is, I don't know myself, and moving in together is just going to make things that much more complicated, and I need you to understand that." *Besides, I'm a Lycan now, and I don't want to accidentally eat you!* He wished he could tell her the truth, but he knew she would just get angrier and think he was crazy.

"Do you even want kids?" She slumped into the booth with a dispirited tone.

Jesus! Here we go again with the fucking kid scenario! He hated to disappoint her, but having a child was not something he wanted, especially now. He reluctantly answered, "Maybe in the future. I don't know. God, why can't we just keep things the way they are?"

"I see." She lowered her head in disappointment.

After a few moments of silence, she raised her voice into a high-pitched shrill.

"Okay, Anthony, great! I stayed with you in the hospital. Dealt with your limp-ass dick and put up with all your bullshit for years! And now, after all that, you're telling me *you don't know! You want to keep things the same!*"

Oh, shit, now you've done it—she's pissed! He cowered in embarrassment as the scrutiny of the surrounding diners fixated on him. *There's no coming back from this.* He was particularly upset after her demeaning of his sexual shortcomings.

Her tantrum festered into rage as she glared at him in disgust.

"Calm down, Sid." He noticed the agitated customers and nodded at them in hopes of diverting their attention.

"'*Calm down*'?!" She sprung from the booth and threw her steaming cocoa, splashing his face.

The hot chocolate burned his cheeks as tiny marshmallows dribbled off his scorched chin.

"Goodbye, Anthony!" She turned her back on him, buttoned her suit, and stormed off.

Before leaving, she put on her coat and took one last searing look back at him as he wiped the remnants of her hot chocolate off his face. She ventured into the cold night, and he desperately watched as his lover became a stranger amongst the crowds. He immediately regretted breaking up with her. He was distraught with a lonesome heaviness that seemed to encumber him. His chest felt as if an anvil had been resting on it for decades.

You're an idiot. You should've just let her move in. And then what? Explain to her that in two days you're turning into a fucking Lycan and could possibly eat her or, worse, turn her into one? Either way, it hurts, and she's gone. He started to feel the weight of his decision bear down on him. An emptiness consumed his soul as he sat stunned and alone.

The burly waitress trudged to the table, clutching her notepad and pen.

"Sir, I'm afraid you will have to order some food. We're going to shut down our kitchen soon due to the curfew," she ordered with a busied look.

Anthony noticed the eye-shifting Kit-Cat Klock on the far wall; it was 6:25 p.m.

"That's okay, ma'am. I'm leaving... Here, for your troubles." He withdrew a twenty-dollar bill and slapped it on the table.

She begrudgingly shoveled it into her pocket and hustled back to the kitchen. Anthony gathered himself with a heavy heart. On his way to the door, the jukebox track suddenly switched records. A moment of silence overtook the diner. The abrupt stillness was broken up by vigorous guitar strumming that he immediately recognized. "Bad Moon Rising," by Creedence Clearwater Revival; the ballad echoed over the eatery.

107

He tramped past the hostess, who gave him an embarrassing look as he removed his coat from the hanger. He escaped into the snowy, neon-lit streets, running his arms through his pockets as the door closed behind him. He could faintly hear John Fogerty singing the last few lines of the chorus while he braved the elements.

He buried his frigid hands in his pockets and slogged along the slush-covered sidewalk, filled with regret. The thought of not seeing Sidney again was unbearable, but he knew that he had to let her go in order to protect her from the evils that lay ahead.

After considering the events that had taken place in the subway, he elected to walk home. Besides, he needed some time to clear his head, and he figured he could make it home before the curfew. Anthony aimlessly strode, listening to the cars zooming by while gracefully eluding pedestrians. His mind wandered. He thought about the upcoming full moon and the hunt that would be commanded of him. The notion of tracking down Kane filled him with exhilaration. Conversely, he reflected on the transformation and how painful it was. Contemplating the pains of his bones breaking and morphing filled him with fear. While approaching his neighborhood, he heard a distinctive cavalry charge-themed horn blare out from the roadway behind him.

The obnoxious melody broke his train of thought, and he knew whose car had sounded that ridiculous racket: it was Rey. He turned to see his purple grooming van, with the moniker "Rey's Stray's" airbrushed on the side above a portrait of him grinning with orange hair.

The van rolled beside him, and the window lowered, revealing his gangly friend. Rey sported a fluorescent-green mohawk and was wearing a white lab coat covered with dog hair. He sneered and did his best John Wayne impression: "Hey there, stranger. What ya' fixin' to do around these parts?"

Anthony laughed before countering with, "Just moseying on home, partner."

He hopped into the van, slamming the door with a loud clank.

He was happy to see him.

"Jeez, man, break my van, why don't ya!" Rey scolded.

He accelerated, swerving down the traffic-ridden streets. Anthony spread his hands under the heating vents and gazed over the fuzzy pink dashboard. His ice-cold knuckles started to defrost. As he warmed himself, he perceived the scents of various dog breeds.

"Wow, nice timepiece, bro!" Rey exclaimed with overzealous eyes while ogling the opulent watch.

"Thanks. Got it as part of my promotion." Anthony withdrew his thawing fingers from the vents and awkwardly stuffed his hands into his pockets.

As Rey drove farther across the neon-hewed Entertainment District, Anthony decided to change the topic.

"So, that's where you do all your hair coloring, huh?" He hinted at the rear wash sink, stained with green dye.

"Yeah, I get bored between pooches. Plus, it's kind of like my brand, I guess." Rey shrugged before stroking his neon mohawk.

Anthony chuckled while viewing the dim tenement buildings of his neighborhood.

"Sidney broke up with me," he announced, keenly observing Rey's reaction.

"What! Why?" He almost rear-ended a car upon hearing the news. He slammed on the brakes, sending Anthony jolting from his seat. "Sorry, Ant." He gawked as the reflection of the stoplight shone on his face.

Anthony leaned back and divulged, "Rey, I got to tell you something, and I need you to believe me."

"Sure, buddy, we're boys for life," he assured him.

Anthony held his breath and confessed, "I'm a werewolf."

"*Blaaaa hhaaa!* Okay, man, whatever you say. Maybe you should lay off those pills, dude." He winked with disbelief, noticing the prescription bottle that had partially dislodged from his pocket.

"It's not the pills, Rey. I can prove it to you." He tucked the vial back inside his coat, concealing it from his childhood friend.

The light turned green, and Rey accelerated.

"Okay. Prove it then," he challenged.

To which Anthony responded by sniffing the air, turning up his nose, and allowing a vast conglomerate of innumerable scents to enter his nasal passages. After a long, exuberant inhale, he revealed, "All right. The last dog you groomed was a border collie."

"Lucky guess." Rey turned down a side street to avoid the gridlock.

"Okay, the dog before that was a Pomeranian. You had a bacon, egg, and cheese biscuit for breakfast, and I can hear the radio playing in the car in front of us."

Rey lurched over the fluffy dashboard, peering at the frost-covered Ford Focus in front of them, and questioned, "Okay, then what's the station, and what song is playing?"

"The station is 98.7, and the song is Frank Sinatra, 'I Did It My Way.'"

After his prediction, Rey turned the dial, and, sure enough, Old Blue Eyes' voice blasted out from the speakers.

He gruffly turned off the radio in shock. "I hate Sinatra!"

He examined Anthony with wide-eyed astonishment and declared, "Well, now I know why you broke up with Sidney."

"Yeah, I can't put her through this." He disappointedly rested his elbow against the windowpane and covered his mouth with the palm of his hand as the van approached his street.

"This is incredible!" Rey shouted.

Anthony gazed out the window, filled with anxiety and despair.

"Well… If you need me, I'm there, bud. Just don't eat me!" Rey laughed in an attempt to cheer him up while stopping in front of his building.

"Just don't get near me during a full moon, and you'll be all right," he jokingly warned as he hopped out.

His feet crunched atop the frosted sidewalk as he held the door ajar and addressed his stunned friend. "Rey, you got minutes to make it home before curfew."

"I'll make it. I'm just glad there's no full moon tonight." He pointed to the half-moon shining down on them.

"You and me both. Not a word of this to anyone, Rey. I mean it!" he cautioned before closing the door.

Rey rolled down the window. "My lips are sealed. Got to go, bud. Curfew. Plus, no one would believe me anyway." He expeditiously drove away, shuttling down the snowy streets while howling from the opened window, "*Oooowwwwwooooowwow!*"

After the van dissipated into the night, Anthony marched up the steps into the warmth of his building. Divulging to Rey about his condition gave him some sense of relief.

He marched down the corridor and could smell his aunt's scent. He unlocked his door and entered his unit to find her sweeping up broken shards of glass that had once been his dinette table.

"Oh, thank heavens!" she shouted, dropping the broom.

Why is she here? He was confused as he tore off his coat and threw it on the couch. He immediately regretted having given her a key; he just wanted to be alone. Gloria brushed tiny crumbles of glass from her floral-patterned blouse and rushed over to hug him. Her hair was a disheveled tangle that resembled an old wet mop.

"I was so worried about you with that murder last night. Then I saw your dining room table was broken. I tried calling you, but you didn't answer!" She cried as they embraced.

"I'm sorry, Auntie, I've been really busy. I just want to take a shower and get some sleep." He dislodged from her and emptied his pockets.

He tossed his cell phone and keys onto the kitchen counter and noticed seven missed calls from her.

"You're walking without your cane!" she sniveled in astonishment after witnessing him stomp to the kitchen.

"Yeah, the doctor said I'm a fast healer." He shrugged.

"That's terrific!"

"Well, looks like you're sleeping over." He pointed to the microwave clock; it was 7:01 p.m.

111

"Oh my, I was so busy cleaning that I lost track of the time. When I heard about the murder this morning, I got here as quick as I could, but you had already left for work. Then I realized that I forgot my key, but your friend Mr. Shepard let me in."

"What? He was here?"

"Oh yes. Sweet man. He works with your company, doesn't he?" she asked while sweeping up the last bits of glass.

"Something like that," he begrudgingly answered while heading for the bathroom, where he noticed a newly installed window, complete with a barcoded inspection tag.

"He said that he was here to replace your window. He told me some kids were throwing rocks when he came to pick you up this morning. I swear, this neighborhood's going to pot."

"Yeah, guess so. You can take my bed tonight; I'll take the couch." Before she could respond, Anthony hurried to the bathroom and closed the door.

He turned on the shower and got undressed, shoving his Rolex inside the medicine cabinet. He stood under the steaming water and closed his eyes. As he washed, he broke down and cried.

After some time, he valiantly composed himself and dried off before putting on his robe. He sulked to the dining room table, where his aunt sat patiently between two steaming cups of tea.

"Come have a seat. Let's visit," she directed.

He reluctantly sat next to her. The last thing he wanted to do was chat. He took a small sip from his tea and complimented, "This is good, Auntie, thank you."

"There's nothing like a hot cup on a cold winter's night," she proclaimed with a satisfied smirk.

"Sidney broke up with me," he confessed, surly and hunched over.

She spit out her tea in shock. "What?! Why?"

"She wants to move in and have kids, and I'm not ready for all that. I just need to figure some things out first, and I don't want her to get hurt. Besides, a life with me would not be the life she deserves," he explained while observing her disappointment.

Gloria wiped the spewed tea with her sleeve before taking another long sip. She doted over him and stated, "If you are lucky enough to find love in this world, you hold onto it and fight for it. You don't just give up and let it slip away, because you may never get that love back again."

"Okay, Auntie. Did you read that on the back of a Hallmark card or something?"

"Fortune cookie," she retorted with a wink.

"Ha, good one. Well, I'm going to hit the couch. It's been a long day."

"Okay, get some rest. I still have hope for you two. Maybe some time apart will make you both realize that you need each other."

"That's one way to look at it, I guess."

"I'll pray for you both. Good night, my little Ant. I love you." She kissed his forehead before shuffling to the bedroom.

Anthony awoke on his couch, wearing only his robe and boxer shorts. His back twinged with a creaking pain from sleeping in an awkward position. He rolled off the sofa and headed to his bedroom, where he discovered that his bed had already been made and a hand-written note was left on the pillow. He picked up his aunt's letter, which read, "Have a good day at work, my little Ant. I'm so proud of you."

He tucked her note next to the pink teddy bear draped with her black-beaded rosary when his cell phone rang.

It was a text from Ben, which read, "Good morning Delta, tonight's Gala is at 6:30 pm the dress code is black tie. I had Brandon pick up your tux, he'll drop it off at your office later today."

"Ok, thanks, see you tonight," he texted back.

He stepped into the bathroom and brushed his teeth. As he studied his reflection, he noticed two small, overlying fangs protruding from his upper gumline. He dropped his toothbrush in disbelief.

What the fuck! I'm getting wolfier as the full moon approaches!
After coursing over the sharp incisors with the tip of his tongue, he shaved and grabbed his Rolex from the cabinet.

He got dressed in his usual black suit (without jeans this time) and slipped on his loafers before clasping his opulent timepiece onto his wrist. He felt rich and was brimming with confidence as he snatched his coat from the hanger and paraded down the hall. He hailed a cab to work, proud of his newly earned status within his pack.

After jostling across the congested lobby and up the sardine-packed elevator, he sauntered to his office, bypassing the rows of cubicle-entrenched employees.

He withdrew his laptop and began his work. After he reviewed his emails, he scanned over the Gene-Con merger for several hours. As he leaned back in reprieve, he heard a knock and immediately smelled Brandon.

"Come in," he shouted.

The door cracked, and Brandon stuck his head in.

"Good afternoon, Delta. Are you busy?"

"I am, but I could use a break. Come in, have a seat."

"Thank you, sir." Brandon entered wearing a light-gray suit with a fuchsia tie. The young associate proudly held a garment bag.

"I have your tux for tonight, sir," he announced while delicately laying it across the booth and closing the door behind him.

"Mr. Morgan said it's yours to keep!" he enthusiastically added before sitting across from him.

"So, what can I do for you?"

"Well, sir, I was just wondering. Who in our pack bit you?"

"That's a really good question. The truth is, I don't know, I blacked out. I was in the woods outside Mr. Morgan's cabin the night I was attacked. What about you?"

"Wow, attacked, huh? That's crazy. Mr. Damien turned me. He gave me an injection, and that was it."

"Must be nice to be chosen or have a choice in the matter," Anthony confessed with confusion. He was still trying to figure everything out;

piecing together the events of that fateful night was especially challenging for him, as his memory was unclear at best.

"Funny not knowing who turned you, but I guess you're a Pureblood now, and that's all that matters." Brandon fidgeted with juvenile eagerness.

"I think I was indoctrinated into the Purebloods long before I was bitten. I should have never gone out to that cabin in the first place, and that paw ceremony was so weird."

"The ritual was just for theatrics. Mr. Morgan has a flair for tradition and spectacle. I guess when you've lived as long as him, things tend to get a little boring," he reasoned.

"Yeah, guess so." Anthony brushed his tongue above his gumline while keeping his mouth closed; he felt the protruding fangs under his lips and hoped that Brandon wouldn't notice.

"Tomorrow night will be my first time turning," the young associate declared with angst while adjusting his tie.

"Are you nervous?"

"I'm terrified." He subconsciously twitched his legs with anxiety.

"Well, it hurts. It feels like your veins are on fire, but after the pain subsides, you feel great power. It's hard to describe." He leaned back in his chair and studied Brandon's naive expression.

"At least we'll all be together," he nervously pronounced, manically rubbing his jolting leg.

"How so?"

"The Purebloods always transition together. At least, that's what Ben told me. We're supposed to meet tomorrow night in the lower level of the building."

"Interesting. Ben never mentioned that to me."

"I'm sure he will," Brandon reassured.

"So, what's your story, kid? Where are you from?" He deliberately changed the narrative; all this talk of transitioning was making him uneasy.

"Born and raised right here in Myrin City. I never knew my parents; I grew up in foster care. It was rough, but hey, I survived, and

I'm here now. I finally have a family with the Purebloods. I belong to a pack, and that's something I always wanted."

"Some family, huh?" Anthony snickered. "I'm sorry you had to grow up like that. Both my parents died in a plane crash, so I can relate." He felt sorry for Brandon, but his difficult past made him feel an immediate kinship.

Brandon beamed with a sense of belonging. "It's not so bad, but you have to learn to live with constant emptiness. You get used to it after a while."

"I suppose so."

"Well, Delta, I'll see you at the gala. It's in the forty-second-floor ballroom."

"Thanks, Brandon, I appreciate you."

"No worries, sir. I look forward to hunting with you tomorrow night," he affirmed with confidence.

"The feeling's mutual, kid."

Brandon glared back at him like a lost dog before he left.

The rest of the day flew by. Anthony was upset that he had not heard from Sidney. He already missed talking to her. He pondered whether to call her but elected not to. It was almost 6:30 p.m. when he shoved his laptop back inside the drawer. He groaned and dressed for the gala, packing his work clothes inside the garment bag before hanging it up.

God, I hate these stuffy events. Social posturing and commingling. I just want to go home! He buttoned his tux and strode down the side-windowed corridor with a deflated reluctance.

His dark shoes echoed a resonating clamor as he trudged across the abandoned workspaces. He dreaded having to partake in these frivolous events but knew it was a requirement now that he was on the board. He felt an ominous tension as he pressed the elevator call button. The lift doors opened to reveal the tall, slender Mr. Damien, sporting a navy-blue tux.

"Looking sharp, Ben," he complimented with a nervous cadence.

"You clean up nice too, Delta," Ben noted upon examining him.

"I thought you only took the private elevator?" he joked before entering.

Ben meticulously studied him as the doors closed. "Oh, that reminds me. We need to get your paw scanned now that you're on the board."

He reached into his pocket and pulled out a bag of coke, displaying the granulated powder with a deviant sneer. "You want some?"

"No, I'm okay." *Jeez, starting a little early, don't you think?* He was taken aback at his flippant offering.

"Suit yourself." Ben spilled a small amount onto the backside of his hand and inhaled.

"Oh yeah, that's the stuff!" His face contorted with a rush of adrenaline as he tucked the bag back inside his pocket while rubbing his nose.

They descended to the forty-second floor. The doors opened to reveal a grand ballroom with crystal chandeliers. A myriad of well-dressed patrons gallivanted about the extravagant hall as a jazz band serenaded from atop a raised platform. White-uniformed servers methodically interwove between the guests, carrying trays topped with hors d'oeuvres. They stepped into the fray, joining the formally dressed masses.

As they advanced through the multitudes, Ben separated from him. Left to his own devices, Anthony grabbed a champagne flute from one of the servers and proceeded to the stage. Suddenly, from deep within the crowd emerged Brandon, wearing a white tux with black polka dots.

"Looking good, sir!" he exclaimed as he patted him on the shoulder.

"Did you steal that tux from one of the servers?" Anthony laughed.

"No, sometimes you just need to stand out," Brandon retorted.

He shook his head. "I like your style, kid, but I prefer to blend in."

The band stopped, and Mr. Morgan took to the stage, wearing a black tux and a blood-red bow tie. The ensemble exited as he stomped to the mic and addressed the gathering.

"Good evening. I hope ya'll are enjoying yourselves. Before we get back to the party, I would like to take a moment and reveal Morgan & Green Enterprises' plans for the future." He signaled for the lights and the room grew dim.

A three-dimensional hologram of a newly developed cityscape spiraled over the stage.

"This, my esteemed friends, is the future redevelopment site of Tenderloin Point, and the Dockside revamp. We will replace the government-assisted housing with high-rise, upper- to midpriced condominiums. Given the Tenderloin's proximity to the port, it will be a desirable place to live once the Dockside revamp is completed."

The holographic cityscape twirled above in a dazzling, illuminating dance as the boisterous CEO proceeded with his address.

"In addition to our redevelopment plans, we are also merging with Gene-Con laboratories. We will be breaking new ground in the genetic engineering space. Their CEO is with us this evening. Dr. Edwin M. Fang, would you please raise your hand so we can acknowledge you?"

A frail hand shot up from the crowd. The gathering applauded as a petite man with short black hair and thin-framed glasses waved.

"Thank you, Dr. Fang. And I want to recognize all of you for your time and patronage; please, enjoy the remainder of the evening." He stepped away from the mic as the twirling hologram disintegrated. The lights brightened and the assembly continued their applause while he descended from the stage.

"Pretty exciting, huh?" Brandon nudged Anthony's side.

He took a long sip from his flute, finishing the libation.

"Thrilling," he sarcastically responded, watching the band retake the stage.

He let out an innocuous belch before departing from Brandon's presence. He strolled to the bathroom, keeping his eyes down as he crossed the dance floor, hoping to avoid any unnecessary conversations. As he approached the seating area, he discarded his empty glass atop one of the tables and intersected among the congregation, advancing through the litany of seated invitees. He scanned over them, wondering which one of these upper-class patrons could be the Lycan that had bitten him.

He suddenly felt a tiny pinch just above his elbow. He turned to see Luna. She was dressed in a flattering red gown that swathed over her curvaceous, athletic frame. Her opulent dress was complemented with red-bottomed high heels. Her flowing auburn hair was greased back and straightened.

"Hey there, handsome." She undressed him with penetrating eyes.

She's a vision. He was taken aback by her beauty as he inhaled her scent. "Hey, Luna. Looking gorgeous as always." He leaned in and pecked her on the cheek.

"So, how do you like your new office?" she enchantingly asked.

"It's definitely retro."

"This building has a history." She sneered before lustfully licking her lips. "Where's Sidney?"

"We broke up," he reluctantly confessed.

"Oh, I'm so sorry." She embraced him, nestling her head on his chest.

Yeah, sure you are, he sarcastically thought. "I'll be okay, thanks." He gently patted her on the back.

"I know you will." She stepped away and blushed. "Maybe we can get together sometime—you know, outside of work?"

Why is she always trying to sleep with me? It seems like she has an ulterior motive. I mean, I know I'm good looking and all, but come on, she could have anyone she wants. Why me? "I'd love that," he agreed, obliging her request with suspicion.

"So would I." She blew him an air kiss before whisking away. After watching her disappear into the crowd, Anthony continued his quest for the bathroom. He weaved past the seating area and entered the restroom. After he relieved himself at the urinal, he washed his hands and admired his reflection in the mirror. He was adjusting his bow tie when he heard a woman giggling.

"Is that you, Delta?" Ben called out from the handicapped stall.

"Yep," he confirmed.

The stall doors swung open, and Ben appeared with his nostrils flaring, crusted with chalky cocaine residue.

"Well then, get over here!" He pulled him inside, where he found Camden bent over the sink with a rolled-up dollar bill.

"Anthony, this is Camden. I believe you two met yesterday."

"Yes, hi," he uncomfortably greeted.

"Hey," she nervously responded after inhaling a line.

She was wearing a sparkly lime-green dress that complemented her bleach-blonde hair.

"Next one's yours." Ben ushered him to the sink where he loomed over two thin lines of powder.

Fuck it. He conceded to Ben's peer pressure as Camden handed him the dollar bill.

Anthony grabbed the cigarillo-rolled currency, bent down, and inhaled.

Holy shit! A euphoric rush tingled his nasal passages before dripping into the back of his throat.

His heart raced with a jubilatory flutter as Ben grabbed the bill from him and snorted the last line, licking his lips with satisfaction.

"That's some good blow, huh?" he proclaimed while tilting his head back.

"Yeah." Anthony's ears started ringing.

They meticulously inspected themselves before leaving the bathroom, quietly laughing to each other. As they reentered the gala, perspiring and coked up, Ben excitedly turned to him and whispered, "Let's check out the roof."

His legs tingled with numbness as he mindlessly followed Ben to the private elevator.

As they proceeded, Ben whispered to Camden and signaled for her to leave. She trolleyed off in an inebriated stupor while they manically zigzagged across the crowd. Ben shoved his palm into the scanner, and the doors spread. They entered the lift, but just as the doors started to close, a hand abruptly shot out. The panels retracted, and Brandon eagerly hopped in.

"So, where are we going, guys?"

"To the moon, Alice!" Ben shouted.

The doors closed, and they let out a unified howl.

Ben pressed the H button at the very top of the key panel. The cab shot up with lightning speed and chimed. The doors opened to reveal the sprawling rooftop of the sixty-six-story tower. A ferocious chilling gust flapped their jackets as they stepped onto the helipad. They crept to Mr. Morgan's idle helicopter with playful enthusiasm.

"Man, this is so cool!" Brandon exclaimed while sliding open the door.

He climbed over the passenger seats and jumped into the captain's chair. Ben and Anthony leaned into the chopper with drug-induced sneers, chattering their jaws while observing Brandon's childlike behavior.

"Be careful! Mr. Morgan's chopper is not a toy!" Ben reprimanded, mocking an elderly woman's voice.

"I know, guys. I'm just having a little fun. I wonder what these levers do?" He shifted a yellow handle forward.

The compressor made a hydraulic hiss. Brandon frantically shifted the lever back, and the blades turned.

"Shut it down!" Ben hollered as the propellers twirled with increasing speed, sending an uproarious twister from under them.

"I don't know how!" Brandon shrieked over the deafening resonances of the fast-churning blades. The helicopter suddenly lifted off the ground.

Ben jumped into the cockpit and pulled back the lever, depowering the aircraft. The helicopter trembled as the foot skids struck the platform with a thud. The blades decelerated and Anthony stepped back, anxious. With his ears still ringing from the cocaine, he became increasingly nervous. The commotion from the chopper triggered thoughts of his parents' plane crash. Brandon and Ben gawked at each other with a combined sigh of relief before exiting with nervy laughter.

"That could've been a fucking disaster." Ben uneasily chuckled as he slid the door shut.

He redirected them over to the roof's ledge. "Check it out, fellas."

They cursorily raced to the edge and leaned over the safety rail, peering down at the cityscape beneath them. They gazed over the bustling metropolis filled with people scattered about the snowy streets and licked their lips.

"The city is ours, gentlemen," Ben arrogantly proclaimed.

"*Ooowwwwooo!*" Brandon howled.

"The night is young, and I have arranged a limo for us. It's time for the Purebloods to hit the streets!" He turned from the guard rail and directed his attention to Anthony. "Or do you need to ask Sidney for permission?"

"I took your advice. We broke up," he stated with his head down.

After his heartbroken declaration, Ben smiled with approval.

Brandon delicately patted his shoulder, consoling him as best he could.

"Cheer up, sir. The night is young!" he encouraged.

"Well, before we get to that, let's talk hunting strategy." Ben stepped away from the ledge. He gave them a keen, daunting glare before describing his battle plan. "Kane is known to patrol the subways near Tenderloin Point."

"Yeah, I know. I saw him standing on the back of a train last night," Anthony added.

"Well, that would make sense then, wouldn't it, Delta? Now, after we transition, we will take the subway line to Tenderloin Point. I will take the lead. You two stay behind me. No matter what happens, always stay behind me. If we get separated, head back here."

"To the roof?" Brandon questioned.

"No, Omega. To the building!" Ben scolded.

"Oh, okay," he apologetically muttered.

Anthony shook his head. "And what? Are we just supposed to walk in the front door, full werewolf?"

"All will be explained tomorrow. Don't worry," Ben reassured.

"Easy for you to say. Last time I faced Kane, I got hit in the head with a fucking brick and fell off a building… He's strong. Taking him down won't be easy," Anthony disputed.

Ben adjusted his tux and sharply countered, "Enough about tomorrow. Just follow my lead, and everything will work out!"

"So what about tonight then?" Brandon asked with teenage enthusiasm.

"Camden has some friends for you both. Maybe they can help you get over your breakup, Delta."

Anthony gave Ben a fictitious half smile. "Where are we going?"

"The Lobo Crank warehouse party."

"Sweet, I love Lobo Crank. They have dope beats!" Brandon exuberantly proclaimed.

"Care for some sugar?" Ben produced the small bag of coke from his jacket.

"I'm good. My ears are still ringing from the last bump." Anthony declined.

"No thanks, Beta. I got my own!" Brandon pulled out a nickel bag filled with powder and poured some onto his knuckle.

Anthony and Ben looked at each other with surprise after observing his bold, drug-induced behavior. Brandon inhaled, wiped the residue from his nose, and they simultaneously let out a wailing battle cry.

They scampered into the metallic lift which carried them back to the gala, where they rejoined the gathering. As they gallivanted through the masses in an attempt to escape from the pretentious ball, Mr. Morgan appeared, stonewalling their departure.

"And how are our new young hunters doing this evening?" he asserted with a grandiose jeer.

"We're ready, sir," Ben confidently reassured.

"Good! Now, gentlemen, let me introduce y'all to Dr. Fang." He cleared a path across the assembly and lead them to the seating area.

Once they arrived at his table, the short doctor adjusted his glasses and stood to greet them. He buttoned his tux before pensively examining them.

"Pleasure to meet you, Dr. Fang." Brandon shot out his hand, and they shook.

Afterward, Anthony and Ben shook hands with him.

"Anthony here has been redlining our merger," Mr. Morgan announced to the pensive geneticist.

Dr. Fang addressed him, his voice soft and low. "I trust that you find our terms most agreeable?" he questioned with an inviting nod.

"For the most part, Doctor. I made some annotations on a few items," he replied with hurriedness as his nose started to drip.

"Very well then. I look forward to reviewing your comments," Dr. Fang stated before sitting back down.

"Okay, gentlemen, behave yourselves tonight. I've instructed Marcellus to drive you," Mr. Morgan warned as he took a seat.

They nodded in unison before making their departure across the congested ballroom. As they anxiously waited for the elevator, Anthony inadvertently made eye contact with Chief Ramsey. The commander was wearing his decorated uniform, complete with his captain's hat. After a brief glance, the tall captain lumbered to them, greeting Ben first.

"Mr. Damien, leaving so soon?" he declared with a deep, husky voice while shaking his hand.

"Yes, sir, we're heading to the Lobo Crank warehouse party. And thank you again for lifting the curfew for us."

Ben turned sharply to Anthony and Brandon, giving them a stern scowl prompting merits, to which they responded in unison, "Thanks, Chief!"

"No worries, gentlemen. A pack always takes care of its own. Look out for one another tonight." He left them with those departing words before rejoining the raucous ballroom.

The elevator chimed, the doors opened, and they filed in. The lift descended to the empty lobby, where they hurriedly exited for the awaiting limo. Upon seeing the board members approach, Marcellus expeditiously rushed to the passenger side and swung open the door.

"Good evening, gentlemen," the scar-faced motorist greeted.

"Thank you, Marcellus. Take us to the Lobo Crank warehouse

party," Ben directed as he hopped in with Brandon.

"Very well, sir," Marcellus acknowledged while standing idlily with a fake smile.

"Glad to see you're doing well, Mr. Montgomery," he recognized as Anthony approached.

"Thanks, it's nice to finally speak with you." He shook his sizable, calloused hand before stepping inside.

Marcellus slammed the door and drove off. Seated on the far end of the limo was Camden, accompanied by two other girls. One was a slim brunette, and the other had a curvaceous frame with short black hair. They both fluttered with nervousness as they adjusted their shimmering cocktail dresses over their knees. They admiringly watched as the board members took their seats. They giggled while greeting the tuxedo-clad executives.

"Ladies, this is Brandon and Anthony," Ben announced.

"Hi. I'm Patricia, and this is Arin," the petite girl introduced.

"Nice to meet you, ladies. Care for some coke?" Brandon eagerly pulled out the half-full bag of powder.

"Right to it then, huh?" Anthony turned to Ben with surprise.

"Sure," the girls accepted with energetic laughter.

"That's one way to break the ice…with snow!" Ben joked, nudging him.

Brandon fervently hopped to the other side of the limo between the girls, while Anthony and Ben poured some whiskey from the neon-lit sidebar. The party ensued as they drove through the barren streets. Ben scoffed and pressed the button above him, opening the sunroof.

The felt panel slowly shifted back, and the chilling night air flowed into the limo. Brandon stuck his torso out of the opening and the three girls excitedly joined him. As they climbed up, they unanimously let out a resounding howl.

Their hollers echoed over the empty streets as the limo crusaded for the Warehouse District.

"Funny guy, isn't he?" Ben took a sip while studying the intoxicated scene.

"Yeah, he's a trip. I see why you turned him," Anthony added.

"He's the perfect candidate: no family and no obligations. No one will miss him," Ben concluded with an aberrant smirk.

"I was wondering, Ben, who bit me?" He probed for answers; given Ben's drug-induced state, he was hopeful that he would divulge.

"That's confidential." He glared at him with harshness.

"Come on. We're all friends here. You can tell me," Anthony persisted.

"Don't worry, Delta. You're one of us now." Ben dismissingly chuckled.

Brandon and the girls ducked as the limo pulled up to the warehouse. A muffled melodic thump pulsated from inside the giant square building. A lone black-suited doorman stood post outside. The limo stopped, and Marcellus got out. The hulking driver stomped to the passenger side and opened the door. Brandon, along with the girls, filed out with Ben following. The slick-haired board member leered back at Anthony, who remained seated.

"Are you coming, Delta?" he encouraged.

"I think I'm going to sit this one out, Ben." He took a long sip before settling back into his seat. He was upset that Ben wouldn't confess as to who had bitten him.

"Come on, Anthony. Don't be a party pooper!" Brandon excitedly shouted while cradling Arin and Patricia on each arm.

"Come on, Anthony. It'll be fun. Are you sure you don't want to party with us?" Camden pleaded.

"Yeah, I'm sure. You guys have fun. I'll see you tomorrow," he reaffirmed.

"Okay. Marcellus, see to it that our newest board member gets home safe," Ben ordered.

"Yes, sir." He nodded and closed the door, leaving Anthony alone to his devices.

As they accelerated past the bass-pulsating warehouse, the concrete building soon became a distant rearview glimmer. The privacy divider lowered, and Marcellus made eye contact with him through the dashboard mirror.

"Not much of a partier, huh, Mr. Montgomery?" he asked.

"I'm not in the mood tonight. Let's just say my life is going to the dogs."

He finished the remainder of his whiskey and slammed the empty glass on the neon-lit counter.

"How's your recovery going?" Marcellus questioned, manning the wheel and slowly turning the titanic vehicle down a side street.

"Very good, actually. Turns out I have good genes," he confided before inquiring, "If you don't mind me asking, how did you get that scar under your eye?"

"I don't mind. People ask me about it all the time." Marcellus took a long pause, gave him a stern, cold-faced stare, and confessed, "Hunting accident."

The limo pulled up to Anthony's redbrick building. He anxiously reached for the door handle.

"Let me get that for you, sir." Marcellus parked and leaned over to get out.

"That's okay, I can handle it from here. Thank you." He nervously shot out of the limo and jogged up the steps. Marcellus' hunting comment did not sit well with him. He felt uneasy in his presence.

The scar-faced driver rolled down the window and shouted, "Mr. Montgomery!"

Anthony turned to face him.

"Good luck tomorrow." He saluted with a menacing grin before driving off into the night.

That was odd. He felt an ill-omened uncertainty after Marcellus' forewarning decree.

Anthony slogged out of bed, still a bit hungover from the night before. He meandered to the bathroom with his head throbbing. While brushing his teeth, he noticed that the newly formed upper fangs had grown. He was thankful that the emerging teeth were still unnoticeable under his gumline. He got dressed in his navy-blue suit, which Sidney had gifted him for his birthday last year.

He adjusted the blazer and grabbed the remote from his couch, turning on the local news. An image of Chief Ramsey cast onto the screen, with the voice of the lawman reciting, "We have issued a citywide curfew for tonight starting at six thirty p.m. Anyone caught outside after that time will be detained and in violation of the city's ordinance under our current emergency protocols. All public transportation and trains will be shut down. I want to remind everyone that the full moon murderer is still out there, and these precautions are in place to protect us all. Stay indoors, stay safe, and if you see something, contact the Myrin City Police Department."

Anthony shut off the TV before grabbing his coat and taking a cab to work.

Confined in his office, he finished reviewing the final pages of the Gene-Con merger, anxiously waiting for the workday to end. His mind was on the transformation ceremony that would soon be taking place. He could feel his internal chemistry beginning to change with the onset of sundown. His belly boiled with the rage of a ravenous stalker as he scanned over his computer and redlined the Gene-Con merger one last time before sending it to Mr. Morgan.

He delved into his work as a way of distracting himself from the fear of turning into a Lycan. His concentration was broken when he smelled the astringent, burning hew of alcohol and there was a faint knock at his door.

"Come in!" he barked.

The door opened, and in strutted Brandon, dressed in a dark green blazer with navy pants.

"Looking sharp, bro. How was last night?" he complimented with curiosity.

"Amazing!" he jovially exclaimed with a hungover drawl before closing the door and jumping onto the manila-cushioned booth.

"I'm still tipsy from last night, but let's just say…three-way!" He raised his hands in victory.

Anthony laughed. "Nice!"

"But that's not why I'm here, sir," he explained. "Ben wanted me to tell you that the transition ceremony will be taking place in the lower levels of the building and that we should meet him in the lobby at five thirty."

"Noted, thanks." Anthony reclined in his seat, scrutinizing him with disbelief.

"What?" Brandon bashfully grinned.

"Nothing, you just surprise me, that's all." Anthony shook his head as Brandon swung open the door to leave.

"I'll have these dry-cleaned for you, sir." He grabbed the garment bag stuffed with Anthony's suit.

"Thanks."

"No worries. I can't wait for tonight! Kane doesn't stand a chance!" he shouted before slamming the door. Anthony could hear him energetically skip down the hall with his garment bag slung over his shoulder.

He worked until 5:15 p.m. With the daunting prospect of turning back into a Lycan soon at hand, Anthony felt an amalgamation of emotions which he could no longer ignore.

I hope it doesn't hurt like last time. Plus, changing with the pack, I hope I don't embarrass myself. I wonder what they all look like as Lycans. Fear, excitement, and anxiety coursed through him as he exited his office and took the overcrowded elevator to the lobby.

He waited for Ben amid the throngs of trampling employees clamoring their way across the atrium. The exiting masses paraded through the turnstiles and filed into the cold streets as evening turned to dusk. He observed the fleeing multitudes when he felt a stern grip on his shoulder. He turned to see Ben, wearing a black pin-striped suit.

"This way, Delta." He ushered him to the private elevator and placed his hand under the scanner.

The shiny doors opened, and they got into the cab. Ben pushed the G button at the very bottom of the key panel. They descended.

"Brandon is already waiting for us," he explained with a serious tone.

"I heard he had a good night last night."

"The kid has potential." Ben smiled as the elevator stopped.

The lift reached the lower levels of the towering building and opened with a chime. They exited and crossed the parking garage to a loading dock. Ben proceeded to the bay and pressed a sidewall-mounted button.

"Hope you're not shy," he warned as the door rattled open.

"What? Why?" Anthony questioned.

The roll-up door stopped, and they walked into the dark loading bay, where Ben proceeded to open a heavy steel door at the far corner of the space.

"After you," he insisted while holding open the large door.

Anthony peered past his hunting partner and viewed a corridor leading to an unmarked red door. He nervously entered the expansive hallway, bypassing Ben, who closed the steel door behind him with a resonating shutter. As they marched down the passageway, they came across a security camera at the end of the hall. Ben waved and the door unbolted, slowly swinging ajar. They proceeded to an expansive shower and locker room area, where purple-hooded robes hung in the far corner. To the left of the showers were rows of metal-barred lockers. Some were filled with belongings, while others lay empty. Stamped above each locker was the name "Gene-Con" in bright yellow letters.

"Hey, guys. You ready for this?!" Brandon called out, donning his purple-hooded cloak.

"As ready as I'm ever gonna be," Anthony nervously rationalized.

He was taken aback at the size of the locker room. Anthony had worked at MGE for years and had never known these chambers existed.

"Time to get dressed, Delta," Ben commanded, grabbing a cloak while heading for the lockers.

Anthony snatched a robe and undressed. He unlatched his Rolex and shoved it inside a locker, along with his suit, phone, and personal items.

"Ben, do you have a lock?" he asked while swathing his cloak.

"No need. Purebloods don't steal from one another. Your stuff is safe here. This is the safest place in Myrin City. Trust me," he announced while thrusting his suit into the cabinet before slamming it shut.

He draped the hood over himself before scrutinizing Anthony with a sharp, authoritative gaze.

"If you can't trust your family, then who can you trust?"

"That's right. Come on, Delta. We're all brothers here. No need to worry," Brandon brayed.

"If you say so." He warily accepted their statements; perhaps this was his new family. The three lavender-robed executives exited the locker room and entered through the blue door on the east side of the changing area.

Anthony followed Ben closely, with Brandon trailing. He led them into a steel-walled chamber. A large window was positioned on the left side of the room. Standing on the other side of the observation booth was Dr. Fang, wearing a lab coat.

Behind him was an expansive laboratory where groups of geneticists overlooked rows of metallic chambers containing assemblies of cloaked men. The scientists hurriedly manned the control panels from behind the safety of the observation bay. They maneuvered about their stations in an organized frenzy, scattering about the passageway with an immediate sense of urgency.

"Gentlemen, if you would take your places. We are about to start," Dr. Fang calmly stated over the intercom.

"This way," Ben whispered as they followed him into the chamber.

He crouched next to Brandon. Anthony followed and knelt at the end of their procession.

"Gentlemen, I will be releasing a mild neuro gas, putting you in a meditative state. This will make the transition into your Lycan form painless."

Thank God. Anthony was relieved after the doctor's announcement.

"Once your transformation is complete, I will initiate the exit passage leading to the subway tunnels. Mr. Morgan and Chief Ramsey have already debriefed you on your directives. Be sure to be back here before sunrise; otherwise, your transition into your human form will take place outside of Gene-Con, which could be problematic. I will release the gas in ten seconds. Please prepare yourself."

Anthony was overcome with unnerving fear as the countdown began.

"Ten…nine…eight…seven…six…"

"Remember, stay behind me," Ben commanded.

"…five…four…"

"What happens if we don't make it back before sunrise?" Brandon shook with dread.

"…three…two…"

"We come looking for you!" Ben warned.

"…one."

A searing hiss sounded as misty gas crept into the air-locked room. Anthony inhaled the vapor and quickly fell into a trance. His consciousness immediately went blank, and he found himself veering into a dark void. Unaware of time and space, he saw the lifeless faces of his parents staring back at him with abysmal holes for eyes. He was terrified as he came out of his stupor and viewed the mist-filled chamber.

Strung along the stainless-steel floor were the purple tatters of the shredded cloaks that had once draped his naked body. He glared down at his clawed hands while snarling, licking his fangs as he admired his comrades' transformed bodies.

Standing beside him was Ben. No longer in his human form, he stood now as an imposing midnight-haired Lycan with a countershaded muzzle. Next to him was Brandon; he was smaller and less impressive. His coat was sable, with black saddle markings along the sides of his ribcage. Anthony caught sight of his beastly reflection in the lab's observation window. His almond coat glistened under the fluorescent lights

132

of the steel-clad chamber.

He observed Dr. Fang's reaction as the geneticist viewed them from behind the safety of the observation bay in amazement. The misty vapor quickly dissipated, and the doctor released the circular hatch.

"Happy hunting, gentlemen," he professed with an accomplished grin.

After his declaration, the steel-paneled door slid open to reveal the darkened railways deep beneath the city.

Ben raised his snout, sniffing sporadically, leading the charge. Their foot talons scraped against the metal floor as they rushed into the darkness. The Purebloods fiercely sprinted across the abandoned railways. The adrenaline of the hunt enthralled Anthony with a euphoric bloodlust. His carnal desire was briefly interrupted when he distinguished a multitude of gleaming red eyes peering out from deep within the dampened side tunnels. He paid them no mind as he rushed ahead.

Dashing through the soot-mired tracks, they came upon the Tenderloin Point platform. Reaching their destination, Ben vaulted onto the landing, leaping through the turnstile and rushing up to the streets.

As Brandon clamored up the stairs in front of him, Ben barked in protest, but he was too enthralled with the hunt and raced ahead, ignoring his authoritative snarls.

Ben and Anthony chased after him, but he was too fast. Brandon ran out of view as they sprinted onto the vacated streets of the Tenderlion. The dimly lit sidewalks were surrounded by high-rise tenement buildings. Ben and Anthony searched the shadowy landscape, combing through the back-alleyways and street corners. They were about to give up when they suddenly heard a sharp yelp.

Ben's pointed ears twitched, homing in on the cries. He raced for the alley, with Anthony trailing. As the lycanthropic search party rounded the corner, Anthony smelled the familiar odor that had been presented to them at the board meeting. It was Kane!

They fervently tracked the scent and sprinted into the alley where they discovered Brandon, latched onto Kane's back. He was transformed into a large, black-coated Lycan. Anthony shuddered at the notion of facing him again.

Kane seemed larger than he had remembered. The Half-Breed bucked and scratched in an attempt to dislodge Brandon, but the young Lycan was undeterred and sank his fangs deep into Kane's neckline. As his incisors penetrated his hide, Kane let out a pain-filled howl. He cried in agony as Brandon bit down and mercilessly clawed at his collar.

Ben leaped to the dueling beasts and swiped at Kane's expansive rib cage, tearing out mounds of flesh with his piercing talons while Brandon somersaulted off of him. The three Purebloods regrouped and encircled the side-gashed Half-Breed. They growled and snarled as they viewed the gushing wounds expel hemorrhaging pools of blood. Kane staggered in a defensive stance while clutching his lacerated midsection.

In an instant and with lightning speed, he scaled the back wall, narrowly escaping his aggressors. Brandon immediately clambered ahead of them, chasing after Kane's blood trail. Ben and Anthony hastily pursued, hurdling themselves over the wall.

Once on the other side, they found themselves on the pier of the Dockside Port. Towering cargo ships lined the concrete channelway as massive vessels ominously ebbed in conjunction with the night tide. They scoured the narrow slips in search of Brandon.

Scattered about the sprawling shipyard were gigantic stacks of containers positioned underneath looming cranes that swayed with a forewarning bob. Ben crouched over Kane's streamlined blood trail, lowering his muzzle and licking the plasma from the concrete. He snarled before taking off, dashing along the dripping line, with Anthony following. The beastly duo tracked the bloody path, which led them to an area of high-piled strongboxes.

A wincing cry wailed from deep within the stacks, resounding over the deserted shipyard. They rushed to the whimpers. As they turned behind a massive container, they discovered Brandon being ripped apart by a voracious pack of Half-Breeds.

His midsized frame was being forcefully torn between two veracious beasts. He desperately yelped as the Half-Breeds bit and slashed into his abdominals. Kane retreated from the slaying, cowering behind a rusted strongbox, while the larger Half-Breeds shredded Brandon's midsection.

Peering down from atop the stacks stood a group of Half-Breeds with shiny yellow eyes. They licked their lips at the sight of the carnage. Some were slender and more curvaceous, while others were dark hulking fiends. They veered down with hunger-fueled ire as their alphas tore Brandon apart.

He was no match for the stronger Half-Breeds, and within moments he was ripped in half. His slime-coated entrails spilled onto the pier as his dismembered torso trembled with a life-fleeing twitch.

Blood splattered over his assailants as they split his carcass with ease. Anthony noticed a distinguishable scar under one of the Half-Breeds' right eye as the beast mounted over Brandon's frayed carcass. The descended pack tore and pulled at his disemboweled entrails with a rapacious, hunger-filled frenzy. As they ensued with their blood-raging gorge, Anthony's chest heaved with adrenaline. The bloodied Half-Breeds abandoned their kill and lurched for them, while the rest of their pack stalked down to Brandon's gut-splayed corpse.

Anthony and Ben retreated as the gore-mired alphas pursued them with a drooling bloodlust.

The Half-Breeds relentlessly charged while Ben fled from the murderous scene, leaving Anthony behind. He scrambled, escaping across the port and over the back-alley wall. He lost track of Ben as he landed on the other side of the stonewalled barrier. He darted through the alleyways, leading to the boulevards of Tenderloin Point.

As he raced across the dimly lit streets, his hopes of losing the Half-Breeds were shattered when he glanced back to see the shadowy alphas trailing him. The murderous Lycans soon gained on him. Noticing that sunrise was approaching, Anthony ran faster. He started to feel his strong lycanthropic body weaken as he swerved for the entrance to the subway station.

He approached the stairway and turned to face his assailants. The scar-faced Half-Breed stepped in front of his hunting partner, growling. Anthony violently snapped in hopes of discouraging their advance. The beast was undeterred and abruptly slashed him across his chest. The Lycan's talons ripped through his torso with a serrating tear that seared his sternum. The forceful strike sent spurts of fleshy blood dashing along the stairwell, causing him to aimlessly fall.

He tumbled, hemorrhaging from his talon-slashed chest. He descended several flights, banging his frame against the hard tile steps before regaining his balance. He was bloodied and beaten, but relieved that, at the very least, he had managed to regain his balance. His roughened foot pads grasped the ledge of the stairs, allowing him to regain his traction and stopping his painful descent just in front of the turnstiles.

He snarled in apprehension of the rising sun while keenly observing the predatory alphas glowering down at him with aggravated disappointment. In fear of dawn, the overlooking Lycans retreated, disappearing into the streets of Tenderloin Point.

The retreating Half-Breeds let out foreboding howls as they weaved between the housing projects.

Anthony was relieved after their departure but felt his body flare with debilitating agony. His chest was mired in tattered flesh as he trembled. He angrily ripped through the turnstile with his meat-shredding claws, leaving an entanglement of slashed metal in his wake. After the dismantling, he tramped over the mangled remnants, leaving a bloody trail behind the contorted wreckage. He was thankful to be alive, but the Half-Breed's attack left him gravely injured. He was frail with the onset of sunrise. Noticing himself growing weaker, he traversed the dark tunnels leading back to the Financial District.

THE
LONE WOLVES

Anthony ensued his wounded limp across the subway's abandoned passageways, attempting to make his way back to the Gene-Con transformation chamber. As he persisted, he felt himself grow fatigued and depleted. His fur shed, his bones started to rescind, and his pronounced muzzle shrank. Only able to maintain a tottering hobble, Anthony slowly turned back into a man. His transformation was surprisingly painless. Cold, naked, and afraid, with his chest slashed, he braved deeper into the depths of the underground pathways.

As he shambled, he broke out in cold sweats. The gash across his chest was deep and he was losing lots of blood. If he did not receive medical attention soon, there was no doubt that he would succumb to his wounds. Enduring his stark-naked limp across the concrete barriers of the soot-filled tunnels, he shakingly grabbed a bundle of discarded rags from the ground and ripped a tattered piece of cloth from the soiled garments. He tied a makeshift bandage around his talon-slashed chest, securing the dressing by trussing a knot under his armpit. He draped the rest of the muck-covered clothes over his shivering body; the reeking, scant rags provided some warmth over his trembling frame. As he forged deeper into the darkened burrows, he thought about Brandon and was overcome with grief. Witnessing the animalistic disembowelment had a devastating effect on him. He was also nervous about returning to his pack unsuccessful and was angry that Ben had abandoned him.

As he tramped, he could distinguish a myriad of shining red eyes lurking deep within the shadowy corners of the underpass. He was filled with dread as he realized that the peering gazes belonged to a surrounding pack of Lycans. As they closed in, the encompassing creatures came into fruition. Anthony was suddenly cordoned off by a hideous, abominable pack. The beasts were scarred and mutated; some were hairless, and others had missing limbs. The red-eyed beasts surrounded him, snarling and growling, exposing their bloodstained fangs. He cowered, scared for his life. With a terrified, doom-filled heart, he waited for the disfigured pack to rip him to shreds.

"Disburse!" a thunderous voice unexpectedly shouted.

The circling mercurial pack scattered into the pitch-black

alcoves. Anthony veered up from his submissive posture to discover an immense, ten-foot tall Lycan with tan fur and red eyes approaching from the darkness.

Holy shit, I'm going to die! He started to hyperventilate as he witnessed the looming beast stomp over to him.

The gargantuan Lycan's head was bald, adorned with a throng of scars that zigzagged from his muzzle to the back of his cranium.

"Come with me," the marred beast instructed as he reached down with his large talons.

He can talk! Anthony was beyond relieved that the domineering creature seemed to be friendly.

He apprehensively grabbed the Frankenstein-like brute's talons, and with the aid of the red-eyed behemoth, he rose to his feet. He aimlessly followed the mountainous Lycan across the barren tunnels, with the freakish pack trailing them.

So these are the Lone Wolves. His thoughts were a conglomerate of fear and wonder as he shakingly followed the gigantic Lycan down the gloomy burrows.

The monstrous brute cleared a path for him farther along the underpass as they approached a homeless encampment. The scar-headed beast ushered him past the tent city, garlanded with foul-smelling garbage. As they marched, more disfigured Lycans watched from the depths of the rubbish-festooned passageway as their alpha lumbered to the far end of the encampment, where a makeshift throne sat. The grand chair was strung together with pieces of plywood and semi-transparent tarps. The large beast took his place atop his throne, peering down at Anthony as he limped to a nearby cable reel.

His chest hemorrhaged with burning agony as he violently shook with a depleted tremor. His body reeked under the soiled rags while he perched atop the wooden reel and timidly asked, "What are you?"

He cautiously observed the onlooking pack, noticing them stealthily huddling around him.

The large beast spoke with an intellectual cadence. "I should be asking you that same question, my boy. Your scent is not that of any

Pureblood I've encountered. So I ask, what are *you*?" the towering Lycan scorned, as Anthony shivered.

"I don't know what I am anymore!" Anthony dropped his head in exhaustion.

The goliath took pity on him. "'All the world's a stage, / And all the men and women merely players: / They have their exits and their entrances; / And one man in his time plays many parts.'"

Anthony lifted his head, quivering and perplexed.

"I see you're not familiar with Shakespeare," the beast acknowledged with disappointment.

"Sorry." Anthony shuddered while miring over his slashed chest; blood had soaked through the tattered rags and spilled over his belly, and he could barely keep his eyes open.

"There, there, now," the beast consoled. He pointed to him and ordered, "Clean!" After his command, a mangy one-armed Lycan with matted hair appeared from the shadows.

What the hell are these things? The sun is out, and they're still in their Lycan form. He was trying to make sense of everything; he was confused, scared, and angry as he watched the horrid pack of disfigured Lone Wolves.

The one-armed Lycan ripped the bandage from his slashed chest and licked the bleeding gashes.

Anthony pulled back in disgust.

"Don't! It will keep your wound from infection," the large beast encouraged.

Anthony reluctantly leaned back and allowed the mutated Lycan to lick his wounds.

This is fucking disgusting. He could feel the creature's slimy tongue glaze over his lacerations with a drooling splatter. After the beast was done, he retreated into the darkness of the surrounding campsite.

The colossal Lycan snarled before proceeding with his oration. "To answer your question, I was a man once, just like you. I was an English professor at Myrin City College, but that was a lifetime ago." He paused with a sigh as he reflected on his former life. "I was unjustly fired for my political views and subsequently ended up homeless. And I was so damn close to tenure!" His aggravated holler resonated across the encampment.

"'The world breaks everyone and afterward many are strong at the broken places.'"

"Huh?" Anthony was confused at the Lycan's random use of literary quotes.

"That's Hemingway, my dear boy! God, the education system is going to shit! But I digress. After I was let go, I drowned myself in sorrow, and when the sorrow wasn't enough to satisfy my self-loathing, I developed a taste for heroin… I saw you in the tunnel a few nights ago. I heard the jingling of your pills. I assure you, you do not want to go down the path I followed."

He waved his clawed hand, signaling for one of his mutilated underlings. A marred Lycan ran up to his dilapidated throne carrying a syringe between its mutated digits. The orating beast outstretched his arm, and the lesser Lycan injected him with a shot of heroin. He briefly nodded, closing his blood-red eyes, before abruptly coming to. "Thank you," he acknowledged. "Now where was I?" The smaller Lycan withdrew the needle and scattered back into the filth-ridden encampment.

"Oh, yes… I was in dire straits and in desperate need of a fix. That's when I signed up for Gene-Con's paid clinical trials. Once I signed my life away for a mere five hundred dollars, I was subjected to Dr. Fang's experiments. They blended my DNA with that of a Lycan, as they did with the rest of my esteemed colleagues you see before you. 'Cry "Havoc!" and let slip the dogs of war!'"

Fuck, he talks a lot. But I guess I would, too, if I was stuck down here with a bunch of lab-tested mutants. He looked over the contiguous pack and felt sorry for them, knowing that Gene-Con was responsible for their condition.

"We were all men once," he explained.

The Lone Wolves all lowered their heads in solitude as they listened to their alpha's discord.

"As part of Gene-Con's bioweapons program, they injected me

with growth hormones and conducted multiple brain-implant surgeries, which allowed me to speak while in my Lycan form, but only after being subjected to a multitude of torturous experiments and numerous pains-taking implants. One fateful night, we decided, enough! My fellow test subjects and I rose up in defiance and escaped from the lab!"

The pack chattered their transfigured jaws, sounding a horrid applause that reverberated across the campsite while their leader held his head high.

"Because of our altered DNA, we are unable to change back into our human form. Dr. Fang injected our eyes with permanent night vision to make us more efficient hunters. As a result, sunlight can cause permanent blindness for us. That is why we remain here, underground, scavenging for what we can and consuming those who would not be missed."

The gargantuan Lycan signaled for one of his underlings. A skinny, wiry-haired creature approached, holding a blender filled with dark sappy blood. The gangly monstrosity tottered to Anthony. He was cold and shivering from blood loss as the creature handed him the grisly mixture.

"Drink!" the colossal Lycan ordered. "It will help you regenerate your wounds and regain your strength."

Anthony held up the blender, smelling the sweet nickel-rich blood, and chugged. Gory rivulets streaked down the sides of his face while he rapaciously emptied the mixer of its contents. As the blood rushed down his throat, his body warmed with the fresh vigor of life. He felt immense strength course through him, and he stopped shivering.

I'm not going to ask where this blood came from, and honestly, I don't want to know. He was pumped with euphoria; his legs and arms tingled with renewed energy as his talon-slashed chest started to heal. The gaping lacerations suddenly transformed into healed-over scabs with thickened skin underneath; only traces of dried blood remained, serving as the lone evidence of his beastly attack. Anthony was shocked at how fast he healed.

After watching him drink, the overbearing Lycan smiled,

revealing rows of razor-sharp teeth. He grinned while feverishly licking his lips and proclaimed, "Blood. It does a body good!"

"What's your name?" Anthony was grateful as he wiped his face and dropped the emptied blender on the soot-covered ground.

"Professor Cody McQuaid," the mountainous Lycan proudly announced with his chest out.

"I'm Anthony."

"I know what you are, hybrid."

"What does that even mean?"

"'We know what we are but know not what we may be.' 'Some are born great, some achieve greatness, and some have greatness thrust upon them.'" Anthony was becoming annoyed with the beast's use of literary quotes in an attempt to avoid answering his question.

"Is that Shakespeare again?"

"Yes! And these are the Lone Wolves!" McQuaid pompously stood and outstretched his massive, brown-furred arms.

The transfigured pack clanked their jaws and ground their teeth in a raucous snapping ovation.

Anthony was astonished and filled with gratitude. These creatures had taken it upon themselves to help him. They had shown him mercy, and even though they were forgotten, tortured monsters, they had not lost their humanity.

"Thank you for saving me." He was humbled by their kindness.

"A good deed never goes unnoticed," McQuaid decreed. "One day we will take our revenge on the Purebloods." He leaned toward him with a wrath-filled stare.

Anthony timidly responded, "Speaking of Purebloods, my pack will be looking for me. I need to get back to MGE now!"

McQuaid scratched his scar-riddled muzzle. "Follow the tunnel behind me. It leads to a manhole just outside your building. I wish you luck, hybrid."

He pointed to a darkened alcove with a metal ladder.

Anthony darted through the tunnel and climbed the rusty steel rungs.

"It's nice to hear my name spoken again," McQuaid revealed. "Parting is such sweet sorrow. You can consider us allies to you, hybrid," he assured as Anthony reached for the underside of the steel plate.

He slid the cover back, sending beams of sunlight shining down.

"Light! Light!" McQuaid warned as the creatures beneath him cowered, taking cover from the intruding sun.

Anthony scrambled onto the cold morning streets of the Financial District. Several pedestrians watched in disgust as they witnessed the rag-covered man emerge from the sewer. He passed the bewildered onlookers and proceeded to the entrance of the tower. As he approached the turnstile, a burly security guard jolted out from behind the gold-framed entrance, standing directly in front of him.

"No shoes, no entry, sir." The guard peered at his soot-covered feet with disgust.

"No, you don't understand. I work here!" he pleaded while shivering on the snow-covered sidewalk.

"Yeah, okay, bud, and I'm the queen of England!" The guard snuffed in disbelief. "Move along, sir!" he commanded, before grabbing Anthony's shoulder in an attempt to usher him away.

"Let him in!" Ben peeked his head out and ordered the guard to stand down.

The officer reluctantly stepped aside, and Anthony entered the crowded lobby draped in mucky rags.

"Not a word!" Ben scolded as he hurriedly escorted him across the congested atrium. The masses turned in revulsion as the reeking, raggedy-clothed executive was rushed to the private elevator, where Ben scanned his hand.

The platinum doors opened, and they filed in.

"It's your fault Brandon's dead!" Anthony belted as the doors closed.

"Not now, Delta!" Ben reprimanded.

He adjusted his pin-striped suit and examined him in repulse. The cab descended to the basement, where Mr. Morgan and Chief Ramsey stood atop an elevated platform awaiting their arrival. They crossed the vacant garage, approaching the silver-suited CEO and the chief, who was dressed in his commander's uniform.

"What the hell happened?" Mr. Morgan shouted as they approached.

"Brandon ran ahead of us, sir. He didn't stay behind me," Ben interjected as they both stepped onto the platform.

"Ben left us behind!" Anthony protested.

Mr. Morgan berated them with furious resentment. "What a mess! We have one of our pack members dead and another dressed like a goddamn street beggar!" he yelled while scratching his white-bearded chin.

After their alpha's scolding tirade, Ben glared at Anthony with a heated scowl.

"Gentlemen, please. I took matters into my own hands," Chief Ramsey calmly interjected while tilting his hat.

The garage gates suddenly opened with a clanking rattle. A barred prison van pulled inside and backed up to the loading bay. The transport sounded a procession of electronic beeps as it reversed. The vehicle came to a stop, and two uniformed police officers exited. One of them clutched an aluminum pole with a slipknot at the end. The two constables unlatched the rear doors to reveal Kane. He was shackled, wearing an orange short-sleeved jumpsuit. He kept his head down, concealing his beaten face beneath his dangling dreadlocks, as the officer grasping the pole fitted the slipknot around his neck. The noose tightened, constricting his airway as the guards led him onto the platform.

The awaiting Purebloods stood atop the landing condescendingly looming over their shackled captive. Anthony noticed the bloody bandages over his ribs, which swelled from under his jumpsuit. Jarring scratches and bites garlanded his neck and shoulders as the officers ushered him to his captors. The brigadiers held the choke-collared convict at bay as Mr. Morgan confronted his hostage.

"Who's your alpha?" he asked with his chest out.

Kane endured, silent with his head down.

"Very well then. We have ways of making you talk, Half-Breed!" Chief Ramsey nodded to the jailer holding the choke stick.

The guard pulled the pole, gagging him. Kane stumbled before gawking at his abductors with quiet rage. The other officer hastily jumped into the rear of the van and rolled out a human-sized cage with silver bars. He wheeled the confine out, sending it clanging onto the landing. The silver-barred enclosure echoed with a metallic chime as the guard rolled it beside Kane.

"Get in!" Mr. Morgan ordered.

"My pack will not abandon me," he declared, scorning his kidnappers with hatred before reluctantly entering the entrapment.

Once he stepped inside, the guard released the slipknot and pulled the shaft from between the bars. He slammed the door, padlocking it shut. As Kane stood inside the cage, he inadvertently brushed his forearm against one of the poles, causing his skin to burn. He jolted from the edges of the enclosure and stood in the center, pensively staying clear of the toxic silver rods.

"Take him to Dr. Fang," Mr. Morgan commanded while pointing at an adjacent loading bay.

The officers rolled the confine up the ramp and pushed the cage into the loading area. Chief Ramsey turned to Mr. Morgan. "I will put out an alert that we have the full moon murderer in custody. That should draw the Half-Breeds out of hiding."

"Thank you, Chief. In the meantime, Dr. Fang and I will devise some creative ways of extracting information from him," Mr. Morgan snarled. The frustrated alpha turned his attention to Anthony and grimaced at him in disgust. "Thank God we have someone like Chief Ramsey among our ranks. Otherwise, your hunt would've been a complete failure!"

Anthony cowered in shame, enduring his alpha's criticism.

"Go get yourself cleaned up and take the rest of the day off. The next full moon is in three days. Hopefully you both can redeem your-selves before then," he fiercely reprimanded.

Ben and Anthony defeatedly marched to the adjacent loading bay.

"Shame about Brandon though," Chief Ramsey mentioned.

"Youth is wasted on the young," Mr. Morgan professed while viewing Anthony and Ben trailing the guarded cage.

"Ben!" he abruptly yelled.

"Yes, Alpha?" Ben turned to face his dissatisfied leader.

"Bring me a list of candidates for Brandon's replacement," he scoffed.

"Yes, sir," Ben enthusiastically avowed.

Anthony viewed Kane being wheeled away, and in that moment, he saw him as a man.

"The Purebloods will betray you, Anthony. They're using you," he muttered.

"How do you know my name?" he questioned while venturing closer to the cage.

"The same way you know my name, hybrid," he responded while glaring through the bars.

"That's enough, Half-Breed! Take him away!" Ben demanded.

The jailers obeyed and wheeled Kane through a double-doored entrance at the other side of the garage. Ben escorted Anthony to the changing area, holding his nose in order to shield himself from the putrid stench emanating from his tattered clothes.

Once inside the locker room, Anthony removed his disgusting, frayed garments and plodded into the shower. He turned the handle and allowed the warm water to rain over his muck-covered face. As he washed, he noticed that his chest wounds had completely healed.

"Don't ever address me in front of Mr. Morgan like that again!" Ben reprimanded from the changing area.

"Brandon's dead because of you!" he screamed while streams of water poured over his face.

"Don't put that shit on me! The kid didn't stay behind me. It's his fault he's dead!" Ben ran his hand through his slicked-back hair as the room filled with steam.

"If you guys weren't out all night partying and doing blow, then maybe he'd still be alive!" Anthony challenged as he exited the shower and wrapped a towel around his waist.

"Hey, I didn't put a gun to his head. And besides, he brought his own coke to the party! Let's face it. The kid was a bona fide degenerate!" Ben rebuked as Anthony trudged past him.

He halted, abruptly grabbing Ben in anger and slamming him against a locker with a boom. As he clutched his jacket with furious rage, the dented locker behind him trembled.

"That's it… I like to see you like this! A true Pureblood!" He smiled before Anthony loosened his grip.

"I'm not a Pureblood! And I'm nothing like you!" He released Ben and paced to his locker, where he viewed the cabinet next to him containing Brandon's hanging suit.

"We'll see about that, Delta." Ben laughed as he exited.

Anthony woefully removed his belongings and got dressed.

"Once you're ready, Marcellus will take you home. He's waiting for you in the garage," Ben explained as he held open the door.

"Okay!" Anthony indignantly retorted while pulling up his pants and tightening his belt.

"Sleep it off, Anthony. Tomorrow's another day." Ben slammed the door and left.

He adjusted his blazer as he sat on the bench in front of his locker. He removed his cell phone and discovered ten missed calls from Auntie Glo in addition to three voicemails from his concerned godmother.

He also had a text from Rey that read, "Hoooowwwwooo'ss it going?" with a wolf's-head emoji.

To which Anthony responded, "It's going."

He slipped on his loafers and called his worried aunt.

"Oh my God! Anthony. I was so concerned about you!" He could sense the panic in her voice, immediately followed by elatedness.

"Everything's fine, Auntie, don't worry. I've just been really busy at work—so busy they gave me the day off!" he lied in hopes of reassuring her.

"I'm so proud of you. Just remember to give me a call sometimes, I get worried."

"Nothing to worry about. I'm fine. I'll have the driver stop by your place on my way home. We can have a visit," he proposed with a tear in his eye as he reached into Brandon's locker and stroked his hanging suit, knowing that no one would miss him.

"That's wonderful! I'll put the kettle on," she responded with relief.

"Okay, see you soon."

"Great!"

He hung up, buttoned his suit, and departed, intentionally leaving his Rolex inside his locker. He needed to speak to his aunt after everything that had happened. He was overwhelmed and just wanted to see a loving face. He marched down the corridor and through the metal door leading to the garage, where a black Lincoln Town Car was waiting for him.

Marcellus remained inside as Anthony hopped into the back. The scar-faced driver glared at him through the dashboard mirror as he closed the door.

"Good morning, Marcellus. I would like to make a quick stop at my aunt's house before I go home. Is that okay?" he asked while scooting atop the leather seats.

Marcellus nodded in agreement, remaining silent as he maneuvered the vehicle up the ramp.

The midsized sedan careened through the bustling streets of the Financial District, slogging along in traffic.

"She lives on 357 Sycamore Drive, near the Nicolo River," he informed.

After twenty minutes or so, they arrived at his aunt's building. His indignation and grief-fueled angst began to ease as he got out of the car; visiting her always calmed his nerves.

"I shouldn't be long. Thanks for stopping," he noted before

closing the door.

He ventured into the lobby and headed down the hall. She lived on the first floor; her building was small, only three stories tall, with a drab painted finish. Gloria lived alone; she never married or had children. Anthony was all she had. He turned the corner and approached her unit. He smelled the fresh brew of Irish black tea wafting in the air as he knocked.

"Hello, my little Ant!" She opened the door with a big smile; she was wearing a Myrin City Knights t-shirt and gray sweatpants with pink slippers.

He stepped inside and wrapped his arms around her, embracing her with a welcoming hug. Her studio apartment was much smaller than his, but she kept her place clean and orderly, which made the unit appear bigger than it actually was. Anthony sat at the small dining room table between two steaming cups of tea and some biscuits. Gloria sat beside him.

"You look so thin. Have you been eating?" she asked with concern.

"Yes, I've been eating." He thought of his recent devouring of flesh.

If she only knew. He elected to spare her the gory details.

"What's wrong, my little Ant? You look worried." She took a sip from her steaming cup while studying him.

"I think I'm going to quit my job."

"What? Why? You just got a promotion. You can't quit now. After all those years of hard work you put in?!"

"The company's not what I thought it was. They're bad people, Auntie." He felt somewhat relieved; divulging his thoughts to her unburdened him, even if it wasn't exactly the whole truth.

"My advice, then, is to stick with it for a few more weeks. Then, if you still feel the same, quit."

"That's solid advice."

She always knows what to say. He felt better; she had reminded him that although he was a Lycan, he still had not lost who he was. She,

152

Sidney, and Rey were the only people keeping him sane in the sea of chaos he now found himself in. They were his only link to his humanity.

"I've learned a few things over the years, my little Ant. Your parents would be so proud." She smiled with a reminiscent gleam in her eye.

Proud of what? That I'm a killer and a monster? He struggled with the thought of what he had become. At first, being a Lycan was exciting, but now his condition was more of a curse than a gift.

"Have you spoken to Sidney?" she asked before chomping one of the golden biscuits with a crunch.

"Not yet. I'm giving her space. She was really pissed."

"I hope you two can work it out. She's a good woman."

"She is." Anthony took a sip from his tea; he missed Sidney and wanted her back, but he knew he had to get out of the Pureblood pack to have any chance at a normal life with her. *Maybe I should give her a call,* he considered while munching on a biscuit.

"Well, I need to get going. My chauffeur is waiting for me downstairs," he announced with his head held high.

"Okay, Mr. Fancy-Pants. Just remember, don't forget where you came from."

"I won't, Auntie. Thanks for the tea." He gave her a departing embrace.

"Don't worry, things always work themselves out in time. Just be patient." She shuffled him to the door.

"Thanks. I will." He marched down the hall as she watched him leave.

They waved at each other before Anthony reentered the Town Car. The glass divider elevated, separating Marcellus from him. Once the partition was in place, his voice broadcasted over the car's speakers.

"How's your chest?" he asked with a fiendish grin.

Anthony shook with fear as he realized that Marcellus was the scar-faced Half-Breed who had slashed him during their hunt for Kane.

153

THE
HALF-BREEDS

Anthony tried to open the door, he hysterically pushed, but the vehicle remained locked. After he thrust himself against the window in a frenzied panic, he came to the revelation that there was no escape.

"Let me out!" he screamed while kicking the glass partition until his foot throbbed.

Marcellus remained silent as the car drifted through the Financial District, making its way to the tenement buildings of Tenderloin Point. Anthony withdrew his cell phone. His heart sank when he noticed that his battery had run out.

"Where are you taking me?" he demanded.

Marcellus stared at him through the dashboard mirror and said nothing.

He's not going to tell you shit. He was trapped, and fighting the situation would only make matters worse.

In a last-ditch effort at salvation, he banged on the windows, hoping to alert the other drivers. His efforts were futile as he remembered that the tints of the Town Car were too dark for anyone to see in. He elected to save his strength and tried to calm himself as he awaited his fate.

The car pulled into the entrance of the port. A yellow-vested longshoreman waved at Marcellus from behind the gates. Anthony broke out in a nervous sweat while Marcellus drove past the dockside workers, venturing into the hectic pier. Anthony studied the scattering masses, looking for a potential opportunity to escape.

The waterfront wharf was a hustle and flow of forklifts loaded with containers and cranes swinging high above, a stark contrast from his experience the night before. The hydraulic booms unloaded sizable strongboxes from the portside barges, clamping them with a clanging racket.

Marcellus maneuvered across the pier, dodging forklifts while carefully zigzagging clear of the working cranes. As he drove, Anthony viewed the myriad of barges lined up along the slips which cast luminous shadows over them. Groups of longshoremen disdainfully glared at him from under their hard hats as they paraded across the bustling seaport.

How can they see me? They must be Half-Breeds! He was deathly afraid.

They ventured to the far end of the dock, where an empty shipping container awaited their arrival. Marcellus pulled into the strongbox and shut off the engine. Two dockside workers immediately ran behind and closed the doors, slamming them shut with a deafening clang. The atmosphere immediately went dark. Fear overtook him as he felt the container lift off the ground. Inside the pitch-black confines of the locked car, he waited in terror, sinking farther into the seats, desperate for any sense of security.

This is it. They're going to kill me. He started to hyperventilate while he sat in the darkness.

The vehicle trembled in conjunction with the hoisted containers descent. The confine shook with a bang as it landed. The doors swung open, sending a beam of sunlight streaking through the interior of the car. Marcellus got out; his black suit was wrinkled as he slammed the door and exited the container, leaving Anthony inside.

He joined a group of blue-uniformed workers who stood on the foredeck of a massive, rusted-out cargo ship. There was an equal mix of men and women aboard the corroded barge. Anthony peered out from the back window with his heart racing.

"Get out!" Marcellus demanded.

He was petrified as Marcellus raised his hand, holding the car's remote and unlocking the vehicle. Upon witnessing the lock pins elevate, Anthony was overwhelmed with fear.

"Get out, Mr. Montgomery!" he sternly shouted over the chattering crew.

Anthony knew there was no escape and got out. He was terrified, but did his best to hide his dread while stepping down from the container. He proceeded onto the foredeck filled with the awaiting pack of Half-Breeds.

"What are you going to do to me?" He approached Marcellus with caution while glaring over the side of the vessel.

He loomed down from the one-thousand-foot tanker at the oily, muddied waters as a possible escape route.

"Don't even think about it," Marcellus warned after observing his wandering eyes; he brushed back his jacket to reveal a wooden-handled revolver tucked into his waistline. "A jump from this high will kill you," he asserted as the Half-Breed crew sneered.

He knew Marcellus was right and reluctantly elected to follow him.

"As you were, people," he dismissed the surrounding deckhands.

Upon his command, they dispersed among the foredeck. Anthony watched with overwhelming anxiety as the crew scattered. The sprawling deck was adorned with shipping containers and a boom crane. He presumed that Marcellus was their alpha as he apprehensively joined his side.

"Follow me." He pointed for Anthony to trail him to the stern of the vessel.

As they crossed the deck, he noticed Mr. Shepard out of the corner of his eye, disguised in a crewman's uniform. The Englishman made inconspicuous eye contact with him from beneath his hard hat. Anthony felt a sense of relief knowing that he was on board and was careful not to look in his direction as he trailed Marcellus.

The escorting alpha trekked to the three-story tower of crew accommodations, where the captain's wheelhouse stood watch over the lively deck. Anthony hesitated, stopping his stride.

"Don't worry. If I wanted to kill you, you'd already be dead. Plus, there's nowhere for you to go anyway," Marcellus warned.

Anthony begrudgingly conceded, noticing the Half-Breeds' scowling stares as they went about their duties. He shadowed Marcellus to the wheelhouse, scared for his life. Once inside, he peeked down the narrow hallway lined with rows of bunks. At the far end of the corridor was a galley, filled with hanging pots and pans. Marcellus stomped down the hallway with Anthony timidly following. Once they entered the dining area, they came upon the ship's captain, who was seated at a round table eating a bowl of grits.

"Morning, Captain Furlong," Marcellus greeted the sizable

skipper with white flowing hair.

"Morning, Alpha." He stood and shook his hand.

So, Marcellus is their alpha. Anthony's suspicions were confirmed. He desperately wanted to run, but he knew if he did, the outcome would not be in his favor.

"Everything is as it should be?" Marcellus asked.

"Yes, Alpha," the long-haired skipper assured before sitting back down.

"Enjoy your breakfast, Captain." Marcellus patted him on the shoulder.

After their brief interaction, they departed from the galley. As they exited, Anthony noticed dark-red blood ebbing from under the sea-man's grits. The captain gawked at him with discernment as they headed for the far end of the galley.

Blood and grits? What the fuck is going on here? He was taken aback as they approached the freezer.

Marcellus lifted the lever, unlocking the cold storage.

"I'm not getting in there!" Anthony protested as he buttoned his suit, shielding himself from the chilling blast.

"Follow me, hybrid," Marcellus scorned as he led them past rows of hanging livestock.

Anthony uneasily straggled behind. As he proceeded under the hanging slabs, he noticed that some of the dangling livestock had large chunks missing, adorned with lacerating bite marks. Others were nothing more than hanging bone and cartilage.

This must be what they eat when they change. His taste buds were triggered as he smelled the suspended flesh. His animalistic desire to hunt was starting to take over as he weaved through the swaying meat.

Marcellus unlatched a hidden door at the far end of the freezer, revealing a massive loading area with a steel mesh floor.

Anthony scrutinized the expansive chamber as Marcellus led the way. Rows of curtained-off cubicles lined the outer walls of the prominent hold.

This must be their medical bay. He was shocked at the

expansiveness of the underdeck cavity.

The sprawling, crude hospital was embellished with rows of beds and medical equipment. Some of the cubicles were vacant, while others had pregnant women resting or being attended to by white-coated obstetricians. Anthony further observed the makeshift maternity ward and was astonished. As he stood in the center of the immense hold, he realized that this colossal tanker was the Half-Breeds' den.

Suddenly, he heard a woman scream from one of the curtained-off beds.

"Make it stop!" the pregnant lady yelled.

Marcellus rushed to the cubicle and pulled back the curtain. Anthony glanced over his shoulder as they both observed her jolt and scream. He contemplated reaching for Marcellus' gun but decided not to. The woman's agonizing shrieks rained over the colossal chamber as her rotund belly contracted. A chubby, short-haired lady, wearing medical scrubs and black-framed glasses, approached Marcellus as her patient toiled in agony.

"How is she?" he asked.

"She's in a lot of pain, but she'll pull through," she assured him.

"Aaaahhh! It hurts!" the woman wailed as her spread legs trembled in the stirrups.

The obstetrician hastily scrambled back to her patient. She reached below the woman's undercarriage, and after a few minutes, she let out one last bloodcurdling scream. The midwife extended farther under her crotch and pulled out a murky, placenta-coated baby. The newborn was blue and lifeless. She frantically hit the baby on the back, but the infant remained still.

"What's wrong?" the sweaty mother questioned.

"Nothing." The midwife desperately struck the baby again.

The child suddenly let out a cough and began to howl. The newborn's wolf-like cries resounded over the tanker's underbelly.

"It's a boy!" she announced as she wiped the baby down.

This is disgusting. I have to find a way out of here. Anthony looked away in repulsion and scanned the large chamber for a possible escape route.

After the newborn's howls had subsided, color flowed through his blue-tinted face. The child's bright yellow eyes glimmered as his animalistic pupils sharpened. The Lycan baby ferociously chewed through his umbilical cord, splattering puddles of dark afterbirth onto the steel floor. Once the infant separated his connection from his mother, the obstetrician wiped the baby's blood-soaked mouth, placing the child in Marcellus' arms.

The pregnant woman jolted again, screaming in agony while continuing to writhe.

The midwife adjusted her glasses and positioned herself back under her.

"I need another set of hands down here!" she hollered from beneath her separated legs.

After her plea, Anthony turned to Marcellus.

"Don't look at me. My hands are full," he announced while cradling his bloody newborn in his arms.

Anthony contemplated reaching for his gun now that his hands were full, but he felt sorry for the thrashing woman and reluctantly crouched beside the midwife. He shoved his hands under her as she toiled. She was drenched in sweat and her face reddened with agony as she pushed. In an instant, two more babies popped out from under her hospital gown.

"Twin girls!" the midwife enthusiastically shouted before shuffling one of the infants into Anthony's arms.

The newborn glared at him with sharpened, wolf-like pupils as she consumed her umbilical cord. The baby Lycan voraciously ripped and tore the connection between her and her mother with her tiny fangs. After the newborn Lycans had chewed through their umbilical cords, the stout midwife collected the infant from Anthony and rested the twins beside their drained mother. He was shocked and revolted at the site of the Half-Breed litter. His hands were mired in dark gooey afterbirth. He was about to hurl when Marcellus plodded to his lover's bedside, cradling his baby boy.

"You see, hybrid, we outnumber the Purebloods by the day." The doting father beamed with accomplishment while surveying the rows of cubicles.

The prominent alpha handed his child to the midwife, who laid the newborn on his mother's chest between his twin sisters. She smiled with joyous relief while cradling her beastly offspring.

"We did good, Alpha," she proclaimed in sweat-mired exhaustion while juggling her newborn Lycans.

"Yes, my love. We did." He kissed her soaked forehead.

"It's best she get some rest," the midwife suggested after wiping birthing plasma from her glasses with a paper towel.

Anthony viewed his afterbirth-stained suit and vomited.

"I'll be back," Marcellus jovially assured the expended mother as they exited the draped-off delivery room.

"You see, we are more human than you were led to believe. We are not the mindless ravaging beasts that your pack has labeled us."

Oh yeah, real humanlike, kidnapping me! Anthony's anger started to fester. "Look, just let me go, and I'll do whatever you want," he pleaded while whiping the puke from his face with the backside of his hand.

"It's not my decision, hybrid," Marcellus revealed.

"Why does everyone keep calling me that? And how come I didn't pick up on your scent?" he shouted in revulsion.

"Because that's what you are! And you didn't pick up on my scent because I injected myself with a pheromone blocker," Marcellus sharply replied as they marched along the rows of curtained-off beds.

He led them to a rusted-out doorway on the far side of the maternity ward. The proud father reached for the corroded entry and swung it open.

"After you." He smiled as he held the hatch ajar for Anthony to enter.

He cautiously proceeded through the doorway leading into a large, vacant holding area with an immense overhead trapdoor. Marcellus closed the hatch behind them, sounding an ominous metallic boom

162

that echoed over the darkened hold. They proceeded to the center of the massive containment area.

"What are we doing here?" Anthony asked, nervously surveying the immense chamber with dread.

"Wait," Marcellus whispered, taking his place next to him.

"I see you have brought the hybrid," an ancient, weathered voice uttered.

"Yes." He lowered his head in servitude.

Anthony peered into the darkened crook and noticed the Half-Breed elder emerge. The being was draped in a black cloak. The elder was hairless, with a wolf-like snout that protruded from under his hooded shawl. The lycanthropic creature was neither man nor beast, but something stuck in between. The cloaked being slowly approached. Anthony was disgusted as the hunched creature's hairless snout extended from under his dark hood and twitched, catching his scent. The wrinkled Lycan scuffled his talon-clawed feet while studying him with his elongated muzzle.

"His scent is that of a hybrid," the elder confirmed while glaring up at him in shock.

The creature's eyes were glossed over with a milky, opaque film, and his jaundice-tinted pupils twitched as he analyzed him. Anthony knew the furrowed Lycan was a primordial being from another time. His scent was old and dingy with decay.

"Now that we have the hybrid, we can exchange him for my son," Marcellus bargained while the elder sniffed.

"No, Marcellus! The time for us to seek revenge on the Pure-bloods will come soon enough," the decrepit Lycan shrieked as he caught his breath.

So they're going to trade me for Kane. That's why they need me alive. He was somewhat comforted finally knowing the Half-Breeds' intentions with him.

"But they're torturing my son right now, as we stand here!" Marcellus protested. "I brought you the hybrid. Now we must rescue my son!" he pleaded.

"Where are the Purebloods keeping Kane?" The elder pointed his feeble clawed finger at Anthony's nose.

"The Morgan & Green Enterprises building, in the basement. That's where Gene-Con has their lab set up," he willingly confessed.

"Spilled the beans pretty quick on that one." Marcellus chuckled.

"Let's just say I don't agree with their company policies anymore," he joked in hopes of lightening the tension.

The elder lurched toward him and explained, "A hybrid has not walked the earth in over two hundred years. There is a prophecy from *The Book of Lycan* that tells of a hybrid that can unite the bloodlines. Stand with us, Anthony, in our fight against the Purebloods!"

This is too much—another talking Lycan! Everyone wants a piece of me! At least the Lone Wolves didn't try to recruit me. He shook his head in disbelief; he just wanted all this to be over. Confusion and rage brewed inside him. "I don't know what to think anymore! First the Purebloods, then the Lone Wolves with that huge monster who calls himself McQuaid...and now this! Some old rat-looking creature telling me I'm some kind of hybrid from a prophecy! What's next? A vampire going to suck my blood?" He was inundated with hopelessness compiled with frustration and ire.

"Don't be silly. Vampires aren't real," Marcellus added with a smile.

"I see you have met the Lone Wolves." The elder interlocked his clawed hands in front of his frail chest.

"Yeah, I met those...things! What about it?" His aggravations grew as his stomach rumbled with hunger; he was beginning to unravel.

"The enemy of my enemy is my friend," the rickety elder quoted as he backed away. "Marcellus, we will wait until the blood moon. Then we will join the Lone Wolves, raid the Gene-Con lab, and rescue Kane," he proposed while trundling deeper into the shadows.

"But the next full moon is in three days. Shouldn't we attack then?" Marcellus implored.

"Our strength will be at its peak during the blood moon. We must wait till then. That will give us enough time to speak to McQuaid so the Lone Wolves can join our ranks. Kane is strong. He will survive," the elder reassured before disappearing into the darkness.

"Okay. So, it's settled then. You guys can let me go now. Right?" Anthony nervously wagered.

"Not exactly," Marcellus replied while looking up.

The overhead port hatch suddenly opened, and the auburn radiance of dusk danced over them. The towering crane's hydraulics hissed in conjunction with a large container being lowered. They stepped aside as the strongbox hit the platform with a bang. Marcellus swung open the doors to reveal a brown-stained mattress, some water bottles, and two buckets inside.

"Get in!" he ordered while parting his jacket, revealing the handle of his revolver.

"Come on. You don't have to do this!" Anthony desperately begged.

Marcellus remained stoic with his hand on his pistol

Now's your only shot. He lunged for the gun, and they hit the floor.

Anthony frantically scrabbled for his waist as Marcellus kicked and withdrew his revolver. He cocked back and pistol-whipped him across his forehead. Anthony stumbled with a debilitating jolt; his vision was blurred as he faltered.

"Okay! Don't shoot. I give up!" he conceded, wobbly and reeling from the heavy-handled strike.

Blood flowed over his eyes as Marcellus aimed down at him with his finger on the trigger. Anthony's heart stopped. He was frozen with fear; one small squeeze and it would all be over.

"Enough!" the elder reprimanded, creeping out from the shadows holding a bloodied slab of meat in his wrinkled hand.

Anthony's primal instincts took over after noticing the blood-dripping cutlet; he licked his lips as his belly turned with a craving famine. The ancient Lycan tossed the raw steak into the container. Anthony mindlessly tracked the scent while Marcellus closed in from behind. As he chomped on the meaty tissue, the bruise inflicted on his forehead shrank, and the blood flow ceased. Tearing through flesh appeased his emptiness.

"You should consider joining us," Marcellus wagered. "We'll give you some time to think it over. Let's say till the next full moon." He kept his aim and laughed.

"Here, this may have the answers you seek." The elder tossed a flashlight and a small leather-bound book into the container.

Anthony diverted from his gorge, viewing the small book lying on the steel floor, entitled *The Book of Lycan*. He paid no mind to his surroundings as he mindlessly consumed, using his concealed fangs to shred the meaty flesh from the shank.

"Maybe once he's eaten, he'll have a change of heart," the elder encouraged.

"Either way, the Purebloods will meet their end sooner or later." Marcellus slammed the doors with confidence, leaving Anthony trapped inside.

He mindlessly ate the rest of the bloodied steak, only concerned with consuming flesh. His mind was that of a feral beast. Once the bloody tissue reached his stomach, he felt a calming satisfaction. He grabbed the flashlight and aimed the small spotlight toward the floor. He picked up a water bottle and chugged the hot liquid before wiping the remnants of afterbirth and blood from his hunger-fueled feast. With his ravenous craving satisfied and his thirst quenched, Anthony removed his jacket and laid on the soiled mattress. He sat with his back against the cold ridges of his entrapment. He shut off the flashlight, exhausted, as his belly swelled with fulfillment. He closed his eyes and started to drift off, fixated on thoughts of Sidney. He missed her smile and the way she used to look at him when he came home from work. He longed for the smell of her hair and her delicate touch. He started to cry, reflecting over all he had lost and what he had become.

After several hours of uninterrupted sorrow, Anthony had come to one absolute conclusion: he had to get out of this container and start over with her. But in order to do so, he knew he needed to get away from all these damned Lycans. His embattled thoughts consumed him.

He was overwhelmed before he slipped into a long slumber.

He was suddenly awakened by a powerful jolt. The container shook. He scrambled to his feet, grabbing the flashlight. He felt the strongbox ascend. The container teetered, sending the empty buckets and mattress sliding for the doors. He steadied himself as the entrapment seesawed before it hit the ground with a tremble. He could hear the crew scatter about the deck as the crane's hydraulics hissed. He waited in anticipation for the doors to open, but they never did. He sat in darkness, listening to the day drone on. Rather than let his mind wander for hours in the dark, he elected to read *The Book of Lycan*.

Fuck it. What do I have to lose? Maybe the answers I need are in here. He shone the flashlight and began:

Before the dawn of civilization, in the beginning, there was the Ultima Lycan. The supreme being and the matriarch of all Lycans. The Ultima possessed the ability to shape-shift at will, regardless of the astrological conditions. In desperate need of a pack, the supreme being turned its sights on the Neuri tribe, an indigenous nomadic race of gypsies. After being bitten by the Ultima, the tribesmen became Lycans themselves. They were the first of their kind, a lycanthropic tribe that could shape-shift at will. Over time, their numbers increased. However, as their pack grew, their bloodline splintered into two distinct subsects.

Those that could transfer their bloodline with a bite were known as the Purebloods. The others were known as the Half-Breeds, which could only reproduce sexually.

Since the Purebloods and the Half-Breeds could only shape-shift during the full moon, the Ultimas had a superior advantage over them. Animosity grew between the factions, and feuds developed between their ranks. The Half-Breeds and Purebloods joined forces, and together they waged war on the Ultimas.

The integrated packs outnumbered the Ultimas, and soon they were exterminated. Centuries passed, and over time the Purebloods and Half-Breeds turned on each other, dividing the once-unified pack.

It is said that every two hundred years, a hybrid will walk the earth, one who can reproduce its bloodline with both a bite as well as sexually. It is also said that the hybrid will bring peace to the warring packs and unify the bloodlines.

This is fucking nuts. Anthony closed the book and noticed that the outside noise had quieted with the onset of nightfall.

He shifted atop the mattress, readying for a good night's rest, when suddenly a loud clank sounded and the doors slowly creaked open. His heart raced with fear, anticipating the torture from his captors.

He shone his flashlight on the crevice and glared up to see Mr. Shepard. His light beam gleamed off the Englishman's bald head as he peered into the container, squinting.

"Mr. Montgomery, we must leave now!" he announced in a panic. "And shut off that damn flashlight!" he belted while adjusting his longshoremen uniform, keenly surveying the vacated deck behind him.

Anthony obeyed his rescuer's command with relief.

"Here, put these on. I grabbed them from the crew's quarters." He tossed him a uniform.

Anthony discarded his placenta-stained suit and hurriedly slipped on the disguise, shoving his dead cell phone into the uniform's front pocket before exiting.

Thank God. I'm getting the fuck out of here! He was beyond grateful as he proceeded across the deserted foredeck, following Mr. Shepard to the stern of the rusted-out barge.

They rushed down the gangway under the cover of night, hastily descending from the towering vessel onto the dock, where a black SUV waited. They both filed into the back seat.

"Thank you," Anthony nervously acknowledged, sweaty and out of breath.

He noticed Ramona in the driver's seat wearing an identical longshoremen uniform.

"Hello, my darling," she greeted with a smirk.

She drove to the port's exit.

"Get down!" Mr. Shepard commanded as he clutched the back of Anthony's neck, ducking him between the seats.

He tensely glared at the wolf's-head ring adorning his savior's finger, mindful to remain hidden as the vehicle approached the guarded exit.

Ramona rolled down the window while an orange-vested port officer advanced. She nodded, producing an ID. He reviewed the card before pressing the button for the gates to open.

"Have a good night, ma'am." He winked while handing her the ID.

Ramona nodded and slowly drove ahead, waving at him with a foolhardy grin.

"Stupid idiot!" she declared while accelerating onto the highway.

Anthony's daunting fears were alleviated as they sped down the snow-slicked freeway. He took a seat and peered out the window, watching the dock slip away.

"Where are we going?"

"I am taking you to Dr. Geani," Mr. Shepard revealed.

"Why?" He was confused as Ramona glared back at him.

"Because it's the only way we can save your bloodline."

"God, what's the big deal about all this bloodline shit! That creepy elder gave me some Lycan bible to read." He was beleaguered with confusion and just wanted to go home.

"Oh, I see. Here, take my copy." Mr. Shepard produced a small book from his breast pocket.

"That's okay, Shep. You can keep your little book. I'm over this shit. All I want to do is go home and take a long, hot shower." He peered out the window in silence.

"Suit yourself." Mr. Shepard shrugged.

They took the exit to St. Josephine Hospital where Ramona

dropped them off. Mr. Shepard accompanied him as they proceeded through the hospital's main corridor, crossing the under-construction wing. As they ventured beneath the scaffolding and tarps, Anthony sensed that he was unusually nervous.

"Are you okay?" he asked before they entered Dr. Geani's darkened waiting room.

"Yes, Mr. Montgomery. It's just that the full moon is soon approaching, and the Half-Breeds may have picked up on my scent when I rescued you from their barge."

"Thanks again. I don't know how I will ever repay you. That's twice you saved me." He whole-heartedly expressed his gratitude as best he could as they sat.

Mr. Shepard studied him, his brow trickling with tiny beads of sweat.

"A war is coming, Mr. Montgomery, and I just hope that we are on the right side when the violence ensues." He reticently tapped his wolf's-head ring on the armrest.

After observing his apprehension, Anthony was worried; he knew there would be casualties ahead.

"Good evening, gentlemen. Nice uniforms." Dr. Geani entered wearing a white lab coat and black trousers, signaling for them to follow him.

The angst-ridden duo got up and trailed the pensive doctor. As they entered his office, an old-style projector stood atop his desk.

"Please, gentlemen, take a seat," he ordered while shutting off the lights and turning on the projector.

They sat across from the rattling machine and both gazed at the blank light shining on the far wall.

Dr. Geani adjusted his glasses while the old-fashioned projector shook with a machine-like clank. A grainy black-and-white image of a naked woman tied to a pole appeared on the wall. Dancing around her was an Indigenous troop of spear-wielding tribesmen.

"This is the first recorded image of the Neuri tribe," Geani explained as the spools rattled. "As you can see here, tied to the pillar is a helpless woman... Now watch."

He removed his glasses and rubbed his eyes. Suddenly, the projected imagery went black.

"What the fuck is this? Some kind of snuff film? C'mon, guys!" Anthony blurted in frustration.

After his brief tirade, the film recommenced, and the pole-tied woman had transformed into a slim, dark-haired Lycan with a brindle-patterned face. The agile beast broke from her bondage and ravaged the tribe. Their spears were no match for the Lycan's strength and speed. In a matter of minutes, the tribesmen were ripped to pieces in a ferocious bloody carnage. The doctor shut off the clanking projector and turned on the lights before sitting at his desk.

"Why are you showing me this?" Anthony asked with vexation.

"Do you recognize the Lycan in the film?"

"Yeah, it kind of looks like the one that dragged me through the woods. But I'm not sure. My memory is a little hazy. If I remember correctly, it was a larger white-haired Lycan that bit me."

"Yes, well, what if I told you there was a way to break your curse?" Geani proposed.

"Wait, what curse?"

"There's a metaphysical element associated with your condition."

"English, Doc."

"It is said in *The Book of Lycan* that once bitten, one can break their curse and revert back to their human form by killing the Lycan that bit them," Mr. Shepard added.

"I guess I missed that chapter." Anthony shook his head and asked, "So if I kill the Lycan that bit me, then I will become human again?"

"Somewhere along the line, we forgot that humans are animals too. But to answer your question, yes," Dr. Geani confirmed.

Anthony felt some reprieve after his explanation, realizing that there was a way out of all this chaos.

"So, it was an Ultima that bit me?"

"I believe so. Your blood samples show that your genetics are in fact commingled with that of an Ultima. However, your specific attributes remain that of a hybrid."

"You lost me, Doc." He just wanted simple answers.

"Let me try and explain." Geani studied him with a sympathetic gaze.

"You were bitten by an Ultima, making your genetics that of a hybrid. An Ultima can only reproduce its bloodline from sexual reproduction, not a bite. However, if bitten by an Ultima, you in turn become a hybrid, whereby your genetic code is altered so that you can reproduce your bloodline with both a bite and sexually. So, if you have offspring, they will be hybrids. If a hybrid mates with an Ultima, then their offspring will be an Ultima, able to shape-shift at will. That is the only way an Ultima can reproduce their bloodline, by mating with a hybrid."

"I think I understand." He was still puzzled, but felt that's what he needed to say.

"Your hybrid genes override the genes of both the Purebloods and the Half-Breeds," Mr. Shepard explained after observing his baffled expression.

"Now I'm even more confused!" He was tired and just wanted all this to be over.

"If you bite a Pureblood or Half-Breed, they will become a hybrid. That is what makes you so special. Your genetics can unite the packs into one bloodline, wiping out the others."

"Okay, I get it. So that's why they all want me to join them. To control the bloodline."

"I believe so," Mr. Shepard confirmed with apprehension.

And that's why the Purebloods don't want me biting anyone. Shit, I could start my own pack. He pondered the possibilities before asking, "So, all I have to do is go to the woods outside of Mr. Morgan's cabin, turn into a Lycan tomorrow night, and kill the fucker that bit me, and I'll be cured?"

"Sort of." Mr. Shepard rolled up his sleeves, peering at him with intensity. "At times, being a Lycan can be an advantage, and sometimes it's not. If you turn, the Ultima that bit you will pick up on your scent.

And as you've seen from the film, the Ultima is much quicker and more powerful than you."

"So, then, how do you propose I go about breaking this curse?" He leered at Dr. Geani, hopeful for a resolution.

"With this." Mr. Shepard reached into his uniform's pocket and held up a black stone amulet attached to a thin chain.

"Holy shit. Is that the amulet that was stolen from the museum? *You* stole it?" Anthony thought of the cash reward as he viewed the smooth glimmering rock.

"No, the Half-Breeds stole it, and I, in turn, nicked it from their ship." He cunningly smiled.

"I see. So what's this amulet going to do for me?" He glared at the dark stone swaying under Mr. Shepard's clenched fist, drawn to its magnetism.

"This is an ancient moon rock dug up from the temple of Anubis during an archaeological expedition in the early 1900s. If you wear it during the full moon, it will stop you from transforming into a Lycan, and it will mask your scent."

Anthony grasped the thin chain and stuffed the talisman into his pocket.

"These are the keys to Mr. Morgan's cabin and the security code to his alarm and gun safe." Mr. Shepard withdrew a small envelope from his side pocket containing a set of keys and a handwritten note with the security codes.

"What are you, some kind of fucking catburglar?" Anthony questioned in surprise.

"I have my moments," he countered with a smirk.

"I thought Mr. Morgan had you both on his payroll?" Anthony was leery; he felt as if he was being set up. He didn't know who to trust, but for some reason he knew he had to go through with this plan.

"If I'm a turncoat, then so be it. I don't approve of Gene-Con's experimentation practices. I took a Hippocratic oath to do no harm, and I plan on keeping that oath," Geani explained with an unnerving cadence.

Anthony knew they were both taking a risk by helping him.

"And you?" He turned to Mr. Shepard.

"My loyalties are to the sanctity of the bloodlines, not to one man or corporation," he clarified with a solemn tone.

This is insane, but what choice do I have? I can't live like this. He was befuddled with skepticism as he grabbed the envelope.

He thought of his safety and the protection of his loved ones, realizing that this was his only way out. If he could break the curse and become human again, the Lycans would have no interest in him.

"Good luck, Mr. Montgomery." Dr. Geani dismissed.

"Thanks, Doc. I hope someday I can repay you both for helping me." He shook his hand.

"Believe me, you already have." Geani gave him a crooked grin as he escorted them out of his office.

"Have a good evening, Doctor." Mr. Shepard saluted.

"Happy hunting, gentlemen." Geani bade them farewell as he closed the door.

They left the hospital and entered the awaiting SUV.

"Ramona, let's take Mr. Montgomery home. It's been a long night for both of us," he ordered.

"Yes, my darling." She stepped on the gas.

They both sat in silence until Ramona pulled up to his building. As Anthony got out, Mr. Shepard leaned over and mentioned, "I don't believe we will be seeing each other again. I wish you luck and Godspeed."

"Same to you, Shep." He shot out his hand, grasping his sweaty palm.

With Anthony's finger grazing the top of his wolf's-head ring, they shook one last time.

"Thank you." He was grateful as he peered into his daggering green eyes.

"The pleasure was all mine, Mr. Montgomery. Take care of yourself. I wish you well."

"Goodbye, Ramona." He was saddened knowing that they would

not see each other again, after everything she had done for him.

"Remember to fukus, my darling."

"I will, and it's pronounced *fo-cus*." He laughed before closing the door. He watched as they ventured off into the night and was grateful that he had been rescued, but realized that new dangers lay ahead.

THE RETURN TO THE CABIN IN THE WOODS

Anthony entered his apartment and removed the amulet from his pocket, along with the envelope Mr. Shepard had given him. He threw off his stinking longshoremen's uniform and slogged over to the bedroom where he plugged in his dead phone, laying the device on his bed. He was exhausted as he undressed and got in the shower.

Warm water rained over him, and as the soothing steam rose, he felt unadulterated rage propagate from deep within his bowels. His wrath was directed toward the Lycan that had turned him into the monster he now was. He thought about all he had lost since he had been attacked in those backwoods. He would have given anything to have his old life back. He punched the wall, smashing the tile, splitting his knuckles. As blood ran over his fist, he let out a rage-filled scream. His holler morphed into an echoing wolf-like wail.

Unadulterated fury flowed through him in anticipation of tomorrow night's full moon. As he glared at his bleeding hand, he realized that he was becoming more Lycan than human.

He got out of the shower, reached for the box of Band-Aids inside his medicine cabinet, and pressed a bandage over his gashed knuckles. He stuffed the package back inside the cabinet and reached for his Oxy-Contin, debating whether to take them. He wasn't in any pain, but he desperately needed an escape, even if it was just to help him sleep.

Fuck it. He dumped two pills into the palm of his bloodied hand and shoved them in his mouth. As he closed the mirrored cabinet and observed his gaunt reflection, he didn't recognize the man looking back at him. He ran his tongue across the overlaying incisors protruding from under his gumline and smiled with a fiendish grin. He dried off and draped a towel around his waist before sitting on his bed. He took a deep breath and noticed his charging cellphone light up with numerous missed calls from Ben, Auntie Glo, and Rey.

It's too late to call them, he reasoned. It was 2:30 a.m.

He knew he could call Rey though. He apprehensively dialed his childhood friend, putting the call on speaker, hoping to get an answer.

He sat half-naked on his bed, nervous with expectancy.

"Hell—Hello," Rey's half-asleep voice creaked with disorientation.

"Rey, wake up!"

"Hey, what's up, Tony? Man, your auntie has been blowing up my phone. Where have you been?"

"I was kidnapped."

"Holy shit!" His voice suddenly livened up.

"Are you okay?"

"I'm good, bro, but I need a favor from you."

"Sure, fam, what's up?"

"I need you to drive me to Mr. Morgan's cabin tomorrow morning."

"Okay, no problem. But first I need you to do something for me."

"What?"

"Call your aunt, man. She's been blowing up my fucking phone for the past two days. She's worried sick!"

"I'll call her in the morning. Be at my place by eight o'clock. Can you manage that?"

"Yeah, sure… So, why are we going to the cabin?"

"We're going hunting." Anthony was determined to put an end to all this, and he knew he needed his friend.

"Right on. I'll see you in a few hours, bright-eyed and bushy-tailed." Rey yawned.

"Thanks, buddy. I owe you one."

"You owe me more than just one. Don't forget to call your auntie, okay?"

"Sure thing, bro. Good night."

He hung up and rolled under the covers. He was suddenly hit with the euphoria of the Oxys and quickly fell asleep without calling his aunt. His phone rang with an illuminating glow, awakening him from his brief slumber. He turned to his phone and saw: "Incoming call from Auntie Glo." He was agitated as he rubbed his eyes and answered.

"Oh my God! Anthony, are you okay? I'm worried sick about you!" she screeched in a panic.

"I'm fine, Auntie, I just needed to get some sleep."

"Are you okay? I feel like there's something you're not telling me," she probed with worry. "Have you been taking more of those pills?"

"No," he lied. "Just do me a favor."

"Sure. Anything."

"Keep your eyes open and be on alert. If you see anything suspicious, like a car following you or any of my colleagues from work show up, call me or Sidney. Don't call the police." He thought of Chief Ramsey and knew the Purebloods would be looking for him since he hadn't shown up for work.

"Anthony, are you in some kind of trouble?"

If she only knew. He was worried himself, but didn't see the point in getting her all worked up over his problems. "No, I'll be okay. Just remember what I said. If you see anything suspicious, call me or Sid, okay?"

"I will. Are you two back together?"

"No, now can I please get some sleep?" he pleaded with half-closed eyes.

"Yes, sorry, I was just worried."

"I know, Auntie. At least I still have someone who cares if I live or die. After me and Rey get back, we'll go out to dinner. Just not at Timmy's Diner. I have bad memories in that place." He cringed while recalling his breakup.

"That would be fantastic! Get some rest, my little Ant. I love you."

"Love you too." He hung up and trundled under the covers; after a few hours, he was unable to sleep. He laid on his back and debated whether to call Sidney but elected not to. She would just think he was crazy and paranoid. Besides, it was too late to call anyone.

He got out of bed and immediately felt anxious. It was 7:46 a.m. He unplugged his phone and texted his aunt: "Remember what I said, I'm leaving the city with Rey, if you need anything call me or Sid."

After he sent the text, he noticed several missed messages from

Ben: "Delta, where are you?" "Call me when you get this." "Mr. Morgan is asking about you. You need to come into the office now! The full moon is tonight!"

Anthony blocked Ben's number and went to the bathroom. He opened the medicine cabinet, admiring the vial of Oxys, and debated whether to take them. He knew he didn't really need them. He thought about what McQuaid had said, and after a few tense moments he decided not to.

Can't be all loopy on Oxys if I'm hunting a Lycan. Plus, guns and drugs don't mix, he reasoned before getting dressed.

He grabbed a pair of jeans and boots with a black nylon jacket. As he slipped on his undershirt, he heard a text chime from his phone. He sprang over to the bedside, half-dressed, hoping it was a response from his aunt. To his dismay, it was a text from Rey.

"Good morning brother, I'll be downstairs in 20 mins."

"Ok, sounds good," he typed with disappointment. *It's not like her to not message me back.* He was concerned but figured that she was probably still sleeping since they had been on the phone late.

He finished getting dressed and draped the stone amulet around his neck. He shoved the envelope Mr. Shepard had given him into his pocket and collected his belongings. He snatched a pair of gloves from his nightstand before rushing outside.

Blistering winds rushed over him as he waited for Rey. He was both anxious and excited, envisioning the hunt that lay ahead. He stuffed his frigid hands through his leather gloves as Rey's audacious van, airbrushed with his grimacing face, pulled up. Upon seeing him, Rey sounded the cavalry-charge horn and rolled down the window.

"It's a beautiful day for hunting!" he enthusiastically shouted.

"More like a cold day." Anthony hopped into the front seat and closed the door.

"Hey, at least it's not snowing," Rey exclaimed with a smile.

Anthony was thankful to have such a loyal friend. He took off his gloves and saw that Rey was outfitted in full camo gear. His spiked hair was his natural brown color. Anthony couldn't help but laugh.

"Wait, no pink hair today?" he jested.

"I'm off doggie duty, bro, and besides, you can't go hunting with bright hair. We would be spotted from a mile away." He snickered while maneuvering through the morning traffic.

"Did you talk to your aunt?" he asked while turning onto Pioneer Bridge.

"Yeah, we spoke." Anthony gazed out the window, peering down at the frozen Nicolo River, peppered with aimless ice-skating sprawls of humanity.

"Good, man. She was really worried about you," he confessed while accelerating across the towering bridge.

Anthony deflatingly viewed the Myrin City Human Services building where Sidney worked.

"Have you spoken to her?" Rey probed after witnessing his sullen expression.

"Nope," he sharply replied.

"So…what happened to your hand?" He attempted to change the topic.

Anthony removed the crusty Band-Aid from his knuckles to reveal a completely healed wound.

"I cut myself last night in the shower," he explained as he marveled in disbelief.

"Wow, man, you regenerate pretty fast. No scab or nothin'!" Rey scrutinized while weaving over the expansive bridge, taking the turnpike to the Alto Vista Mountains.

"You're like Werewolverine!" he cackled.

"I'm more like Beast than Wolverine," Anthony snarled.

They both let out a nervous laugh as they ensued with their northerly course for the white-capped mountain range. The surrounding cityscape slowly melted away, and they found themselves encircled by pine-scented woodlands.

"It's nice to finally get out of the city. You know, I feel like I can breathe again." Rey cracked the windows, leaving a small crevice between them and the outside world. He inhaled deeply before exhaling slowly.

"Smell that fresh mountain air!"

Brisk gusts swirled throughout the interior of the van, gently brushing the pink shag dashboard.

"Okay, so where do we go from here, dude?" he asked while surveying the countryside.

Anthony lifted his nose and inhaled the chilling breeze, taking in the smells of the surrounding forest. He caught a peculiar rancid scent. "Take the next exit on your right."

Rey peered at him awestruck before exiting the turnpike and venturing onto a two-lane highway bordered by looming redwood trees.

"Shit, I need to get gas!" he shouted with urgency.

"There should be a rest stop a mile or so ahead," Anthony calmly assured.

"You can smell it, huh?"

"Better than any GPS," he scoffed while tapping his nose.

A small gas stop suddenly appeared over the horizon with two rusted-out pumps.

Rey pulled into the dirt-bottomed station, stopping beside one of the corroded pumps.

"Jeez, this place could use a facelift," he commented.

They entered the quaint, slightly leaning general store. The small bell chimed as they marched inside. The quick stop was comprised of timber shelves covered in thick layers of dust. Two humming refrigerators were positioned in the back, displaying cold drinks.

"Mornin', gentlemen," a stubble-bearded elderly man wearing a trucker hat greeted from behind the rickety checkout counter.

"Good morning," they responded in unison as they weaved across the aisles and headed for the refrigerators.

Rey reached in and grabbed some bottled water. As he cupped the jugs under his arms, the doorbell sounded. An imposing Native American man with white dreadlocks stomped into the establishment wearing a chalky camouflage poncho. His matching cargo pants were splattered with blood.

"Yo, check this guy out," Rey whispered while creeping down an aisle, pretending to inspect the snacks and magazines.

"Good morning, Hunter. I see Mother Gaia has blessed you yet again," the clerk greeted.

They watched from behind the shelves with childlike curiosity. As they peered across the aisles, they glanced out the storefront to see an old, muck-and-blood-covered truck parked alongside Rey's van. Sprawled over the flatbed was a bloodied buck carcass with an arrow through its neck.

"Yes, the great spirit has been close with me." The mysterious Native's voice was low and crackled.

He produced a Ziploc bag from under his poncho. Inside was a bloody heart.

"Bro, what the fuck?" Rey nudged Anthony as they both peered over the shelves at the bizarre transaction.

"People up here are different," Anthony whispered while his mouth watered at the sight of the bloody organ.

"Thank you, Hunter. This will not go to waste." The shopkeeper accepted the heart from the towering tribesman.

"Thank Gaia. She is the one that provides. I am merely a harvester of her bounty."

The strange Native draped the hood back over his hoary dreadlocks and exited the shop, the bell chiming upon his exit. They watched as the Indigenous hunter sped off in his blood-and-muck-covered truck. The storekeeper dropped the bagged heart into a knee-high freezer behind him as Anthony and Rey squeamishly approached the kiosk, shoving their water bottles and some beef jerky onto the counter.

"Will that be all, gentlemen?" he asked while tallying their purchases.

"And thirty bucks in gas, please, sir." Rey slammed the money onto the wobbly counter.

He shoveled the cash into the register as Anthony nodded for Rey to exit.

"I'll meet you outside, I have to use the restroom," he dismissed with a fake monotonal intonation as Rey collected the provisions.

"Thank you, sir. Have a good day." Rey juggled the bottles and jerky under his gangly arms while pushing open the door with his backside, bumbling his way to the van.

"The bathroom is just behind the fridges." The shopkeeper pointed.

"Yeah, on second thought, I don't have to go... So, how much do you want for that heart?" Anthony peered into the old man's eyes with belly-churning hunger.

"Oh, sorry, youngster, I'm afraid that's not for sale. You see, only Indigenous people can hunt this late in the season. The heart was a gift. And besides, it's illegal to sell meat from an Indigenous hunt," he reluctantly explained while tipping his hat.

Anthony presented his wallet and slammed $300 on the shaky counter.

"Well...you look like a nice enough fella!" the clerk hastily recanted while creeping his hand over the stack of bills. "I'm sure I can make an exception."

He transferred the currency into his pocket before turning to the freezer behind him. He bent down and slid the bloody bag over the counter.

"You didn't get this from me." He winked.

"Thank you, sir." Anthony nodded with satisfaction as he swiftly collected the heart and left.

"Happy hunting!" the shopkeeper shouted with an ill-omened grin as the bell chimed behind him.

While Rey pumped gas, Anthony hopped into the van with the bagged heart concealed under his arm. After he was done fueling, Rey got into the driver's seat to see Anthony gnawing down on the bloody organ.

"Bro! What the fuck?!" he shouted as his friend viciously tore through the slimy heart, using his concealed incisors to cut into the thick, juicy meat.

As he mindlessly ravaged, dripping spouts of thick plasma fountained onto his hands and gushed onto the floor.

"What? I'm hungry," he growled while rapaciously devouring the fleshy organ.

His mouth was smothered with blood. Ripped flesh dangled from his teeth as he delightfully chewed on the tender chunks of oily tissue.

"You're getting blood all over my floor, dude! Wash that shit out over the sink, man! I can't believe you!" Rey scolded as he peeled out of the gas station, heading north onto the two-lane highway.

Anthony clambered to the rear wash sink where he insatiably engulfed the rest of his snack. As the lurid remnants of torn flesh ran down his gullet and into his stomach, he felt an unadulterated swell of verve emanate through him. His physique was pumped with animalistic vitality.

After he was done, he washed the last bits of flesh from his hands and face. As the blood trickled, he observed small rivers of watery plasma swirling around the shiny drain.

God, please save the beast in me. He knew he was losing himself.

"Hey, Cannibal Lecter, any idea where we go from here?" Rey hollered, speeding down the highway.

Anthony wiped his face with some discarded rags.

"Make your first right a mile ahead," he announced before retaking his seat.

"I guess it's better you eat that heart than me… Please don't eat me, dude," he nervously pleaded.

"I won't… You probably taste like shit anyway."

"Probably."

"Sorry, bro. I just couldn't control myself anymore," he stated in shame before slipping his gloves over his bloodstained fingertips.

"It's okay. Let's just get to the cabin." Anthony could tell that he felt sorry for him.

As they drove, he smelled the fresh dew of incoming rain. Within a few moments of his detection, they heard the pitter-patter of raindrops. The light flutters soon turned into a torrential downpour. Rey rolled up the cracked windows and turned on the wipers in a feeble attempt to combat the incoming storm.

A thunderous bolt of lightning struck with a sudden boom, illuminating the darkened skies as Rey turned off the highway and onto a dirt road.

"The cabin is ahead on the left," Antony instructed while peering through the deluge.

"If you say so, boss," Rey replied, hunching over the steering wheel as they advanced down the winding road leading to the chalet.

Rey stopped in front of the cabin's porch, aligned with three rocking chairs. He parked and shut off the engine.

"I guess we better make a run for it. Last one to the porch is a rotten egg!" he playfully shouted while gathering the provisions.

He galloped through the fierce storm, reaching the dry safety of the porch, where he waited for his friend. Anthony draped the hood of his jacket over his forehead and bolted, sprinting across the rainy muck before jumping under the porch.

"So now what, dude?" Rey questioned, soaking wet while balancing the water bottles and jerky.

As they both stood under the overhang, looking out at the incoming squall, Anthony removed the envelope from his pocket and unfolded the letter inside. Written on the small note were two four-digit codes: "Alarm: 6114. Gun safe: 4161."

"Here goes nothing." He nervously placed the key into the knob and pushed the front door open.

"Intruder alert! Intruder alert!" the alarm sounded with an ear-piercing blare.

Flashing strobes compiled with the deafening screech of a buzzer frantically sounded throughout the three-story chalet. Anthony burst inside and rushed to the panel, where he hurriedly typed in the code: 6114. The earsplitting alarm muted.

"That was one hell of a burglar alert. I hope we don't catch a case," Rey boldly announced as he entered the spacious cabin while awkwardly balancing the supplies under his arms.

Anthony stuffed the key and the note back inside his pocket while Rey rushed ahead, sauntering past the lumber staircase into the kitchen, where he laid out the provisions on the counter. He flipped on the lights, illuminating the scullery.

"No, Rey! Shut them off!" Anthony roared.

"So, like, what? We're just supposed to stumble around in the dark?" he protested as he hit the lights.

Anthony could see him perfectly across the dark with his night vision. "We need to look for flashlights and the gun safe. We can't turn on any lights. I don't want anyone to know we're here. That's the last thing we need right now!" he reprimanded as he scrummaged around the kitchen, searching for a flashlight. Even though he didn't really need it, he knew Rey did, so he played along.

"Got 'em!" Rey announced from the corner pantry.

"Nice! Now, if I was a gun safe, where would I be?" Anthony probed as he grabbed a flashlight, clicking it on.

"My bet is the master bedroom," Rey suggested.

They navigated the gloomy chalet and climbed up the stairs. The cabin seemed larger than Anthony remembered, but, of course, this time it wasn't overstuffed with MGE employees. As they crept up the steps, the relentless drumming of the rainstorm echoed over them. A flashing bolt of lightning brightened the sky as they persisted with their climb.

"I can't believe you talked me into this." Rey shook his head as they came to the landing.

"Bedroom's this way." Anthony shone his light and opened the door.

"Aaaahhh!" Rey screamed in horror.

Anthony turned in a panic and saw a fanged beast. Posted next to the doorway was a stuffed mountain lion.

"Come on, Rey. We got to find the safe," he hastily encouraged, thankful that the fierce cat wasn't a Lycan.

"Bro, who has a stuffed cougar in their bedroom?" Rey flashed the spotlight on him.

"C'mon, man, you stuffed plenty of cougars uglier than that!" he joked while shining his beam back over his face.

"Ha, you got me on that one." Rey squinted with a fool hardy smirk. "I've done plenty of shaggin' in that wagon!"

"Too much info, bro. I'm going to check the closet," Anthony redirected, opening the bifold doors across the bedroom.

"Jackpot!" he excitedly proclaimed while viewing the large safe secured to the back wall.

He brushed past the rows of clothes to the safe's keypad. He typed 4161. The thick door unbolted with a clank, revealing an armory of shotguns and various high-caliber handguns. Stockpiled on the bottom were stacked boxes of ammunition.

"Sweet baby Jesus! That's a lot of guns!" Rey shrieked while peering over his shoulder.

"Mr. Morgan is an avid hunter... Keep the light on me," he ordered while dropping his flashlight and collecting two pump-action shotguns from the rack.

"You know how to use those?" Rey asked while steadily aiming his flashlight on him.

"Yeah, my dad used to take me shooting, but that was a long time ago," he explained with glossy eyes as he handed Rey a shotgun.

He grabbed the barrel with a shaky hand before Anthony collected a rifle for himself, along with a box of bullets.

"What about you? You know how to use that thing?" He adjusted the rifle over his shoulder while tucking the box of slugs under his arm.

"Yeah, just load, pump, point, and shoot."

"That sounds about right. Just don't forget the safety," he advised while handing him a handful of shells.

"Safety first," his gangly friend ignorantly stated as he shifted the barrel over his shoulder.

They proudly toted their weapons as the relentless downpour quieted. The violent drumming transitioned into a sprinkle as they marched to the kitchen, where Anthony carefully loaded his shotgun.

"Locked and loaded!" Rey exclaimed as he followed his example, shifting the forestock.

"So, what are we hunting?" he asked, resting the loaded gun over his shoulder.

"*We* aren't hunting anything," Anthony replied, stuffing some shells into his coat pocket.

"Really? Then why the fuck did you drag me out here! To be your chauffeur?" Rey exclaimed with a fiery tone. "I even bought this camo outfit and everything!"

"Rey, I need you to stay here and hold down the fort. If I don't come back by tomorrow morning, then don't come looking for me," he instructed, observing his heated gaze.

"C'mon, let's take a seat outside, and I'll explain everything."

"You go ahead. I'll be right out," Rey dismissed while wandering through the kitchen.

Anthony proceeded to the porch and laid his gun on the floor beside him.

He was unnerved while surveying the surrounding forest. Contemplating the rigors of the hunt consumed him. The rain had stopped just as the sun made its descent over the tree-capped horizon. Anthony pensively swayed on the rocking chair as his anxieties took over.

God, I hope this works. His worried inhibitions were a jumbled, terrified cluster. His fears were heightened with the anticipation of the moonrise.

Suddenly, a loud bang sounded from inside the cabin. He scrambled for the door. With his heart racing, he reached for the knob. As he grasped the handle, Rey abruptly swung open the door with an embarrassed look on his face.

He had a disquieting expression, toting his recently fired gun over his shoulder while carrying an opened bottle of wine coupled with a package of jerky.

"Sorry, bro. Forgot the safety," he embarrassingly stated before slumping atop one of the rocking chairs with his chest heaving.

"Man, that scared the shit out of me!" Anthony belted as he sat next to him.

"Don't worry. The…s-shot…h-h-hit the ceiling. No…b-b-big… d-d-deal, but my ears are still ringing," he defended with a trembling stutter while trying to play it off. Anthony hadn't heard him stammer like that since high school.

"Jerky?" He offered the hickory-smelling bag with a wobbly hand.

"No, I'm good, thanks."

"Oh, that's right. You already ate," he whispered with a creeped-out smile.

"What happened to safety first?" Anthony couldn't help but laugh.

"Wine first. Care for a swig?" He passed the bottle to him.

"Fuck it." He took a long gulp in hopes of alleviating his anxieties and handed it back.

"Mr. Morgan definitely knows his wine," Rey complimented before taking another swig. He held up the libation, inspecting the vintage. "Who says alcohol and guns don't mix?"

"Everybody," Anthony countered while gazing at the picturesque sunset.

"You got a point there." He bit into a jerky strip.

"The reason we're here, is because I'm hunting the Lycan that bit me," he explained, watching Rey become more intoxicated with every swill.

"A little revenge hunting, huh?" he added as he sipped the bottle, washing down bits of jerky, before passing the libation to Anthony.

"Something like that. If I kill the Lycan that bit me, then the curse will be reversed, and I will become human again." Anthony took another chug.

"I don't think you can ever go back to what you used to be, but I understand. So, what happens when the moon rises tonight?" Rey grabbed the bottle.

Anthony unzipped his jacket revealing the onyx stone dangling over his chest.

"This amulet will stop me from changing."

"Thank God. I don't think I could deal with you as a werewolf." Rey took a long sip in reprieve.

191

"I hope this works. This is my only shot at getting my old life back."

"No pun intended." Rey chuckled as he patted his rifle.

"Come on, Rey. Be serious. There's something else I have to tell you."

"Okay. Shoot." He chuckled.

"C'mon, seriously." Anthony loomed over his inebriated friend with nervous angst; he wasn't sure what his reaction would be, but he needed to tell someone.

"Okay, okay. I'm all ears." Rey stopped rocking and listened with intent.

"Remember that murder near my place?" he asked, ashamed.

"Yeah. Poor woman was ripped apart. Saw it on the news. But they caught the guy that did it. His name was Kane or something, right?" Rey looked into his eyes for reassurance.

"I did it... I killed that woman," Anthony confessed.

"Fuck." Rey stared at him with disappointment.

"I couldn't help it. Once I turn into a Lycan, the beast takes over. The hunger and blood lust is uncontrollable," he cried, hoping Rey would understand.

"So, I guess this really is your only shot... No pun intended," he lightheartedly jested.

"May God have mercy on my soul." Anthony was humiliated as he glared through the redwood trees amid the setting sun.

He grabbed the bottle and took a long drink before shamefully handing it back. He solemnly removed his gloves, zipping them into his front pockets, stuffing them alongside a handful of shells. The two childhood friends drank and rocked, watching the sun set. Soon, the bright orange hew of dusk transitioned into nightfall.

"Well, it won't be long now." Anthony turned and saw that Rey was fast asleep.

The empty bottle rolled off the porch with a hollow ping. Anthony beheld the radiant moonrise with tense anticipation. The full moon shone down on him as he tucked the amulet under his shirt, allowing the stone to touch his bare skin. Shooting pains suddenly coursed through him. He jolted from his chair and shook uncontrollably.

Shit, this isn't going to work! The fiery hurt inside him permeated as he tremored with encumbering pain.

He quaked in fearful agony as the beast inside him emerged. Without warning, the amulet shined with an emanating pale light. The onset of the stiffening seizure melted away, and Anthony felt the growing beast inside him dwindle.

The amulet's light faded as he grabbed his shotgun. After clutching the cold barrel of the stock, he zipped his jacket and pulled out his gloves, draping them over his bloodstained fingertips.

He was reinvigorated with determination as he stepped off the porch with a clear sense of purpose, leaving his slumbering friend behind. He ventured farther into the thicket. The hunt was on.

Although he had not physically changed, his senses had become more wolf-like. The surrounding darkness reflected off his retinas, adjusting to the pitch-black woodlands, allowing him to see with canine-like night vision.

As he trekked over the rain-soiled muck, he picked up on a pungent feral aroma. He instinctively followed the scent, tracking the sour smell farther into the undergrowth. His ears perked as he detected the sound of a faint running stream.

He adjusted the barrel over his shoulder and ventured across the moonlit forest. He hiked deeper into the uncharted thicket, following the sound of the babbling brook which led him to a clearing.

He abruptly stopped. A succession of ominous howls splintered the silence of the gloomy night. He shivered as the incessant wails echoed across the forest. The woodland hounds' forewarning cries resonated with an unrelenting discord. Anthony peered up at the menacing glimmer of the full moon and debated whether to turn back as the hollers dwindled.

He hesitated before finally deciding to proceed. He forged deeper into the dense thicket, stepping over bulbous extruding roots, motivated by a carnal desire to kill. After painstakingly traversing the uneven landscape, he finally came to the shallow stream.

The turbulent rivulet reflected the distorted radiance of the moon as he approached the creek. He took cover under a nearby brush, observing the rock-strewn shoreline without detection. From behind the safety of a prickly shrub, he scanned the outer banks of the river. His night vision allowed him to conspicuously scour the shoreline in search of the foul-smelling Lycan.

After studying the outer banks, he saw what his senses had led him to. There, across the ankle-high stream, was the white-haired Lycan. His heart raced as the colossal beast lowered its massive head and drank from the ford. The faint shimmer from the amulet masked his scent, and the beast was unaware of his presence as it slurped.

Anthony wedged his rifle on a nearby branch, aiming at the guzzling monster. Once the hulking Lycan was between his sights, he shifted the safety.

The massive beast unexpectedly stood from its crouched position. Its daunting red eyes vigilantly examined the wooded countryside as it snarled, exposing pearl-white fangs. Anthony knew he had to take the shot. He exhaled and squeezed the trigger. The blast jolted him. A spark of gunfire lit up the forestry with a resounding blast. The beast abruptly turned, and the slug struck a nearby tree, splintering the massive redwood's trunk. The giant Lycan swiftly retreated, disappearing into the enveloping maze of redwoods. Anthony frustratingly shifted the pump, expelling the fiery shell. The slug sizzled as it hit the rain-soiled muck.

"Shit," he whispered in disappointment before shouldering his gun.

With his ears ringing, he drudged across the brook, ensuing his relentless pursuit. As he traversed, the cold flowing waters seeped over his boots, soaking through his socks.

Fuck, I can't believe I missed. He thought of his dad. He would've been so disappointed with him. All those years hunting bucks and boars, now he could barely tag a huge Lycan. His aim wasn't what it used to be. He had gotten rusty; city life had made him civilized. With an unwavering resolve, he crossed the ice-cold stream and forged into the bordering thicket, following the sizable Lycan's muck-stamped footprints.

He painstakingly tracked deeper into the bellows of the shadowy forest, bringing him to a clearing, where he observed the behemoth with his back to him.

Anthony readied himself again and took aim. The shot rang with a pulsating boom. He peered through the smoky discharge to see the creature retreating as the shot whizzed by. He kicked the expelled shell in frustration.

"Fuck," he winced under his breath, discouraged, as he watched the brooding monster retreat deeper into the forest.

He unzipped his pocket and begrudgingly loaded two more slugs into his rifle.

Come on, Anthony. You can do this. You have to. He knew that killing the beast was his only chance at salvation.

He followed the Lycan's footprints deeper into the heart of the woodlands. As he trampled onward, he felt the chilling freeze of his river-soaked socks penetrate his feet. His toes grew numb with each bitter step. Anthony knew that he had to finish his hunt soon or run the risk of hypothermia. Nonetheless, he urgently pursued, tracking the sizable paw prints deeper into the rain-dampened woods.

Click. He suddenly heard the triggering sound of a metal latch as he stepped down, followed by an agonizing sharp pain that penetrated above his right ankle.

He screamed in torment as he viewed a rusted bear trap clamped over his shin.

The jaws of the bone-nerving snare penetrated his leg with a snapping stab.

"Aaaahh...*fuck!*" He fell to the soggy earth in excruciating pain.

Blood fountained over his boots, mixing into the mossy ground. He dropped his rifle and desperately reached for the clamped teeth. As he tried to pull the eroded snare open, he noticed a litany of radiant yellow eyes encircling him. While struggling, he witnessed a formidable pack of wolves quickly surrounding him. They prowled closer, in hopes of an easy meal. The stalking pack bellowed with a gut-churning growl as they lurked toward him.

Anthony desperately reached for his gun and scooted along the muck. He fearfully inched back, causing the snare's chain to tighten. The sharpened teeth tore through his flesh as the clamping blades dug deeper into his leg, cutting through his muscle. He whimpered under his breath as the nerve-ending pain coursed through his ensnared limb.

He painstakingly maneuvered against a trunk. With his back pressed firmly against the coarse bark, he fired another shot into the darkness, hoping to ward off the encroaching wolves. The stalking pack was unphased by the blast and advanced toward their wounded prey. Anthony shifted the pump, expelling the shell. He readied himself again, aiming over the pack's approaching alpha.

He stared deep into the lurking wolf's hungered eyes as it snarled at him with a feverish drool. He wrapped his finger over the trigger and waited.

He held his aim with a trembling hand, but the large wolf unexpectantly retreated, as if spooked by an unforeseen specter. The rest of the pack followed, dissipating into the wilderness. Anthony was relieved as he lowered his aim. He laid against the trunk, bleeding in anguish, when he smelled a rancid aroma. The beast had returned. He was filled with dread as he heard the crunching of approaching footsteps.

Shit, he's coming back! He raised his gun, anticipating the return of the hoary-haired Lycan.

Vulnerable fear coursed through him as he canvased the darkened woodlands, desperately aiming toward the sound of forthcoming steps.

Clutching his gun, quivering with panic and excruciating torment, he noticed two shimmering red eyes peering at him from the forest. He aimed between the being's bloodthirsty gaze. As the dark figure approached, the ominous creature came into fruition. To his surprise, it wasn't the white-haired Lycan he had anticipated. He leered into the darkness and saw the dreadlocked Indigenous man from the general store.

"Help!" he cried while lowering his aim.

The Native rushed to him, wearing the same bloodstained poncho he had donned in the general store. As the mysterious man approached, he tightened his belt around his pants.

"Hold still," he commanded as he bent down and released the trap, positioning his feet over the side springs.

The corroded jaws opened, and Anthony removed his limp, flesh-torn leg.

"Thank you." He trembled with gratitude as he beheld his gashed limb.

"You're lucky I was just over the hill taking a piss when I heard your gun go off... We have to hurry. The wolves will be back soon," he urgently explained while helping Anthony to his feet. "Can you walk?" he further questioned, slinging his arm over his shoulder.

"I think so." Anthony took an agonizing step, leaning most of his body weight against his rescuer's broad shoulders. "Ahh. Hurts like hell." He stumbled, hobbling on his frayed leg.

He collected his shotgun from the mud before they limped across the forest. Anthony noticed the brown-eyed Native's facial markings. Underneath both his eyes, just above his tanned cheeks, were arrowhead-patterned scars accompanied by rows of tiny, imprinted dots. His forehead was adorned with tribal markings that ran down to his eyebrows. His chin was tattooed with dark thin lines running from under his bottom lip to the base of his mandible.

After a succession of lingering howls rained over the darkened woodlands, Anthony tripped, suspending their limping slog.

"Come on, we have to move faster!" the dreadlocked brave asserted, ushering him along the shrub-cleared trapline.

"I can't feel my feet." Anthony could tell that frostbite had set in as he glared down at his bloodied leg.

They staggered across the brush-cleared path, coming to an octagon-shaped cabin with a sheet-metal roof and chimney. Prominently displayed in front of the modest hut was the strung-up, fleshed-out hide of the buck that the mysterious brave had killed earlier. Parked next to the hide was his old mucky truck. They hobbled for the safety of the cabin, with the bloodthirsty pack stalking them.

The forewarning howls rang closer as they approached the front door. Anthony glanced over his shoulder to see a swarm of yellow eyes reemerge from the forest behind them.

"Get inside!" The Native trapper flung open the door and pushed him through.

He turned to face the encroaching wolves, aiming the shotgun at their leading black alpha. The feral hound growled at the site of the weapon-toting brave. He took aim and squeezed the trigger. The blast rang out, causing the surrounding pack to scatter into the thicket.

Their alpha remained unphased, standing boldly as he pumped the shotgun. A smoldering shell ejected from the chamber as he retook his aim, holding tight on the growling wolf. The creature of the forest paused with a diabolical sneer before deliberately reeling back into the darkness.

He entered his home and latched the door behind him before hanging the shotgun's sling on a nail beside the doorway. The small windowless cabin was designed with an open floor plan, constructed of plywood and harvested lumber. An alcove fireplace with hanging pots was notched in the far corner. Alongside the nook was a picnic-style table with attached planks for seats. Anthony collapsed on a wooden chair in front of the fireplace.

"That's my chair!" he disdainfully scolded while stomping his heavy boots on the plywood floor.

"Sorry, Hunter. But I kind of got a situation here," Anthony apologetically pleaded while glaring at his flesh-torn leg covered in blood.

He winced while painstakingly removing his boots and socks.

"How do you know my name?" the dreadlocked brave questioned, positioning a log from the fireplace in front of him, angling the timber upright for him to elevate his wounded leg on.

"From the gas station. I saw you give that heart to the clerk," he nervously replied while Hunter aided him with the removal of his socks.

The trapper stepped over to the inglenook and lit some firewood, tossing a match into the tinder.

"And you are?" he asked after removing his waterlogged socks, hanging them over the slow-burning fire.

"I'm Anthony." The flames crackled with warmth.

His gashed shin and calf were mired in blood; he watched as the droplets puddled atop the smooth log. Hunter turned from the growing fire and pulled off his poncho, revealing a dirty sleeveless shirt underneath. Anthony noticed a swarm of keloidal scars along his tanned arms that resembled Lycan scratches. Hunter hung his poncho next to the swaying shotgun as Anthony shifted his bleeding leg atop the stump, exposing his frozen feet to the warming flames.

"I was in the middle of a hunt when I heard your gunshots. Nearly woke up the whole damn forest. What were you doing out there?" he asked while plodding to the fireplace, sounding a drumline procession with each step.

I guess I should just tell him. He might be able to help me. I'm sure he knows every nook and cranny of this godforsaken forest. He debated before divulging, "I was hunting the Lycan that bit me."

The kindling embers turned into a crackling blaze. Anthony felt warmth penetrate his toes and permeate to the soles of his feet. After his confession, Hunter bent down and grabbed a fresh cut of buck meat from a nearby pot.

"Here, this should help you regain your strength." He tossed the cutlet over to him.

That went better than I thought. He snatched the bloodied steak midair and tore into the flesh with animalistic fervor.

He beheld the juicy meat in his black-gloved hands and viciously chomped through the stringy tissue. As he violently indulged with voracious hunger, Hunter looked down on him with awe.

"Just as I suspected… You are a Lycan!" he shouted.

Anthony bit down on the succulent filet with blood dribbling from his mouth, grateful for the generosity Hunter had shown him. If not for him, he would surely have been ripped to shreds by those wolves, and for that reason and that reason alone, he trusted him somewhat. Anthony knew he needed all the allies he could get, and for now he deemed Hunter as someone he could rely on.

"But you're still in your human form. Why haven't you turned?" he asked with a puzzled expression.

"This amulet." Anthony unzipped his jacket and unveiled the onyx stone.

"Amazing!" He gazed at the talisman; his eyes grew wide with wonder.

Hunter treaded to a removable wall in the far corner of the cabin and shifted back the partition, revealing a storage room filled with guns, dirty bombs, and a bow accompanied by a quiver stuffed with silver-tipped arrows. On the far end of the concealed room hung three snarling taxidermied Lycan heads.

Holy shit, that's a lot of ammo! Anthony's jaw dropped.

"I hunt Lycans also," he proclaimed while proudly standing in front of his trophy wall.

"I can see that." Anthony was shocked; the sight of the severed Lycan heads amid the assortment of armaments was daunting.

He nervously tucked the amulet under his shirt before finishing his feast. An immediate satisfaction radiated throughout his body as the fleshy remnants brewed in his gut.

This is the guy I need to put an end to all this. Plus, he hunts Lycans, and I know where to find plenty of those. There's a deal to be made here. His business acumen kicked in as he sat quietly and observed the Native's pensive mannerisms.

He analyzed the weapons closet while Hunter admiringly stood in front of his stash. The three snarling Lycan heads were all varied in color.

"The brown one is a Pureblood, the black one is a Half-Breed, and the gray one is an Ultima," he smugly explained.

Before Anthony could comment, Hunter lunged toward him, clenching an arrow.

"Wait, don't!" he pleaded with his mouth full of stringy deer meat.

Hunter laid the arrowhead over his exposed foot. His skin sizzled as the silver-tipped projectile tinged his warming metatarsals.

"Stop!" he pleaded as the shiny barb scalded his foot.

"Give me one good reason why I shouldn't kill you right now, Lycan!" Hunter withdrew the singeing arrowhead and redirected the point under his chin. He had rage in his eyes and Anthony knew he had to think fast.

"Wait…wait…" he nervously implored. "I know where all the Lycans in Myrin City will be on the next blood moon!" he desperately bartered in a panic.

Hunter withdrew the arrow from his jaw and dropped it back inside the quiver.

"I'm listening," he asserted.

Anthony hoped his explanation could sway him.

"On the night of the blood moon, the Half-Breeds are joining up with the Lone Wolves, and both packs are going to raid the MGE building in Myrin City to rescue Kane, the son of the Half-Breeds' alpha."

"Lone Wolves?" Hunter scoffed.

"Yes, their alpha is named McQuaid, and he can talk. The Purebloods experimented on them, but the Lone Wolves eventually escaped and now they live in the subway tunnels."

Hunter reeled in closer. "There is much to fear in this world, but nothing scares me more than the deeds of men."

After his decree, Anthony noticed that his ankle was no longer bleeding. The once frayed, torn gashes had completely healed. His skin had regenerated over the jarring wounds with the aid of the digesting venison stewing in his belly.

"What type of Lycan are you?" Hunter asked with a wonderous look in his eye.

"Apparently, I'm a hybrid," he explicated, in hopes of not becoming the newest addition to his trophy wall.

"And what about you? What's your story?" he delved while balancing on his newly healed ankle.

Hunter lowered his head in solace.

"I'm a direct descendent of the Neuri tribe… The Ultima Lycans decimated my people and killed my family… But I got my revenge." He pointed at the gray Lycan head.

"I can see that." Anthony was uneasy, but he decided to compliment his stash. "With all those guns and bombs, we can destroy all the Lycans in Myrin City," he explained, hoping Hunter would agree with his sentiment.

"The less Lycans there are in this world, the better," he stated before rolling back the partition with a hollow thud.

"So, you'll help me?" Anthony hopefully pleaded while ringing out his socks.

"I will. But after, I want you to give me that amulet as payment."

"Okay, on one condition," he proposed after slipping on his damp socks.

"And that is?" Hunter sat at the picnic table in the corner of the fire-lit cabin.

"I need you to help me kill the Lycan that bit me. Then I will give you the amulet." He stepped into his boots, awaiting his answer.

"Okay, deal," Hunter agreed, and approached with his hand out.

Anthony peered into his dark brown eyes, and they shook.

"Let's get you back. The sun will be coming up soon."

Anthony was grateful for his kindness; he still didn't fully trust him, but he knew Hunter was his only chance of him breaking his curse.

"I can't believe I'm actually helping a Lycan." He shook his head in disbelief as Anthony strung up his boots.

Hunter grabbed a handful of flour from a bag underneath the table and tramped to the fireplace, smothering the blaze with the powdery dust.

Anthony snatched his rifle as Hunter draped his bloodied poncho over himself. They exited the cabin with the morning sun peeking over them. As they got into the blood-and-muck-smothered truck, beaming hues shone through the outstretched buck's veiny cartilage as flies danced around it, picking the last bits of fatty tissue.

While he sat atop the torn, spring-coiled seats, he took notice of dog tags dangling from the rearview mirror. The name on the tag was "H. Wolfson."

He wedged his shotgun between his legs and waited for Hunter to start the truck. He reached under the steering wheel and turned the keys already lodged in the ignition. The starter stammered, struggling to turn over. Hunter turned the key again, and the engine rattled with a boom.

"She's a classic!" He shrugged with embarrassment as the chassis of the old truck tremored.

"Yeah, a classic piece of shit," Anthony yelled over the loud clanking.

Hunter sneered before accelerating. The rickety truck meandered for the two-lane freeway, surrounded by thick shrubs and redwoods.

"The cabin is a few miles ahead on the right," Anthony instructed.

He nodded in acknowledgment as the sun inched its way over the horizon. He was still suspicious of Hunter and decided to depose him further.

"You served?" he asked while gazing at the dangling dog tags.

"I was in the army," he answered with pride.

"Let me guess. Infantry?"

"Aviation officer. I flew Apaches." He exited the highway onto the dirt road leading up to Mr. Morgan's chalet.

"Huh. I thought only the air force flew helicopters?"

"Air force. Ha! I was going to join the air force, but then I found my balls and joined the army instead," he jested as they pulled up to the lodge.

Anthony elected not to mention his parents' military background; he wanted to keep Hunter on a need-to-know basis until he fulfilled his end of their bargain.

"Well, thank you for your service," he saluted with a half grin.

"Don't mention it, kid… Who's that guy?" Rey was fast asleep in the rocking chair with his shotgun by his feet.

"That's my friend Rey." He hopped out and slung his rifle over his shoulder, facing Hunter.

"Okay, hybrid. I'll meet you at your place in the city, the night before the blood moon," he proposed.

"Sounds like a plan. Let me write down my address." Anthony

scanned the dilapidated vehicle for a pen and something to write on.

"No need. I'm a Lycan hunter, remember? I'll find you," he pledged while eyeballing his amulet.

"Okay, suit yourself. Thanks again for saving me." Anthony was wary as he zipped up his jacket, concealing the pendant from Hunter's penetrating gaze.

"Take care of yourself. I'll see you soon." He confidently nodded as Anthony closed the door with a metallic clang.

Hunter backed up and sped away. Anthony watched with unease as the truck disappeared down the dusty path.

"Wake up!" Anthony shouted while jumping onto the porch.

Rey sprang from his chair with fright.

"What?! I'm up!" he barked while rubbing his eyes, disoriented.

"Let's put these guns away and head back to the city," Anthony ordered while entering the cabin.

"Did you kill any werewolves?" Rey eagerly probed after collecting his shotgun and flashlight.

"Not yet...but I will."

Rey zealously trailed him. Anthony's gawky friend strode into the kitchen, where he collected the boxes of shells while glaring at the scorched ceiling he had accidently fired into.

"You think Mr. Morgan will notice that?" he asked with a bashful grin.

"Definitely. Come on. Let's get the fuck out of here. I'm tired." Anthony was feeling woozy from a lack of sleep.

They bypassed the taxidermied cougar and hurriedly tossed the munitions back inside the safe, locking the heavy door. After jogging down the stairs, Anthony activated the alarm. They got into the van and commenced their drive back to the city.

"Myrin City, here we come!" Rey fervently announced, turning the ignition and shifting into drive.

He reached into his camouflage jacket and withdrew a .38-caliber revolver. He smiled before tossing the gun inside his glove box.

"I can't believe you stole a gun!" Anthony was amused at his emboldened thievery.

"Best to have and not need than to need and not have." He slammed the glove box and raced onto the highway.

As their journey ensued, Anthony became drowsy, resting his head against the windowpane. His eyes closed as reflections of the rising sun shone onto his brow. He quickly fell into a deep slumber.

As his subconscious dwindled into a dreamlike state, he saw the face of his aunt glaring back at him from a darkened, endless abyss. Her eyes were hollow voids, and her face resembled a ghoulish, obscured likeness of herself.

"Wake up!" Rey screamed, jolting him from his lurid nightmare.

He abruptly shot up and peered out the window. They were in front of his building.

"Your phone has been blowing up, dude," Rey explained as he yawned before hopping out of the van.

He pulled his phone from his pocket to see four missed calls from an unknown number.

"Here, I need you to take this for safe keeping." Anthony unzipped his jacket, removing the stone amulet from his neck.

He handed the talisman to Rey.

"No problem, bud." He leaned over and snatched the chain before draping the stone over himself.

"Does it suit me?" he questioned with a bold-faced smile.

Rey's whacky mannerisms reminded him of a rooster. "It looks great. We'll talk later," he acknowledged before closing the door.

Rey lowered the window and shouted, "Hey! Maybe you should call Sidney?"

"Yeah, maybe I will. Thanks for everything."

"Don't mention it!"

After his salutation, he drove down the traffic-jammed streets, blaring the van's obnoxious cavalry-charge horn. Anthony stepped inside and took the elevator to his floor. He entered his unit and sat on his sofa. After throwing his jacket and bloodied gloves on the floor, his phone rang.

"Hello?" he answered.

"Hello, Anthony?" The low, baritone voice on the other end was that of Chief Ramsey.

"Good morning, Chief," he apprehensively greeted as he got up from the couch.

"Son, I'm sorry to tell you this, but…your Aunt Gloria is dead."

After hearing those devastating words, Anthony's head went into a tailspin. His heart sunk with despair, and he started to hyperventilate.

"Hello…? Anthony…? Are you there?" the chief asked with a woeful tone.

"Yes…" He could barely respond, desperately trying to catch his breath.

He was inconsolable as his knees buckled.

"What…happened?" he mustered the strength to ask.

"She was murdered last night, coming home from the train… Her body was found in the back alley behind her building… Don't worry, son. We'll catch whoever did this… Purebloods take care of their own."

He was disheartened, in a state of confused rage.

"I need you to come to the morgue to identify her body. I'll be here waiting for you." Ramsey did his best to sound consoling.

"Okay…" Anthony hung up and collapsed.

He let out a gut-wrenching wail as he felt a part of himself die. As he lay on the floor in a paralyzed state of agonizing grief, he stared at the blank ceiling in a daze. He couldn't help but feel responsible for her death. The guilt was overwhelming. He should have stayed with her instead of going to the cabin. He had thought of himself instead, and now she was dead. He would never be able to forgive himself for that.

Hours passed. Anthony was barely able to gather enough strength to pick himself up off the floor, wishing he could go back in time so he could tell his aunt how much he loved her. He was alone now; she was the last biological connection to his parents, and she was gone. He felt ashamed as he reflected on all the things he had done since he had become a Lycan. He painstakingly collected himself, exhausted with heartache. He snatched his hoodie from the floor and headed for the morgue.

He wiped his tears as the cab stopped in front of the windowless building. Anthony reached into his pocket and grabbed his wallet. The driver took notice. "Don't worry about it... I'm sorry for your loss."

"I appreciate that," he acknowledged before exiting.

He shakily approached the tombstone-colored building. As he entered under the artificial lights, he felt cold and lightheaded. Waiting to greet him in the reception area was Chief Ramsey, wearing his usual decorated uniform and captain's hat.

"I'm so sorry, son," the tall commander comforted, grabbing his shoulder.

"Let's just get this over with." He was inconsolable and kept his head down.

"Follow me." They paced through a set of double doors at the end of a long hallway.

The cold storage room smelled of formaldehyde accented with the stale stench of death. The medically sterilized tomb was bordered with a lineage of stretchers draped with sheets resting beneath drawers that warehoused the dead. Waiting for them was a coroner dressed in an apron wearing a face mask and latex gloves.

"This is Mr. Montgomery," the chief announced to him.

He nodded and led them to a stretcher on the far end of the morgue. Anthony's heart raced with dread as he approached the sheet draped over his aunt's body. The medical examiner slowly lowered the covering, revealing Gloria's pallid face.

"That's her." He staggered while looming over her dead stare. It was difficult for him to breathe as he deflated with sorrow. "What was the cause?" He was barely able to ask as he felt a tightness constrict over his chest.

"Multiple lacerations," the coroner explained.

He inched down the sheet revealing grisly claw and bite marks dug deep into her neck and chest. Anthony immediately recognized that the deadly lacerations were from a Lycan. He scanned over her torn torso and noticed dark clumps of brindled hairs wedged between her gaping wounds. He smelled the distinguishable scent of Ben Damien, and he knew who had killed her. Agony and wrath churned inside him as he valiantly composed himself.

"Don't worry, son. We'll catch whoever did this." Ramsey was doing his best to console him.

This is my fault. If I had just stayed with her or answered Ben's texts, this would've never happened. He was lost and alone; his despairing sorrow was only soothed by the thought of revenge.

The coroner covered her up, masking her dead face.

"Mr. Morgan has agreed to pay for all the funeral arrangements," Ramsey assured him.

"Tell him he can keep his fucking money. I can bury my own!" Anthony vehemently decreed with clenched fists.

He wiped his tears and left the morgue with vengeance on his mind.

THE
BLOOD MOON
RAID

The next few days drummed on in a grief-stricken blur. Anthony monotonously went about making his aunt's funeral arrangements, picking out the casket, and consulting with her priest. Then the dreadful day finally came. It was time to lay his last living relative to rest.

With a heavy heart, he got dressed in a black suit and tie. He grabbed her rosary and stuffed the prayer beads into his pocket. He slipped on his loafers, left his apartment, and hailed a cab to the cemetery.

The drive was quiet. Anthony was overcome with sadness as the cab crept under the ornamental gates of the burial grounds. As the taxi approached the plot, he noticed a procession of cars lined up alongside the road down from the small hill. Atop the grassy knoll was his aunt's plot, where an oakwood coffin was suspended above a six-foot-deep hole. Amid the cavalcade, he noticed Rey's grooming van, along with a jet-black limo.

He paid the driver and got out. As he trudged up to the procession, fresh cut blades of grass stickered onto his loafers. He approached the plot and noticed Rey, wearing a black suit with no tie and sunglasses, standing in front of a small group of coworkers and friends of his aunt, who he barely knew. He was ashamed as he marched to the casket. Rey gave him a big hug.

"I'm so sorry." He noticed tears edging from underneath his sunglasses.

She was like a second mother to him, and he knew Rey was hurting.

"Thanks for coming." He did his best to hold back his emotions while engulfed in his childhood friend's embrace.

Anthony turned and noticed Sidney making her way to him from the crowd. His heart fluttered at the sight of her. She was wearing a black dress that complemented her dark hair and pale skin.

"I'm sorry... She loved you so much." She broke down while draping her arms around him.

Her hug comforted his grief-stricken soul.

"Thanks, Sid... She loved you too." He grasped her hips and backed away, looking deep into her weeping eyes.

She kissed his forehead.

"I miss you." She shuddered after wiping away her lipstick imprint with a handkerchief.

"I miss you too," he whispered.

"If you all would please take your seats, we are going to start." The priest raised his hands before adjusting his collar.

The attendees all sat as Anthony walked beside the coffin. He spread his aunt's rosary over the bridge of the casket. After letting go, he knelt beside her coffin and made the sign of the cross before sitting between Rey and Sidney.

She grasped his trembling hand as the priest began his eulogy.

"We are gathered here today to celebrate the life of Gloria Agnucci. She is survived by her nephew, Anthony. She was a child of God, and as with all children of God, she was called home. Though her life was cut short, we know for certain that she is in God's kingdom smiling down upon us. She was a devout Catholic and loved all those who she came in contact with. We commend her body to the earth from which she came... 'Yea, though I walk through the valley of the shadow of death, I shall fear no evil: for thou art with me; thy rod and thy staff they comfort me. Thou preparest a table before me in the presence of mine enemies: thou anointest my head with oil; my cup runneth over.'"

The priest produced a vial of holy water and splashed the casket as it slowly lowered into the pit.

"Ashes to ashes, dust to dust. In the name of the Father, Son, and the Holy Spirit." The minister signaled for the gathering to pay their last respects.

The procession lined up, tossing roses into the ditch and consoling Anthony as they went by. Sidney comforted him as best she could. After the attendees retook their seats, Anthony retrieved a white rose from under his chair. He stood and tossed the stem into the hole, glaring down at the fully lowered casket with a heavy heart. The finality of death struck him like a sledgehammer; his movements were slow and weighted with grief.

"Goodbye, Auntie." He sighed as he retook his seat.

"This concludes our service. We have some refreshments in the reception area for those who would like to join. Thank you all for attending as we bid Gloria farewell one last time."

The priest made the sign of the cross before departing to the reception area. Most of the assembly followed, while others tramped down the hill to their vehicles.

"Come on. You need to eat," Sidney encouraged while cupping his hand.

"Yeah, come on, buddy. Some food would do you good." Rey did his best to sound upbeat.

"Go ahead. I'll catch up to you," he instructed while keeping his head down.

"Okay, we'll see you inside." Sidney joined Rey, attending the small gathering.

Anthony sat for a while as two gravediggers shoveled dirt from a nearby mound. He watched in heartbreak as his aunt's coffin was covered.

I'm so sorry, Auntie. He was devastated. He put his hands over his face, trying to find a reason to go on. After the gravediggers left, Anthony smelled the familiar scent of Ben Damien.

He turned to see the tall, slender Pureblood wearing a solid black suit.

"I'm sorry for your loss," he falsely consoled with a deviant chuckle.

Anthony was enraged. Ben and the Purebloods had destroyed his life; he was ready to kill him right then and there.

"Now, now, don't get all heated up, Delta. Mr. Morgan would like a few words with you," Ben calmly stated while pointing to the limo parked at the bottom of the hill.

He was furious as he turned from his aunt's grave and broodingly followed Ben. As they approached, he noticed Marcellus in the driver seat. Fear and anger inundated him as Ben opened the door. Mr. Morgan was seated in front of the glass divider wearing a navy-blue suit with no tie. His winter-white hair was combed back. The menacing alpha scowled at him. As he entered, Ben closed the door. Mr. Morgan scratched his manicured beard, studying Anthony with an inquisitive scorn.

While observing the backside of Marcellus' bald head through the marginally lowered divider, Anthony knew he was listening, and chose his words carefully. They convened in the back of the limo, sizing each other up before Mr. Morgan spoke, oblivious to Marcellus eavesdropping.

"Remember, son, when you're a Lycan, the wolves are always at your door," he proclaimed.

"I'm not your son!" Anthony hollered.

"Remember that contract you signed," he calmly reminded him.

Anthony nodded as Ben smiled.

"Well, in the fine print, it states that if you miss more than one transition ceremony, we can terminate you from our pack... I don't think you want to become a Lone Wolf, do you?" he questioned with glaring intensity.

Anthony shook his head no in response.

"And you've already missed one ceremony and look what happened. Your aunt died. I'd hate to see what would happen if you missed tomorrow night's blood moon transformation... Who knows? Maybe your girlfriend will be next," Ben implied with an aberrant sneer. "Lest we forget, you killed someone. That late-night snack of yours was someone's aunt, mother, child. Funny how karma has a way of getting back at you," he elucidated.

"Okay! I'll come back... Just don't hurt anyone else!" Anthony fervently agreed as he examined their expressions.

"A wise decision, Delta," Mr. Morgan assured with a leering grin.

He was surprised at how calm and unphased they were. Unbeknownst to them, the Half-Breeds' plan to raid the building with the Lone Wolves would assuredly seal their fate. He took comfort in that.

"We know where the Half-Breeds' den is. After some physical convincing, Kane confessed that their lair is on a barge docked at the port," Ben revealed while Anthony viewed Marcellus obscurely listening in.

215

What fools. They don't know what's coming. He knew he had the upper hand as his alpha ensued with his ignorant discord.

"That's correct. Tomorrow night we're all going to transition together, head over to the port, and descend upon the Half-Breeds with the full strength of our pack!" Mr. Morgan announced with unwavering determination.

Anthony observed the backside of Marcellus' head twinge as he revealed his battle plan.

"I'll be there, sir!" Anthony avowed with certainty, playing along with their demands.

"Good… We believe the Half-Breed that murdered your aunt is their alpha, so you will have your revenge," Mr. Morgan misleadingly implored.

"I look forward to it, sir," he falsely assured, playing up to his wishes.

He knew the Purebloods' methods of deception and did his best to make them believe he was one of the boys again.

"I'm glad you see it that way, son." He snickered.

I'm not your fucking son, asshole!

"It's good to have you back, Delta." Ben patted him on the shoulder with anomalous enthusiasm.

"It's good to be back," he insincerely concurred with retribution on his mind.

Mr. Morgan tapped on the divider, and Marcellus stepped out. He stomped over to the passenger side and held the door ajar for Anthony to exit.

"You're making the right decision. Tomorrow night you will have your revenge!" Mr. Morgan guaranteed.

"I will, sir. That is certain." Anthony exited, watching Marcellus with a nervous glare.

The towering Half-Breed closed the door behind him.

"Sorry for your loss. See you tomorrow night, hybrid," he whispered, brushing his jacket, displaying the handle of his revolver.

"I'm looking forward to it," Anthony cunningly challenged while staring deep into his eyes.

Marcellus broke from his fiery gaze and got back into the limo. Anthony watched as they drove away.

What fools. He envisioned the outcome of tomorrow night's raid, hoping to finally put an end to all of them.

"Hey, you okay?" Sidney called from over the hill.

"Actually, Sid, I'm not, but thanks for asking." She rushed to him.

He was entranced by her beauty; she was a vision, even in a graveyard.

She wrapped her arms around his neck. They embraced, and for Anthony, time stood still. He knew he needed her and was willing to give her whatever she wanted just to have her back.

"There's something I need to tell you. Can we go somewhere to talk?" she murmured.

"Yeah, let's go to your place. I need to get the fuck out of here." He leaned back, gazed into her eyes, and he knew that she had missed him.

"Hey, wait up!" Rey came jogging down the grassy knoll.

"Hey, bud, me and Sid are going to hang out for a while. Take the key to my place, and I'll meet you there, okay?" He tossed him his keys.

Rey fumbled the catch. "Yeah, sure thing." He nodded at Sidney with a bashful chortle, saluting them before hopping into his van and driving off.

"My car's over here." She pointed to her small white sedan parked near the curb.

They got in and Anthony peered up at his aunt's final resting place one last time. He wiped a tear from the corner of his eye, silently vowing to avenge her.

"You've been busy, I see." He peeked in the back and noticed stacks of folders spilling over the seat.

"Yeah, I have. I don't think I'll run out of work anytime soon," she coyly stated while driving over the Pioneer Bridge. "Do the police have any leads?"

"Yeah, I think they are onto the guy who did it."

217

"I swear this city is going to the dogs. Literally." She exited and approached her neighborhood.

If she only knew. He was happy just to be with her again.

"God, there's never any parking around here." She cowered over the steering wheel in search of a spot.

"There's one!" he shouted.

She accelerated and parked. They got out and entered her studio apartment. Her unit was a clutter of clothes sprawled on the floor amid stacked files and random papers. She was messy, which was one of his concerns regarding their living together, but he was willing to overlook her shortcomings. He just wanted her back.

"Have a seat." She shoved some files off her sofa, allowing him to set next to her.

"So, what did you have to tell me?" He looked at her with doting eyes.

"Okay, here it goes." She took a deep breath.

Anthony was nervous; he knew she had something important to divulge.

"I'm pregnant."

"Fuck! Really?!" He was shocked and immediately thought of the abominable offspring of the Half-Breeds.

His heart raced with panic. He wasn't ready for all this. After everything he'd been through, having a child terrified him the most.

God! I just buried my aunt, and now this! He was caught off guard, sweating uncontrollably.

"That's not the reaction I was hoping for." She glared at him, disappointed.

"It's not that, Sid. It's just…"

"Just what, Anthony? I mean, I didn't make this baby by myself!"

"You have to get an abortion," he claimed in haste.

"What?! I don't have to do anything! And if you don't want to be a part of your child's life, then so be it! I'll do it alone! My mom was a single mother, so go ahead and be a deadbeat. I don't give a fuck anymore! I'm sick of your noncommittal bullshit!"

He immediately regretted what he said and tried to calm her. He rested his clammy hand on her knee, hoping to sooth the tension.

"It's not that, Sid. I want us to move in together and have a family. Just not now. There are some things I have to do first. Or else we will never be safe."

"I don't understand." She swiped his hand away.

There comes a point when you can't hide who you are anymore, he reasoned. She deserved to hear the truth. "Okay, Sid, I'm going to tell you something, and I need you to believe me."

He was tense; what he was about to disclose would not be well received, but he had to tell her, especially if she was carrying his hybrid offspring.

"Here it goes... I'm a werewolf."

"Oh, wow, really?! That's your excuse?! Come on! I know you just lost your aunt, but this is crazy!"

"I am, Sid! Look!" He raised his lips, showing her the canine-like incisors concealed beneath his gumline.

"Come on, really? Those are wisdom teeth. You should get them pulled. This is pathetic!" He realized that she would never believe him based on his words alone.

"Listen, Sid, that baby inside you is a Lycan. I was bit by a were-wolf in those backwoods. I have hybrid blood in my veins. You think all that howling at night are stray dogs? They're not! This city is crawling with Lycans, and I'm one of them!"

"A bear attacked you. I think you need to lay off those pills."

"I haven't been taking any lately."

"Then maybe you should start! God, do you even hear yourself right now?"

"Listen, I don't expect you to believe me, but tomorrow night there's going to be an attack on the MGE building. If, after that, you still don't believe me, then we can consider having the baby." He hoped his explanation would change her mind.

"Oh, I'm keeping the baby, with or without you!" She was upset, and Anthony knew she would soon grow angrier.

"You don't know what you're saying. That baby inside you isn't human. If you've seen the things I've seen, you wouldn't want to go through that. Our child is cursed! It's an abomination!"

"Get out!" she shrieked.

"Okay, but hopefully you will believe me after tomorrow night." Anthony headed for the door and glanced back at her. "I just want you to remember that we're in this together." After his failed attempt at reconciliation, she slipped off her stiletto and threw it at him. He ducked as the shoe whizzed by his ear, hitting the door, leaving a mark. He conceded, hoping that after tomorrow night she would believe everything he had said.

"I'll call you later, Sid." She rushed toward him and slammed the door in his face.

He sighed and decided to take a long walk home. As he paced down the snowy sidewalk, thinking about his unborn child, he became uneasy. He pictured the monstrous offspring of the Half-Breeds and didn't want that future for him, his kid, or her. As he approached his building, he smelled the synthetic scent of the Lone Wolves. He inconspicuously viewed a nearby storm drain, where he saw red eyes peering back at him. It was McQuaid. He sat on the curb with his legs over the inlet.

"I'm sorry for your loss," his booming voice echoed from under the drain.

"Thanks… The Purebloods are going to attack the Half-Breeds' barge tomorrow night." Anthony kept his head down, mindful to not draw any attention to himself.

"The war to end all wars." The Lone Wolf's cadence was low and ominous.

"Guess so. I just hope I'm on the right side," he stated with worry.

"There never is a right side. One can only hope to survive." Silence ensued as McQuaid retreated into the depths of the sewer.

"Hello? McQuaid?"

He was gone.

Anthony entered his building, approached his unit, and knocked.

Rey opened the door. He collapsed on his couch, anxiously looking up at him.

"You okay, bud? Do you need anything?" he asked with concern.

"Sidney's pregnant."

"Holy shit!"

Anthony knew Rey didn't fully understand the gravity of the situation and elected to spare him the details.

"Yeah, I guess I'm going to be a dad." Even though he didn't want to be a father, he felt it was the right thing to say.

They were interrupted by two stern knocks. Anthony opened the door to see Hunter standing before him wearing a wolfskin pelt. A timber wolf's upper cranium and jaws extruded over his forehead. His black cargo pants were stained with mud, as were his thick, brown boots. He was carrying a large duffel bag as he pushed his way through the door. He stomped into the living room, dropping his bag on the floor with a metallic thud.

"Nice fur," Anthony complimented, closing the door behind him while Hunter scrutinized his apartment.

"What's this guy doing here?" Rey shouted.

"Hello... You must be Rey," Hunter greeted from the kitchen.

"Yeah... And you're the guy from the gas station," he recognized with a perplexed tone.

"My name's Hunter... Why are you guys wearing suits?"

"Why are you wearing a wolf?" Rey countered.

"Keeps me warm," he sharply explained with a smile. "Anthony, do you have anything to eat?"

"Yeah, Tony, I'm kind of hungry too. The food at the reception was horrible."

"Okay, guys, why don't we all have a seat? I can explain everything," Anthony suggested while loosening his tie.

Rey and Hunter both sat at the dining room table while Anthony opened his fridge. After gazing at the empty shelves in disappointment, he opened the freezer to see the half-eaten bear cake from when he had come home from the hospital. He reluctantly removed the dessert from the iced-over freezer and laid it out in front of them with some silverware and plates. He reminisced over that day; he could almost hear his aunt's cackling laugh. He nearly broke down, realizing that those get-togethers were long gone, and he would never hear her voice again.

"Dig in." He did his best to hold back his grief while serving them.

"You sure about this?" Rey asked.

"Yeah. It's time to finish the cake."

He sat at the head of the table and served himself a slice. Hunter cut a piece, as did Rey.

"The reason Hunter's here is because tomorrow night we're going to raid the MGE tower and kill all the Lycans in Myrin City."

"What?" Rey spit out frosted bits of cake while Hunter sauntered over to his duffel bag.

The two childhood friends watched as the looming tribesman unzipped his bundle. Stuffed inside was a pump-action shotgun, dirty bombs, a chrome-plated Desert Eagle, boxes of bullets, and his bow, accompanied by a quiver cradling silver-plated arrows.

"Holy shit!" Rey exclaimed in astonishment while viewing the spillage of armaments.

Hunter reached in and pulled out a bushel of flowering wolfsbane.

"Those Lycans don't stand a chance against my bow," he assured before zipping the bag. "Oh, I forgot to mention that my truck died on the way over here." He marched over to the table, clutching the bundled flowers in his hand.

"Maybe you can pawn some of those guns and get yourself a decent ride," Rey roasted as he retook his seat.

"Perhaps," he rebutted, tossing the plumage next to his half-eaten cake.

"Well, either way we're going to need your help, Rey," Anthony informed. "Tomorrow night I will be joining the Purebloods in their transformation chamber. Once the transformation portal opens, the Half-Breeds and Lone Wolves will raid the lab."

"Lone Wolves? Half-Breeds?" Rey looked at him baffled.

"They are rival packs," Hunter added. "Hopefully I can get my hands on a Lone Wolf. Another Lycan to add to my trophy wall," he expounded with a vengeful gaze.

"So once I transform with the Purebloods, the rival packs will storm Gene-Con. During the attack, I will make my way up to the lobby and let Hunter inside through the main entrance."

"But you will be in your Lycan form," Hunter stated with confusion.

"Yes, that's why you need to wait outside. Pretend to be a homeless beggar until I transform, then I will get you in."

"Shouldn't be a stretch for you," Rey teased.

"Sounds like a solid plan," Hunter added while peering at Rey with a demeaning frown.

"So where do I come into play in all this?" Rey asked.

"I need you to park your van by the Pioneer Bridge and wait for us. We'll need to get as far away from the city as possible after the raid. We will meet you at the bridge and drive back to Mr. Morgan's chalet until things die down," Anthony instructed while studying him, hoping that he would agree.

"Okay. I'll be there," Rey guaranteed with confidence.

"I'm going to give you my boots and a change of clothes."

"Should I bring some raw meat too?" he jokingly suggested.

"Couldn't hurt." Anthony shrugged.

"So, what's with those flowers?" Rey questioned, viewing the purple blossoms from across the table.

"This is wolfsbane." Hunter stood and held up the long-stemmed plant. "My tribe would use this as protection before a hunt." He reached into his pants and withdrew a lighter.

He ignited the lavender-budded plant and started chanting while wafting the smoldering wolfsbane overhead.

"Great spirit Gaia, we ask of you. May this wolfsbane awaken the power within each of us as we prepare for battle." He bowed, waving the burning stems over them. "*Hey hey, hey hey, hey min-ga-la. Min-ga-la-hey!*" he chanted before throwing the fiery plant onto the floor and stomping it out.

"Hey, that's going to leave a stain!" Anthony scolded.

"Hey. Hey, hey… We like to partay!" Rey jokingly mimicked his blessing by wiping cake batter under his eyes, resembling war paint.

"Mocking the great spirit will no doubt have grave consequences for you," Hunter sternly warned as he retook his seat.

"Well, this ain't the reservation, dude. I'll take my chances." Rey wiped the red syrupy markings from his face and got up. "Well, look at the time. Jeez, six thirty already. I should be getting home. Goddamn curfew! I guess I'll see you guys tomorrow night at the bridge then?" he confirmed as he plodded for the door.

"Yeah, Rey. Hold on. I'll walk you to the elevator." Anthony rushed to his closet.

He grabbed his black hoodie and blue jeans. While cradling his garments, he trailed him, collecting his boots on his way out. As he opened the door, he looked back at Hunter seated at the table next to the stomped-out ashes, wondering if he could trust him. He closed the door and handed Rey his clothes. They both quietly paced down the hall to the elevator.

"Dude, what the fuck?" Rey whispered.

"Listen, Rey. Hunter saved me back at the cabin. I need him, and he needs me, but I need you to keep this for me." He reached into his suit pocket and gave Rey his cell phone. "The Purebloods make me put all my belongings in a locker before we transform. That way they make sure you come back. But after tomorrow night, it all ends," he stated with unwavering resolve.

"Okay…" Rey warily agreed and tucked his things under his armpit while pressing the call button for the elevator.

"Those bastards killed my auntie, and now they're going to pay."

The doors opened, and Rey hopped inside.

"Don't worry, bro. I got your back… I'll be at the bridge waiting for you—nine o'clock sharp!" He stuck out his fist between the closing doors while balancing his clothes and boots under his arm.

Anthony reached in and bumped his knuckles.

"Oh, Rey. Don't forget to bring the amulet," he yelled as the doors closed.

"Don't worry. I will!" he shouted back as the lift descended.

Anthony was anxious and grief-stricken as he marched back inside his apartment.

"Your friend is strange," Hunter announced while cleaning the charred wolfsbane from the floor and tossing it in the trash.

"Says the guy wearing a dead wolf on his head." Anthony locked the door and proceeded to clear the plates from the table, aimlessly throwing them in the sink.

"Rey's an acquired taste." He lowered his head as he sat.

"You lost someone, didn't you?" Hunter probed.

"The Purebloods killed my aunt," he tearfully blurted.

"I know all too well the pain you're going through," he consoled, removing his pelt from his shoulders.

The preserved wolf's glass eyes stared at him as Hunter shook out his hoary dreads.

"The Ultimas killed my wife, my two kids, and my dog." His eyes welled up while reminiscing over his murdered family and tribesmen.

"From that day on, I vowed to kill all Lycans that came across my path. For my tribe and for my family."

"I, too, am the last of my family," Anthony mournfully confessed, realizing that Sidney and his unborn child were all that he had left.

"Then we are brothers in loss." Hunter laid on the couch, kicking off his boots. "We should get some sleep. We will need all of our strength tomorrow." He crossed his scarred arms over his chest.

"Okay."

"*Osda sv hi ye.*" He bid him good night in his native tongue.

Anthony plopped on his bed and tried to fall asleep. He tossed and turned thinking of tomorrow night's raid. He questioned himself, wondering if his alliance with Hunter was enough to take down the Purebloods. He thought about Sidney and the future he had to make for them. He would have to be successful tomorrow night, or all would be lost. His worrisome contemplations and the grief of losing his aunt inundated him. After hours of mental torment, he eventually fell asleep.

He rolled out of bed and saw Hunter loading his shotgun and Desert Eagle with silver-tipped bullets. His weaponries were sprawled over the kitchen counter.

"Good morning." He smiled while stuffing the loaded shotgun into his duffel bag.

"Morning," Anthony greeted before entering the bathroom. As he brushed his teeth, the soft bristles gently stroked the back of his concealed incisors. He rinsed, opened the medicine cabinet, and gazed at the vial of OxyContin.

Fuck it. He grabbed the bottle. While considering the pills with an unsteady grip, he decided to flush them down the toilet, again thinking of McQuaid's forewarning backstory. He watched as the green pills swirled the bowl in a turbulent dance before flushing into the sewers.

He got dressed in a gray suit with a black shirt and tie. He glanced out the window, noticing snow beginning to fall. Hunter was adorning his wolf pelt, anxiously waiting for him by the door, clutching his duffel bag.

"I guess this is it."

"Mother Gaia, we ask that you protect us on this day," Hunter declared with his head down.

Anthony grabbed his pea coat from the hanger and slid on his loafers, wiping off the dried blades of grass from his aunt's funeral.

"Come on. Let's get the fuck out of here." He took one last look at his apartment before closing the door.

The Lycan hunters made their way onto the snow-laden streets, where Anthony hailed a cab. The taxi pulled up and Hunter popped the trunk, tossing his bag of arms inside while Anthony slid into the backseat.

"We're going to the MGE building. Financial District," he

instructed the dumbfounded driver.

"Sure thing, boss," the overweight cabbie acknowledged while scrutinizing his odd-looking passengers.

Hunter got in and they dredged through traffic. The voice of Linda Haskins suddenly came onto the radio with an announcement.

"Citizens of Myrin City, tonight Police Chief Ramsey has placed a seven p.m. citywide curfew."

"Goddamn politicians! How can anyone make any money when you shut down the city at seven o' clock? Especially us cabbies!" The driver turned the knob in disgust.

"Will your friend be able to meet us at the bridge if there's a curfew?" Hunter whispered.

"Don't worry. He'll be there. Rey's solid." Anthony did his best to hide his apprehension.

"So, are you guys like in show business or something?" the driver asked while turning down a side street, viewing Hunter adorning his wolf's head pelt.

"Yeah, we're, uh...in a band," Anthony jokingly stated.

"Oh, nice... Maybe I heard of you. What's youse guys' name?" The driver made eye contact with them through the dashboard mirror.

"Silver Bullet," Hunter interjected with a grin.

"Yeah, we're a heavy metal band," Anthony added.

"Oh, nice... I'm not into heavy metal myself. I like Sinatra," he professed as the cab approached the Financial District.

"You can pull over anywhere along here, sir." Anthony instructed for him to stop a few blocks away so none of his coworkers would see him stepping out with the oddly dressed Native.

"Sure thing, boss!" The obese cabbie pulled over, and Anthony paid him as Hunter got out and retrieved his duffel bag.

"Good luck with your band!" he encouraged.

"Thanks. We got a big show tonight." Anthony nodded before joining Hunter on the curb.

As they strode for the sixty-six-story bronze-and-silver tower, Anthony was mindful to keep distance between them.

"Okay, this is where I leave you." He turned to face him.

"The next time I see you, you'll be a Lycan," Hunter noted with trepidation.

"Yeah, so don't shoot me with your arrows." He snickered.

"As long as you don't try and eat me, I won't."

"When the full moon approaches, wait for me outside and I'll get you in."

"See you tonight," Hunter acknowledged before lumbering away.

Anthony witnessed several bystanders gawking at them. The sight of the clean-suited man speaking to the dreadlocked Native was odd and drew unwanted attention. As he departed for the tower, Hunter removed a crunched cup from a nearby trashcan and took a seat on the curb with his duffel bag beside him. Some people threw change into the cup, while others hurried by in disgust. Anthony observed his ruse from a distance while marching up the steps.

Before entering, he looked back at the bustling, snow-covered sidewalks to see gleaming eyes peering at him from the drainage inlet across the street. He felt the Lone Wolf's foreboding gaze as he pushed through the turnstile and weaved across the flocks of professionals inundating the lobby.

He merged with the horde and headed to the private elevator, where he stuck his hand under the scanner. A red-light came on; he was denied. He frustratingly traversed to the communal elevators, where stockpiles of admins anxiously waited for the lifts.

After a few moments, the doors opened with a chime and the migration clamored their way through the opening, spilling into the elevator. Anthony pushed his way past the corral and inched inside. Sardined, he desperately called out, "Fifty-five, please!"

The doors closed. After a laborious climb, he finally reached his destination. He tore from the crowd and approached the reception desk, where he saw Camden outfitted in a slightly less-revealing dress than the night of the gala.

"Good morning, Mr. Montgomery... I'm so sorry to hear about your aunt," she broadcast with pity while peering over her desk.

"Thanks, I appreciate that. Can you remind Ben to have my fingerprints scanned for the private elevator?"

Not like it's going to matter after tonight. He envisioned the outcome of the raid, hoping that he would survive.

"Sure thing, It's good to have you back!" she bubbly encouraged.

"It's good to be back," he falsely stated as he headed for his office, bypassing the rows of cubicle-entrenched employees.

He couldn't help but think of Brandon as he glared at his name and delta symbol embossed in gold leaf before pushing his door. While hanging his coat, he saw his returned garment bag encasing his dry-cleaned suit. The pick-up slip had "Brandon" written on it. He paused with grief before sitting at his desk. He withdrew his laptop and started reviewing his emails. He scrolled and noticed that the contract for Gene-Con had been fully executed by Dr. Fang.

His focus was interrupted by a knock.

"Come in!" He peered up from the screen.

The door opened, and in strutted Luna, wearing a white suit with a red turtleneck. Her curly auburn hair was tied back in a ponytail.

"I'm so sorry for your loss." She sat on the manila booth, studying him with sympathy.

"Thanks, Luna. What can I do for you?" He was anxious and wanted to get her out of his office as soon as possible.

"Ben wanted me to tell you that you should meet him in the lobby at six o'clock."

"Okay, thanks."

"But that's not why I'm here." She crossed her legs and brushed back her hair.

Of course not. He was becoming annoyed with her unwarranted advances, but nonetheless he was still flattered that a woman as beautiful as her was even remotely interested in him.

She looked deep into his eyes, her pupils sharpened.

"I'm here to take you up on my offer. Would you like to go out for drinks sometime? I know a great place for happy hour in the Entertainment District."

"Actually, Luna, me and Sidney are talking again."

"Oh, I see. Well, I wish you two the best," she championed with a despondent tone.

"Thanks. How have you been?" He suddenly felt bad and wanted to change the topic.

"Ah, you know. Mr. Morgan is always busy. He definitely keeps me on my toes." She got up and buttoned her jacket.

"You and me both." He chuckled.

"I pray for the day when I will no longer have to listen to the mindless rantings of cowardly old men desperately trying to remain relevant." She shrugged. "Well, I've got to get back to work. I'll see you later. It's good to have you back." She leered at him with an uncomfortable stare before leaving; he knew she was disappointed with his rejection.

After she left, Anthony proceeded with his work, anxiously watching the hours advance to six o'clock. He peered out from his floor-to-ceiling windows, admiring the view overlooking the Nicolo River. The frozen waterway had warning signs posted around the perimeter indicating thin ice.

You better be there, Rey. He was uneasy while observing the lineage of cars crossing over the sprawling bridge.

It was 5:50 p.m. The blood moon would soon rise. He packed up his laptop and plucked his coat from the hanger. As he hiked for the elevators, the rows of cubicles emptied. The once diligently working staff abandoned their workstations in a departing march.

"Have a good evening, Mr. Montgomery," Camden called out from behind her desk as he joined the rest of his colleagues stuffed inside the elevator.

Anthony nodded at her in acknowledgement. "You better get going if you want to make it home before curfew," he cautioned as the doors closed.

"I will. Ben asked me to stay late," she nervously claimed with a fabricated smile.

The jam-packed lift descended in awkward silence. The cramped elevator arrived at the lobby with a ding and the myriad of employees rushed out, jutting their way through the gilded turnstile. Anthony watched as the hurried masses made their journey onto the snowy streets, anxiously rushing home before the curfew.

He waited in the lobby for Ben. As he scanned over the exiting crowds, he noticed Hunter seated on the steps in front of the building. The wolf-pelt-sporting brave caught a glimpse of him and gave him an inconspicuous nod. Anthony turned, noticing Ben amid the multitudes. He was wearing a blue suit, with a young man by his side.

"Anthony, this is James." Ben closed in with a young blond associate donning a brown suit with no tie.

"Pleasure to meet you, Delta." The youthful admin had an ignorant eagerness as he stuck out his hand.

"Nice to meet you," he rebutted while clutching his sweaty palm.

"This will be his first time transitioning," Ben explained as they approached the private elevator.

Anthony felt sorry for him. He knew that James would more than likely be killed by the invading Lycans.

"Must be nice to take the private elevator," Anthony sarcastically stated while Ben removed his hand from the scanner before they entered the lift.

Ben responded with a shit-eating grin as he pushed the B button. They descended to the garage, where they marched across the concrete underbelly and into the Gene-Con locker room.

The changing area was filled with men getting dressed in their purple hooded robes. Anthony was shocked as he witnessed the multitudes preparing for their transition. He separated from Ben and vigilantly crept to an empty locker with a robe hanging inside. He unlatched the cabinet before getting undressed. As he removed his clothes, he looked over at Brandon's old locker to see James, fully cloaked.

"Tonight, we will avenge your aunt, Mr. Montgomery," the low voice of Chief Ramsey alerted him as he shot his arms through his robe.

Anthony faced the towering commander, concealing his fury.

"Without a doubt," he responded.

"Gentlemen!" Mr. Morgan's booming voice suddenly rained over the packed room.

The congregation of hooded men stayed at attention as he proudly stood over a bench, donning a silver robe with black embroidery. The hood of his cloak was slung back so his pack could observe him. The locker room went eerily mute.

"Tonight, we will transform together as one united pack. First, we'll feast on the Half-Breed known as Kane. Once our bellies are filled with his flesh, you all will follow me through the subway tunnels to the port, where we'll advance onto a barge at the far end of the dock. We will board the Half-Breeds' lair and bring death to those mongrels once and for all!"

The cloaked assembly raucously howled in response.

"Our hunt will be dangerous. The Half-Breeds outnumber us, but we are smarter than them. As long as we stick together and don't break from our formation, we can overtake them. You men have been specifically selected because of your strength and intelligence," he encouraged. "Tonight, when the blood moon rises, we will hunt down the Half-Breed scourge that plagues our city!"

The hordes applauded after hearing their barrel-chested alpha's call to arms.

"After tonight...the city will be ours!" Mr. Morgan climbed down and opened the door at the far end of the locker room.

The tyrannical mogul draped the hood over his head and stomped into the metallic chamber with the cloaked procession following. Chained to the far corner, near the exit portal, was Kane.

He sat defeated with his head down, his blood-drenched locks draped over his face, concealing the bruises and lacerations inflicted by his captors. His orange jumpsuit was ripped and splattered with blood. His face was swollen from the torturous beatings. He was shackled with mechanized restraints over his wrists, which allowed for the handcuffs to remain secure after his beastly transformation. The futuristic confines were connected with heavy metal links that bolted into the wall. A digital pressure monitor displayed the PSI poundage on the face of the bulky cuffs.

As the cloaked consortium piled into the vast chamber, Anthony remained in the rear of the cavalcade, where he observed Dr. Fang looking on from behind the safety of the separating window. He dropped a pen into his lab coat pocket and adjusted his black-framed glasses as he viewed the spillage of Purebloods filing into the chamber.

"Gentlemen, if you would take your positions, the blood moon is approaching, and soon I will be releasing the neuro gas," he announced over the intercom while a scatter of geneticists frantically manned the control panels behind him.

He admiringly observed the litany of cloaked men as they positioned themselves about the expansive space, readying for their transformation. Some of them kicked and punched Kane as they took their places along the room's back wall. The hooded pack lined up, with Mr. Morgan in the center of the procession. Ben took his place next to him, with Chief Ramsey on the other side of their alpha, while James knelt beside him.

The pack faced Dr. Fang while he leered at them from behind the glass. The hooded convoy slowly knelt in unison, awaiting the release of the innocuous gas. Anthony situated himself next to the observation window, in the rear corner, before kneeling.

Here goes nothing. He lowered his head; he was tense and filled with adrenaline.

"Ten…nine…eight…seven…six…five…" Dr. Fang commenced the countdown.

"…four…three…two…one." An exfoliating hiss echoed over the chamber as misty vapor filled the space.

Within minutes the haze enveloped the room. Anthony inhaled the gas, quickly falling into a deep stupor. He suddenly found himself glaring into a shadowy void, where he saw a mirrored image of himself staring back at him with wolflike eyes and razor-sharp teeth. He jarringly awoke from his brief terror to see the fully transformed pack circling Kane.

Anthony gazed at his hands to discover talons and brown fur. He had transformed into a lycanthropic brute. Hunger and unadulterated rage coursed through his veins as he witnessed the discarded tatters of the cloaks scattered over the titanium-paneled floor. He marveled in horror at the lineage of beasts. He viewed Mr. Morgan, debating whether to attack.

The stocky, tyrannical businessman was a charcoal-haired Lycan with dark saddle markings down his back. Next to him was Chief Ramsey, altered into a towering black-haired Lycan with gray swirls peppering his face and midsection. He further examined the room to see Ben, who was a midnight-haired beast with a countershaded muzzle. Standing next to him was James, transmuted into a brown Lycan with white spots along his back.

The corralling Purebloods grumbled with a gut-churning hunger while they admired one another's transformed physiques. The vaporized mist dissipated as Mr. Morgan joined the encircling pack, stalking toward Kane.

The tortured prisoner had morphed into a fierce, black-coated Lycan, with the remnants of his orange jumpsuit strewn onto the floor. Kane snarled, desperately pulling at his shackles. As he tugged, the pressurized restraints tightened around his wooly appendages.

He snarled, growling with a belly-trembling warning as Mr. Morgan and the brooding Purebloods circled him.

The restraints tightened over his black-furred carpus, halting his movements. As he desperately pulled, the bloodthirsty pack licked their lips and sneered, exposing their daggering fangs.

Anthony stood against the back wall while Kane chomped and growled in defense. Mr. Morgan and Chief Ramsey pounced on him, breaking from the rest of the pack. They snapped and clawed, tearing out mounds of flesh, while Ben and James looked on. Blood splattered about the chamber as Kane let out a pain-filled whimper. The shackled Half-Breed yelped while enduring the flesh-tearing onslaught. The sight of blood triggered the rest of the pack.

Anthony watched as Ben and James approached Kane. He was suffering as Mr. Morgan and Chief Ramsey ensued with their relentless assault. Suddenly, a loud bang shook the room. The other side of the circular door trembled. The pack froze from their devouring ambush as the iron-clad portal bent.

The Purebloods all froze with apprehension as another thunderous bang sounded. The portal abruptly caved in, revealing a rushing trove of Lone Wolves led by McQuaid.

Anthony observed Dr. Fang looking on in horror from the other side of the lab, while his fellow geneticists raced for the stairwell in an attempt to escape from the intruding Lycans.

McQuaid shattered the overhead lights, punching them into crystallized remnants that let off a blinding spark. The room went dark. Anthony angrily snarled while scanning the pitch-black chamber with his night vision.

He scoured over the unadulterated melee of flesh-tearing carnage, holding his position near the separation glass. The warring Lycans relentlessly tore each other apart. Animalistic howls and cries echoed over the chaos. He remained on guard, snarling, waiting for the right moment to attack as the droves of disfigured Lone Wolves collided with the Purebloods. Loud snarls and barking whimpers resonated amid the bloodshed.

As the ambush persisted, two encroaching Lone Wolves broke from their pack's formation and pounced on James, knocking him to the ground before tearing out his throat. Fountains of blood splattered into the air. James gargled in desperation, went limp, and died.

Dr. Fang viewed the onslaught with ignorant fascination. The ravaging Lone Wolves wasted no time in disemboweling their kill. McQuaid turned his gargantuan frame from the frenzy and punched through the separation glass, shattering the window with a crash.

After the gigantic Lycan's breach, alarm buzzers sounded and strobes flickered. McQuaid reached through the opening and seized Dr. Fang by his neck, pulling him into the chamber with the rest of the bloodthirsty Lycans. The doctor trembled within the outstretched clenches of his taloned grasp.

"What's up, Doc?!" McQuaid snickered as he pushed Dr. Fang's head inside his gaping jowls.

"Please…don't!" the geneticist helplessly begged as the disfigured Lone Wolf chomped down on his forehead, piercing his cranium with his jagged fangs.

In a panic, the doctor withdrew a syringe from his pocket and stuck McQuaid in the neck. He injected the thick blue serum into his bloodstream as the hulking Lycan crooked his head and crushed his skull like a watermelon. McQuaid delightfully chewed on the doctor's severed head, pulverizing his cranium into bits before devouring his brains. The red-eyed beast released his headless body and toppled over. McQuaid's immense physique hit the ground with a bang.

The fallen brute shook the embattled chamber, briefly bringing the surrounding massacre to a pause. Anthony noticed Mr. Morgan and Ben cowardly retreating through the shattered window, fearfully escaping into the lab, leaving their pack to fend for themselves against the invading Lone Wolves.

The effects of the fatal injection delivered by Dr. Fang had begun to course through McQuaid's bloodstream. The colossal beast lay on the floor next to the headless, blood-oozing torso of his assailant. The Lone Wolves formed a barrier around their leader, protecting his dying body from the onslaught of fiendish Purebloods.

"Death, how I've longed for your embrace," McQuaid winced with a deteriorating quiver as he caught a glimpse of Anthony.

"Godspeed, hybrid," the Lone Wolves' alpha decreed as he took his last, labored breath and died.

McQuaid's pack let out a series of long, mournful howls in acknowledgment of their fallen leader, ushering a brief pause to the ensuing slaughter.

After their sorrowful wails dwindled, they broke from their formation and ensued with their attack.

Anthony noticed a small group of Purebloods discontinue their assault on Kane. As they backed away, he perceived a second wave of black-coated Half-Breeds flooding into the chamber, led by Marcellus.

The drove quickly overwhelmed the battle-worn Purebloods, and soon they were overrun by the invading Lycans. Marcellus charged into the flesh-strewn chamber, making his way past the battling packs over to his son. He forcefully snapped the metal-bound links, freeing him from his bondage.

After witnessing the impressive feat of strength, Chief Ramsey rushed Marcellus, facing off with the scar-faced alpha while Kane hastily retreated with the pressurized restraints secured over his wrists. He bolted across the darkened tunnels with a desperate, bleeding limp.

Marcellus gave his wounded son an encouraging nod before facing the lycanthropic commander. As he circled the chief, another wave of Half-Breeds flooded the chamber, joining the Lone Wolves in their assault.

Chief Ramsey lunged, striking Marcellus, slashing his chest. He abruptly countered and slapped the chief across his maw. After his tumultuous swipe, the chief's snout dislodged from his face. A cascade of butchered flesh careened from his shredded facade. The snout-less lawman helplessly whimpered as Marcellus bit down on his neck, tearing out his jugular. Decimated, the chief fell as the surrounding Half-Breeds, together with the Lone Wolves, descended upon him. The brooding Lycans angrily feasted on his body, ripping his flesh with childlike glee until there was only a fur-and-bone-torn carcass.

As the war ensued, Anthony snuck through the shattered window, escaping from the ravaging melee.

He trudged across the lab, viewing the sprawled-out bodies of frayed geneticists strewn atop the flickering control boards. It was apparent that Mr. Morgan and Ben had killed them as they spinelessly abandoned their pack.

He picked up on Ben's scent while cautiously creeping to the stairway. As he approached, the door jarringly swung open. Ben pounced on him, digging his talons deep into his shoulder, knocking him to the floor. He ferociously kicked with his clawed feet, scraping Ben's midsection while catapulting his aggressor's beastly body off him.

Ben stumbled and let out a foreboding growl. He snarled before retreating up the stairway. A trail of blood dripped from his serrated belly as he made his ascent.

Anthony picked himself up, profusely bleeding. Ben was stronger than he had expected. After he collected himself, Anthony valiantly tracked the bloody trail up to the lobby.

He nudged open the stairway door with his gashed shoulder and passed the communal elevators to see Ben crouched over the ripped-open chest cavity of the night security guard. He growled, veering at Anthony with ravenous eyes. His muzzle was plastered with blood. The feasting beast tore from the ripped carcass of his kill and lurched for him.

The bloodied Lycans circled each other, posturing about the grand lobby, sizing each other up before their impending duel. As they faced off, Anthony observed Hunter outside the turnstile.

The wolf-pelt-sporting brave peered into the lobby from the snowfall outside. He rashly opened his duffel bag, jammed a suction cup bomb onto the storefront, and hurriedly backed away. Anthony lunged at Ben, slashing his neck with a bombastic swipe. His talons ripped through his collar like a hot knife through butter.

Ben retreated, sneering with anger as his wounds hemorrhaged. Blood mercilessly gushed from his neck and stomach while Anthony encircled him.

Ben pounced, knocking him to the floor. Spouts of blood splattered onto his snout as he crouched over him. Anthony looked up in horror as Ben opened his jowls and dove for his neckline. He lowered his fanged jaws, sinking his razor-sharp teeth deep into his jugular. He let out a desperate moan as he felt Ben's incisors cut through the side of his neck.

Suddenly, a loud crash sounded. The storefront windows crumbled in a thunderous explosion, followed by a chilling rush of cold wind. The rapacious gusts ripped through the lobby with a hollow, deathly chill.

Ben withdrew his fangs from Anthony's neck. He turned from his prey as Hunter jumped over the explosive flames. He skirted his duffle bag across the floor and nocked his silver-tipped arrow, taking aim.

Anthony scrambled to his feet, bleeding and wounded. He looked on at the confrontation between the wounded Pureblood and the archer.

Ben raced for him, grumbling with a bloodthirsty growl as he angrily stomped. Hunter was steadfast and released his arrow. The soaring projectile cut through the air with accurate precision, striking Ben through his chest. The dark-haired Lycan fell back, stumbling against the granite reception desk.

As Ben's bloodstream came in contact with the silver arrowhead, he morphed back into a human. His dark fur shed, and his hulking, lycanthropic physique crooked.

He painstakingly bent and twisted in unnatural ways, agonizingly transforming back into a helpless, naked man. Ben lay dying in a contorted bloody mess with his back against the desk's stone facade. The once-imposing Lycan had been reduced to nothing more than a bare and defenseless man, hardly able to breathe. Blood flowed from his gaping wounds. He tried to pull the arrow from his chest, but he was too weak. All he could do was shudder as dark blood gargled from his mouth. He withered with each dying breath.

Hunter stomped over the mortally wounded executive, while Anthony limped behind. They both closed in on their prey. Anthony had lost a lot of blood and was beginning to feel the effects; an unnerving chill consumed him. He trembled while looming over Ben.

Murky bile dribbled from Ben's mouth as he attempted to speak.

"Your...aunt...was...delicious," he confessed with a smile.

Hunter stomped his boot heel atop his chest and plucked the arrow from his breastbone. Rivered streams of blood flowed from his sternum. With each gasping inhalation, his chest compressed with a shaking death rattle.

Anthony opened his jaws and ate him alive. He devoured Ben with feverish anger, tearing through his muscle tissue with ravenous delight. He felt his burning desire for revenge leave his soul with each satisfying bite. His neck and shoulder wounds healed as Ben's meaty tissue digested in his belly. As he consumed the innards of the decimated board member, he felt an unadulterated strength course through him. He broke from his gorge and spotted Hunter unzipping his duffle bag while slinging his bow and quiver over his shoulder.

He withdrew his shotgun from the sack and aimed for the

stairway. Anthony's pointed ears pivoted as he turned from Ben's eviscerated carcass. His furry lobes detected the sound of a Lycan's foot talons scraping over concrete.

Hunter took notice of his renewed alertness and, with pensive tension, kept his aim steady. After a few moments, the door swung open, and out jumped Marcellus. Hunter squeezed the trigger. The blast reverberated over the expansive lobby. Marcellus ducked, and the slug whizzed by his ear, hitting the wall.

Hunter frustratingly pumped the shotgun, expelling the shell in hopes of firing off another shot, but it was too late. Marcellus was fast. He forcefully pounced over him. The Half-Breed's lunging attack dispelled his wolf pelt from his head, causing him to drop the rifle before he could get off another shot. The gun misfired with a disorienting bang. As Hunter fell, his bow and quiver dislodged from his shoulder. In desperation, he withdrew one of his silver-tipped arrows.

Marcellus lowered his snout and reeled over him, opening his jowls, attempting to bite the scrabbling brave. Hunter held his arrow horizontally in front of him, impeding the black-haired beast's assault. Marcellus chomped on the shaft as Hunter struggled beneath him, holding him at bay with the arrow's rod wedged inside his drooling mouth.

Anthony rushed to the tussle and grabbed Marcellus. He dug his talons deep into his wooly hide and tossed him off his Indigenous brother-in-arms. As Marcellus tumbled to the floor, Anthony noticed the silver-tipped arrow sticking out from his midsection. Hunter had stabbed the scar-faced alpha through his abdomen.

Marcellus let out a long, pain-filled howl. The lodged arrow exuded gushing spouts of plasma from his belly. He sank to his knees, unable to stand. As the silver arrowhead came in contact with his bloodstream, Marcellus transformed back into a human. His black coat shed, and his hulking lycanthropic frame bent and distorted, painstakingly reverting into a man. Anthony stomped over the fallen Half-Breed while Hunter collected his bow from the bloodstained floor.

Marcellus looked at him with fear and desperation.

"Join us, hybrid… It's not too late… You can still have a family," he helplessly bargained.

Anthony reached back and swiped at his neckline with earth-shattering force. His head dislodged from his neck and somersaulted against the back wall, where it exploded on impact. His headless body went limp and toppled over.

Anthony caught Hunter nervously witnessing the grisly decapitation from the corner of his eye while shaking out his dreads.

Marcellus' decapitation alerted the rest of the Half-Breeds still fighting in the transformation chamber below. Anthony heard the grumblings of the lycanthropic horde ascending the stairwell. The scratching of talons striking concrete resonated inside his lobes as the pack vehemently clawed its way up to the lobby. Hunter noticed his tense body language as he crouched over his bag and apprehensively waited for the onslaught of vengeful Half-Breeds. He rifled through his sack and held up a tubular bomb.

In an instant, the stairwell doors flew open, and a sea of dark-coated Half-Breeds spilled into the lobby. Hunter pulled the pin from the canister and rolled the bomb toward the charging Lycans.

"Get down!" he shouted as they both leapt from the rolling explosive.

The frenzied Lycans paused from their vengeful charge and watched the rolling tube, puzzled. The bomb exploded with a deafening blast. Large scraps of silver shrapnel spewed from the arresting discharge. The jagged fragments lodged inside the surrounding Lycans, changing them back into blown-up, dismembered men. Those who did not perish from the blast lay on the corpse-strewn floor screaming in pain. Hunter withdrew his Desert Eagle and shot the wounded, putting them out of their misery. With each resounding boom, a Half-Breed lost his life.

The lobby had transformed into a deadly, carnage-riddled battlefield. Anthony's ears were still ringing from the discharge when he picked up on the scent of Mr. Morgan near the private elevator. After Hunter dispatched the last of the Half-Breeds, he noticed Anthony gnawing off the right hand from Ben's half-eaten carcass.

Once his hand was severed, he nudged the detached appendage across the floor with his blood-stained snout, inching the severed limb to Hunter. As he skirted the bloodied palm, they both heard the incoming clamor of the Lone Wolves making their way up the stairwell.

Hunter grabbed Ben's hand before reaching into his duffel bag, withdrawing a grenade. They rushed to the private elevator. Hunter had no choice but to abandon his armaments as the Lone Wolves breached the stairwell.

The invading drove careened into the blood-spattered lobby, chattering their jaws as Hunter shoved Ben's severed palm under the scanner.

Ding! The elevator doors opened.

He threw Ben's hand at the rushing Lycans before jumping inside, with Anthony following. He pulled the pin from the grenade and rolled the explosive toward the charging pack. Just as the doors closed, Anthony pressed the PH button with his clawed finger.

The cab quaked. Something had impeded their ascent. The elevator stalled. Rows of claws breached the doors, prying them open to reveal a consortium of snarling Lycans.

Hunter unholstered his Desert Eagle and opened fire on the infringing pack. An explosive flash rained over them as a Lone Wolf's head exploded. Brain and skull fragments showered the compartment. After the gunfire ceased, the rest of the pack backed away. They had no time to react before the grenade exploded.

A fiery deluge engulfed the mutilated Lycans, incinerating them into ash. The doors closed, shielding Hunter and Anthony from the rolling flames. The lift shook with a thunderous rattle before it soared to Mr. Morgan's penthouse.

Hunter stood in awestruck silence, admiring Anthony's lycan-thropic physique with fearful wonder.

"Please don't eat me," he pleaded.

Anthony nodded while panting. Drooling drabs of bloodied saliva dribbled from his bloodstained maw as the gore-splattered elevator climbed higher. Hunter shook out his locks, dispelling skull and brain fragments from his hoary, interwoven dreads.

"Damn, that was close!" He brushed brain matter off his shirt. "Never seen a Lone Wolf before. Man, those things are ugly." He was covered in blood as he reloaded his pistol, grabbing a handful of bullets from his pockets.

"These aren't dipped in silver," he begrudgingly stated as he cocked back the slide.

The elevator unexpectedly came to a stop just below the fifty-fifth floor of Anthony's office. The cab jolted and the lights cut off. He could smell the distinguishable scent of Mr. Morgan as they lingered in the dark. He knew his alpha was close. In an instant, the ceiling caved in, and the grey-haired Lycan crashed inside.

Mr. Morgan slashed Hunter across his chest before he could unholster his gun, sending a spray of blood across the lift. His strike left a brash, gaping wound across Hunter's breastbone. The domineering Lycan turned and kicked Anthony, splitting his abdomen with his flesh-tearing talons.

After his rapid assault, he pried open the doors and escaped into the office space above, climbing over the slab and disappearing into the rows of vacant cubicles. While reeling from his attacks, they heard a series of explosions that shook the building. The elevator quaked with each shattering bang. They were badly wounded but still managed to collect themselves as they climbed over the slab's edge in pursuit of the elusive alpha.

Bleeding and injured, they surveyed the pitch-black office space. Anthony was losing a lot of blood. His stomach was severely gashed. He felt his midsection swell with an agonizing hemorrhage as his innards gaped out. His lungs burned with fiery pain, scorching his airway.

Another thunderous explosion rocked the building, and the elevator crashed. Anthony looked back at the barren shaft, relieved that they had escaped in time.

As they canvased the empty rows of cross-stitched cubicles, Hunter withdrew his gun. Blood flowed from his slashed chest as another blast rocked the building's foundation, triggering the sprinklers.

Pressurized water rained over them as they manically searched.

A terror-filled shriek suddenly broke them from their hunt. The wail emanated from the reception desk. Anthony immediately recognized Camden's horrified shrill. After her cry, rows of flimsy partitions hurled into the air. Mr. Morgan charged for her, knocking the dividers aside while forcefully sprinting on all fours.

Hunter took aim and squeezed the trigger. The blast resounded across the downpour, grazing the tip of Mr. Morgan's ear. Upon impact, blood sprayed from his clipped lobe. He halted from his unadulterated charge, stumbling. Anthony mustered his strength and leapt over the ear-struck alpha, landing on his back, knocking him to the ground.

As the Lycans brawled, Hunter aimed through the showering deluge. Anthony was no match for his alpha's strength. Mr. Morgan quickly pinned him while lowering his gaping jaws over his neck. He was helpless under the weight of his alpha's brooding physique. Anthony was about to pass out from blood loss when he heard an arresting boom. Hunter fired, striking Mr. Morgan in the shoulder, suspending his assault. Blood gushed from the explosive wound as he backed away and bolted for Camden.

The terrified receptionist crouched under her desk as Hunter kept his aim on the charging Lycan. He was unable to get a clear shot. His chest unceasingly bled, leaving him weak and out of breath. Anthony could sense that their time was limited as he bravely scrambled to his feet. Injured, soaked, and bleeding, he stalked after his alpha. The rushing Pureblood burrowed his snout under Camden's desk and mercilessly slashed as she frantically kicked.

"Noo! Please… Help!" she hysterically cried while recoiling from the beast's snapping jaws.

The desk-burrowing alpha pushed ahead and bit down on her calf. She let out a painful wail as the beast's fangs penetrated her soft tissue. She cried in agony, grabbing her displaced pumps and stabbing down. Mr. Morgan yelped as her heel firmly lodged in his eye socket.

Anthony barreled into him, sending both of them tumbling over the desk and spilling into the foyer. He thought of his alpha's words as they tussled.

"*Purebloods don't bite women or children.*" The hypocritical statement reverberated in his mind and angered him. Witnessing the unadulterated attack on Camden fueled his rage.

He slashed the side of Mr. Morgan's midsection, causing him to leap off him. Anthony knew he was badly injured as Mr. Morgan slowly pulled the blood-soaked heel from his eye. He dropped the bloody footwear onto the puddled floor, leaving a fleshy hole where his right eye once was.

He stood back, allowing Anthony to rise amid the raining sprinklers, growling as he picked himself up from the blood-soaked tiles.

Hunter took another shot. The booming discharge halted them as the bullet whizzed by Mr. Morgan's head, just missing its target. After his misfire, the wounded alpha bolted through the stairwell and retreated to the safety of his office.

Hunter disappointingly holstered his gun and rendered aid to Camden. She was cowering under her desk in terrified shock. Anthony glanced back just before entering the stairwell. While peering from the doorway, he observed the cavernous slashes sprawled across Hunter's chest as he ripped off his shirt.

"Go! I'll meet you on the roof!" he yelled while fashioning a tourniquet from his torn shirt, tying her calf as Anthony ran up the stairwell.

A mixture of blood and water dripped from his serrated wounds as he proceeded with his agonizing climb.

He shook out his coat, akin to a wet dog withdrawing from a ravine, sending spouts of watery blood into the atmosphere. He valiantly ascended with a renewed sense of vengeance. He was bleeding profusely, and immense pain radiated from his innards; nonetheless, he carried on. He was cold and dying, each step weak and shaky. He was losing his strength as he followed his alpha's blood trail up the stairs to the rear entrance of his penthouse office.

He nudged open the door with his snout and cautiously crept inside the opulent chamber. As he clambered past the black stone bar next to the seating area, he noticed the blazing fireplace crackling with flaming embers. The taxidermied animal heads adorning the wall had a red glow cast upon their snarling faces.

The threatening stuffed grizzly next to the fireplace seemed to glare at him with a demeaning sneer. Anthony limped across the firelit space, debilitated and hemorrhaging as he scoured with labored breath. He heard an inconspicuous rustling when, suddenly, Mr. Morgan dove at him from behind his desk.

The one-eyed Lycan pounced over him, knocking him into the stuffed bear. The mounted grizzly teetered before toppling in front of the fireplace.

Mr. Morgan lurched on top of him, scratching and biting, delivering an onslaught of gashing strikes. Anthony was helplessly pinned. While enduring the assault, he caught a glimpse of the bear's fur catching fire.

The crackling blaze instantly spread over the fallen grizzly and engulfed the office space. Shooting flames kindled, rolling onto the walls. He started to lose consciousness, fading in and out amid the barrage of lacerating attacks.

Mr. Morgan ruthlessly chomped and lowered his head over his throat, ignoring the fast-building pyre around them. Anthony opened his eyes with rage. He felt his lifeforce dwindling under the strength of his menacing alpha. In desperation, he rallied his strength and managed to kick Mr. Morgan off him, sending the bloodied brute's body into the blazing inferno.

Mr. Morgan's lycanthropic physique instantly caught fire. He wailed as the flames consumed him. Anthony stood, observing his alpha being burned alive. Mr. Morgan let out a shriek that resembled a wolf-like howl as he flailed.

The Pureblood's agonizing, unnatural screeches resonated over the chamber as the flames melted the skin from his snout and extremities. He floundered in a spastic, deathly tango, singeing and twitching in agony as the flames meticulously ate him. Anthony retreated from the inferno, out of breath. He watched with satisfaction as his boss seared and toppled over. The flames rose, and he exited, making his escape to the roof with a wounded sprint.

With each blood-dripping stride he grew colder. Anthony knew if he didn't stop the bleeding soon, he would surely die. Chilling, voracious gusts coursed through his bloody muddled coat as he limped for the helipad. He fell over and glanced up to see Hunter inside the helicopter. The passenger door was slid open for him to enter. The blades violently spun, kicking up a torrent of wind. He ducked under the forceful inertia, stumbling his way closer to the hovering chopper. As he approached, he noticed that Hunter's wounds had completely healed.

"Anthony! Behind you!" he shouted from the cockpit.

He turned, witnessing Mr. Morgan lunging for him. His fire-singed body was nothing more than scorched flesh that slid off his bones. Anthony dropped and rolled, kicking his clawed feet, sending Mr. Morgan soaring into the blades. His scorched physique instantly pureed into a gelatinous cascade of flesh that rained over him.

The chopper wobbled after the gory collision. The once-domineering Lycan had been reduced to nothing more than a confetti-like meat splatter. Another explosion sounded, shaking the building.

"Come on! Get in!" Hunter screamed while piloting.

Anthony crouched, showered in the shredded flesh of his alpha, and grabbed the foot skids, wrapping his bloodied claws over the bar. He pulled himself inside just as the aircraft took flight. He scrambled over the back seats and noticed that Camden was missing.

"Close the door!" Hunter commanded.

Anthony barreled over and slid the door shut with his foot. As they flew away from the towering inferno, he viewed the cityscape below. It was hard for him to breathe. Sprays of gushing blood spouted from his snout, staining the windowpane of the soaring chopper.

As he looked through his partially closed eyes, he could see a caravan of blaring police cruisers and fire trucks streaming to the building. It took all his energy just to remain conscious.

The flames relentlessly billowed from the tower, casting a smoky haze over the blood moon-illumined skyline. He shifted to the other side of the chopper, where he observed the pier.

He viewed the Half-Breeds' barge leaving the dock, propelling for the open ocean, with the black-cloaked elder standing on the bow of the rusted-out tanker. Without warning, an alarm blared.

"We're going down!" Hunter yelled as the aircraft rapidly descended in a disorienting corkscrew. "Hang on!" He jarringly manned the controls in an attempt to keep the wavering chopper stable.

Anthony clutched the seats, tearing through the stuffing with his talons. He was terrified. He couldn't help but think of his parents, who had perished the same way. Now his fate would be the same.

Fear engulfed his soul as they fell over the Nicolo River, peppered with thin ice caution signs. He peered out of the fluttering chopper with pure dread and noticed the beaming headlights of Rey's van shining in the parking lot, overlooking the mouth of the river.

"Hold on!" Hunter hollered in terror.

A deafening boom accompanied by a jolting impact tossed them about the cockpit as they shattered through the ice and sank. Hunter struck his head and lost consciousness, as did Anthony.

Anthony creaked opened his eyes as freezing water rushed in. Though he was close to death, he was able to maneuver himself and slide the door open just as the aircraft took on water. The freezing river flooded over them as Anthony cut the unconscious brave's shoulder strap with his talons.

He pulled Hunter from the sinking wreckage and cradled him, relieved that they had not perished. As he cautiously crept over the ice, he noticed Rey on the other side of the river, standing in front of the shimmering headlights of his van. His childhood friend was outfitted in an inconspicuous black jacket and black jeans; his hair was spiked and dyed red.

"Holy shit!" he excitedly shouted.

Anthony meticulously stepped. With each harrowing stride, the ice beneath his clawed feet cracked. Blood poured from his wounds, staining the picturesque waterway. He stumbled as he felt the adrenaline from the crash wear off. He was shivering uncontrollably but still managed to hold Hunter. An explosion sounded. He ducked amidst the fiery blast, shielding them from the booming discharge. The smoldering helicopter ebbed before it sank. As he ensued with his wounded march across the ice, he glanced back to see the flaming tail sink into the icy abyss. He was thankful to be alive.

BREAKING
THE CURSE

Anthony crossed the frozen river, grateful that he had survived. Rey awaited with fearful astonishment at the edge of the parking lot. He was stunned with disbelief as he observed the bloody Lycan that was once his friend.

Anthony wobbled onto the snow-covered parking lot. He could barely hold Hunter as he slogged to Rey's van, relieved to be on solid ground. Rey scrambled and slid open the back door.

Anthony laid Hunter inside before collapsing. Rey pulled his hulking physique as Hunter creaked open his eyes. He tore off his jacket, revealing the black-stoned amulet draped over his shirt.

"Well, don't just lay there. Help me!" he belted while tugging Anthony's furry hide.

The dangling stone twinkled below his chest, tempting Hunter. He sat up, gripping Anthony's thick neck, and they collectively heaved him inside. The van sunk under the weight of his sizable frame.

After he was secured, Rey draped his coat over Hunter, noticing him shivering from hypothermia. The quivering brave viewed him with a vehement, possessed stare as the amulet wavered over his chest. Hunter was woozy and shook on the floor while clutching onto his donated overcoat, keeping his steadfast gaze affixed on the swaying amulet.

"Let's get the fuck outta here!" Rey's voice cracked with fear.

He slammed the door, jumped into the driver's seat, and drove for the exit.

As he approached, he perceived a barrage of police cars streaming toward them.

"Get down!" he shouted over his bloodied passengers laid out in the back of his van. He shut off the headlights as a litany of cop cars whizzed by, streaming for the smoldering tower.

"So much for enforcing the curfew." Rey shrugged with relief.

He turned onto the highway and drove over the Pioneer Bridge. Anthony barreled to the front, poking his bloodied snout over his shoulder.

"Please don't eat me, dude." He removed the amulet from his neck while keeping one hand on the wheel.

Hunter jostled between them, starring at the pendant with a greed-filled look in his eye as he ran his scarred arms through Rey's jacket.

"I'll take that!" Hunter snatched the talisman from him.

Anthony immediately turned and championed enough strength to growl, revealing his bloodstained fangs. Hunter reluctantly slipped the chain over his wolflike skull. The stone drooped over Anthony's gouged neckline, touching his bloody furred chest. As the stone came in contact with his frame, a blinding light emanated from the dark rock. Rey swerved in reaction to the dazzling radiance.

Anthony's lycanthropic physique started to shed. His battered body transitioned back into its human form. His snout rescinded, and his pointed ears shrank into human lobes.

"Holy shit!" Rey shouted upon witnessing his friend effortlessly shape-shift.

Anthony laid on the floor of the racing van, covered in shed hair, naked, and bleeding. He smelled the sweet, rancid scent of store-bought meat. It was hard for him to breathe as he desperately crawled to the sink.

He pulled himself up and discovered two packages of defrosted steaks as Hunter climbed into the seat next to Rey.

"Yeah, I picked those up for you, buddy. Top choice sirloin!" he nervously decreed while coming to the bridge's exit.

Anthony reached in, shaking and clammy. He enthusiastically tore the packaging off the steaks and gluttonously gnawed the bloodied cuts, ripping through the tenderized shanks with animalistic intensity.

Upon consuming the store-bought flesh, his serrated body started to heal. His bloody gashes repaired with each satisfying bite. Within moments, the lacerations that had adorned his wounded body were nonexistent, and he felt like his former self again with the meat stewing in his belly. His breathing became easier and the swelling from inside his gut was gone. No longer shielded from the elements with the aid of his furred coat, his nude frame shivered.

"Rey, can I get some clothes back here? I'm freezing!" he pleaded, with steak blood plastered over his mouth.

"Here you go, bud." Rey uneasily tossed the hoodie and jeans he had given him prior to the raid, with the keys to the cabin and his cell phone tucked inside.

They commenced with their fleeing journey along the redwood-encompassed highway leading to Mr. Morgan's cabin.

"What happened to Camden?" Anthony inquired after getting dressed and cleverly tucking the amulet under his hoodie.

"Who's Camden?" Hunter ignorantly stated as he flipped down the visor.

He inquisitively stared into the small mirror in order to discern the large bruise protruding from his forehead.

"She was the girl under the desk!" Anthony was angered as he slipped on his boots.

"Oh, she didn't make it," Hunter dismissively revealed as he warmed his hands over the air vent.

"What do you mean she didn't make it! She died from a leg wound?" Anthony screamed in rage.

"Look, she was bit by a Pureblood. She would have turned into a Lycan anyway. Sometimes death is better," Hunter justified.

"That's not your call to make! And how did your wounds heal so fast!" Anthony lurched between his childhood friend and the Indigenous brave, furiously awaiting his answer.

Hunter had a wrath-filled look on his tattooed face.

"We killed all those men back there! Purebloods, Half-Breeds, and Lone Wolves! Why is she any different! Don't put yourself on a pedestal, white man! You're a killer too!"

Rey quickly interjected in an effort to diffuse the tension.

"Jeez, guys, come on! We're all alive, and I'm sure you both don't mean what you're saying right now... I don't know what happened inside that building, but I can take a guess, and you guys survived. Our plan worked!"

"You mean *my* plan worked!" Anthony exhumed with a fiery tone while glaring at Hunter.

Silence overtook the van as Anthony peered out at the redwood trees rushing by. Rey drove onward, accelerating down the two-lane highway, racing past the old-fashioned gas station where they had first encountered the mysterious Native. He sighed before making another attempt at easing the conflict.

"Come on, my dudes! You both really set the town on fire tonight! We make a good team! Werewolf hunters for life!" he jested with an empathetic smirk. His enthusiastic proposal fell on deaf ears.

"Once Hunter helps me kill the Lycan that bit me, we are done, and you can have your precious stone! I'm done with this shit!" Anthony bellowed.

Hunter loomed back at him; his silence spoke volumes. He washed the steak blood from his face as Rey turned off the highway. As they pulled up to the cabin, Anthony couldn't help but think, *This is where it all started.*

They exited the vehicle without saying a word. Anthony produced the key from his pocket and opened the door. As they entered, the alarm sounded. He rushed over to the panel and typed in the code, muting the system.

"The sun will be up soon. We should get some rest," Hunter suggested as they filed past the fireplace, corralling into the kitchen.

"What happened here?" he asked while looking up at the scorched ceiling.

"Forgot the safety." Rey embarrassingly shrugged. "I'll sleep downstairs by the fireplace. I got my sleeping bag. You guys can take the bedrooms. Figured you deserve it after what you've been through."

"Thanks, Rey, I'm exhausted. I'll see you both in the morning. Then we can talk more about breaking my curse, okay? Hunter?" Anthony assertively questioned.

"A deal's a deal. I will uphold my end as long as you uphold yours," he nobly stated with a calming tone as he withdrew his Desert Eagle from his holster, boldly resting the firearm on the kitchen counter.

"I'm glad to hear that." Anthony climbed the stairs, not sure if he could fully trust him.

"Good night, bud." Rey saluted as he sprawled out his sleeping bag in front of the fireplace.

"Thanks for everything, you're a good friend. I couldn't have done it without you, buddy." He glinted at his gangly comrade, knowing that Rey was a better friend to him than he was.

"I know! Boys for life!" he enthusiastically claimed before Anthony entered the bedroom.

Rey's unquestionable loyalty was a constant in his life and was something that he treasured. He took a minute to reflect on their undying bond as he passed the taxidermied cougar and hopped onto the bed, exhausted. He yawned while kicking off his boots and sprawling over the sheets. His mind was a hectic jumble; processing everything that had just happened was overwhelming. His thoughts kept coming back to Sidney. He missed her and wanted to be with her. He reached into his pocket and removed his cell phone.

He was disappointed that she hadn't called him. His heart sank as he thought of how he could make up for what he had said. He contemplated calling her but realized that it would just make her mad. He knew one thing for certain: he had to break his curse. After mulling over his thoughts, he eventually fell into a deep, uninterrupted sleep.

He woke with a renewed eagerness and tucked the amulet under his hoodie.

"Okay, Hunter, time to uphold your end of our deal." He rubbed his eyes while stomping down the stairs.

As he removed his knuckles from his blurry sockets, he saw a large white-haired Lycan gorging on the cracked-open chest of his best friend. He witnessed the carnal scene in horrified panic as the hunched beast devoured the insides of Rey's lifeless corpse. He was wedged inside the fireplace. The talon-ripped remnants of his sleeping bag were shredded over the living room floor in a frenzied, gore-trampled splatter. His limp body was lodged deep inside the alcove, bent in an unnatural way. Anthony figured he had tried to escape by climbing up the chimney. He called for Hunter in a terrified wail.

"Hunter! Come quick! Hunter!" he cried in desperation as the feasting Lycan crooked its head.

The hulking creature broke from the gutted hollow of Rey's frayed body, with his heart pulsating inside its jaws. The beast consumed his torn organ with delectable zeal, chomping Rey's beating heart within its maw, extruding a dark, oily deluge that dribbled down its bloodthirsty jowls.

After swallowing, the Lycan let out a ferocious howl.

Anthony was in a grief-stricken panic as he rushed to the kitchen and grabbed Hunter's Desert Eagle from the countertop. He stumbled over the shredded tatters of his black cargo pants atop Rey's shredded jacket.

Stunned with horrified shock, he was able to discern the Lycan's facial features as it lurched for him. The menacing beast had a bruise on its forehead and distinct tattoo markings under its eyes.

He shook with dread, realizing that the monster pursuing him was Hunter.

He was the beast that had attacked him on that fateful night, the Lycan that had tracked him through the forest, leading him to his cabin. Able to shape-shift at will, the charging Ultima was unphased by the rising sun. The lycanthropic Hunter snarled with a drooling, blood-pasted grimace. He was a powerful beast; his stalking advance was undeterred by Anthony's gun-wielding threat.

He aimed at the charging Lycan and pulled the trigger. The blast rang with a deafening boom, striking Hunter's belly.

He jolted back, clutching his bullet-struck abdomen with his clawed mitts as blood gushed from his hoary midsection. Anthony pulled the trigger again.

Click! The emptied chamber sounded with a deflating tick. The gun had run out of ammo.

Hunter leered from his gut-blown belly and angrily stalked him, slapping the misfired gun from his hand as Anthony bolted for the stairs.

Anthony desperately scrambled up the timber steps heading for the gun safe. As he climbed, Hunter stalked him. He could feel the monster's hot acidy breath linger over him as he frantically rushed for the bedroom.

The wounded Ultima seized his ankle. Hunter's serrating talons sliced through his flesh, scraping down to the bone. Anthony screamed in agony as his claws ripped through his leg. The pain was excruciating. He fell facedown before reaching the bedroom. He desperately kicked as Hunter snapped at his heels.

As Anthony wildly flailed, the amulet inadvertently dislodged from under his hoodie. The talisman emitted a blinding light, stunning him. Hunter staggered, rolling down the stairs in reaction to the arresting discharge.

He was in a stupefied state as Anthony kicked his snout. The heavy strike sent him tumbling farther down. Anthony sprung to his feet and plodded into the bedroom with a wounded limp.

As he hobbled for the gun safe, he pushed over the taxidermied cougar, wedging the base of the stuffed mountain cat between the doorway, serving as a blockade. He tottered to the safe and typed in 4611. The safe chimed with a red light.

"Fuck!" he screamed, realizing that he forgot the code.

As he contemplated the numeric possibilities, he noticed the angered Lycan approaching from behind the stuffed cougar. Hunter's snout spewed blood as he grabbed the large cat and wedged it farther inside the doorway. Anthony knew it would not be long before he negotiated the barricade. He suddenly remembered the code and immediately typed in 4161. The safe unbolted with an electrified clang. He grabbed a shotgun and hurriedly loaded the rifle, confronting the tattoo-faced Ultima.

Hunter crushed the cougar against the door frame and rushed for him. Anthony took aim. Just before pulling the trigger, he thought of Mr. Morgan's haunting words: *"A shot to the heart is still a shot to the heart, Lycan or not." Time to break the curse... This is for you, Rey.* He pulled the trigger with a tear in his eye.

A deafening blast resounded as Hunter's chest exploded in a flesh-spouting burst. He flew over the banister and tumbled down the stairs. His body hit the floor with a bone-shattering bang. Anthony caught his breath. With his ears ringing, he cautiously crept down.

He aimed the barrel of the shotgun in front of him as he made his limping descent; his leg was mired in blood and hurt like hell. As he entered the living room, he observed Rey's lifeless eyes staring back at him from deep within the crook of the fireplace. His heart broke with rage as he shuffled to Hunter. The lycanthropic brave had collapsed over the banister and was dying. As he desperately gasped, his beastly body tremored. He gargled labored inhalations while laying against the bottom run of the stairs. Pools of blood flowed from his buckshot-riddled chest. He quaked, helplessly watching Anthony stand over him.

With the barrel held over his snout, Anthony removed the amulet from his neck and draped the necklace over Hunter's white-furred head. When the stone touched his blown-out sternum, he reverted back into a human.

His hoary coat shed, and his snout rescinded. His canine ears returned to hairless lobes as he struggled to breathe.

"A deal is a deal," Anthony proclaimed, knowing that he would soon be dead.

"You…will…pay…for…your…sins…white   man!" Hunter blurted between dying wheezes.

"Yeah, but not before you do." He staggered over to Rey's corpse and reached into his ravaged jean pocket, removing the bloodstained keys to his van.

Sorry, Rey. He deflatingly looked into the dead stare of his childhood friend, placing his bloody fingertips over his cold eyelids, lowering them shut one last time. He wept, knowing that he would never again hear his encouraging words or see his awkward smile.

Devastated with grief, he nervously jangled the keys while tucking the shotgun under his armpit. He hobbled to the door, turning his back on Hunter as he made his way outside.

He lumbered onto the porch. The beaming glow of the morning sun glared over him with a warming radiance. He examined the wooded landscape and saw a pack of feral black wolves standing between him and Rey's van. He nervously took aim on the unwavering pack. They paid no mind to his threat and calmly marched past him.

Anthony lowered the rifle while the pack paraded by. They funneled inside the cabin and consumed Hunter. The hungry wolves pounced on him, gnawing and tearing his flesh, dismembering his limbs from his torso.

"Aaaaa... No... Help!" His desperate cries were useless as the wolves ripped him apart.

Anthony got in the van and tucked the shotgun behind the passenger seat. He turned on the ignition and took one last look back at the chalet before driving off.

His guilt was overwhelming. He broke down, weeping uncontrollably with his hands over his face. Rey hadn't deserved to die like that; it was all his fault. All he had now was Sidney. He needed to get to her. He sped off and glanced back to see the alpha wolf standing guard over the porch. The creature of the forest lingered between the teetering rocking chairs, ominously swaying amid the morning gusts. The large wolf raised its head and emitted a saluting howl as Anthony drove away.

He pulled off the dirt road, continuing down the tree-adorned highway. With his mind swirling in a grief-stricken blunder, he decided to call Sidney. He frantically removed his cell phone and placed the device inside the cup holder as he raced for the city.

"Hello?" she answered with a tired drawl as he put the call on speaker.

"Sid, I'm so sorry. I need you to meet me at my apartment right now! I have to tell you some things. You still have your key, right?" he questioned.

He was in a frenzied, sorrow-filled state and wasn't thinking clearly. As he furiously drove across the Pioneer Bridge, he viewed the crash site. He observed a consortium of rescue trucks and crewmen scattered about the riverside parking lot, staging an effort to tow the chopper from the frozen depths.

"Yes, I still have it. Anthony, what's going on? I'm worried." Her voice elevated with fear.

"Rey's dead!" he tearfully gasped.

"Oh my God! What happened?!" She started to cry.

"I can explain everything. Just get over to my place now! We have to get out of the city!" he demanded, almost crashing into the car in front of him.

"You're scaring me. What's going on?"

"I'm ready to be the man you want me to be. I'm sorry for all the things I said. I want a family now more than ever, but we have to get out of the city. It's not safe!" For the first time in a long time, Anthony was sure about his future.

"Okay, I'll head over there now," she agreed amid her tearful sniffles.

"All right. I'll see you soon. I'm just getting off the bridge." He was rattled as he veered for his neighborhood.

"I love you."

"I love you too," he decreed before hanging up.

While manically weaving across traffic, he turned on the radio.

"Good morning, citizens of Myrin City. This is Linda Haskins with a live report. We are here in front of the MGE building, where last night a domestic terrorist attack left several employees dead and significant damage to the building's structure. Among the deceased was Franklin P. Morgan, the CEO of Morgan & Green Enterprises, and Chief Benjamin Ramsey. Police and local authorities are on the lookout for a Native man with white dreadlocks and tattooed markings on his face. If you have any information regarding this attack, please contact the Myrin City Police Department. This is Linda Haskins, signing off from the Myrin City Financial District, where last night a domestic terrorist bombing claimed the lives of several employees of the firm."

Anthony turned off the radio, relieved that his name had not been mentioned. He drove down a side street leading to his building. He noticed that no cars were on his block; his street was empty except for

Sidney's white sedan, which was unusual, especially in the morning. His phone rang.

"Hey, I'm here. Where are you?" Her voice crackled with nervousness.

"Yeah, Sid, just parking. I'll be right up."

"Okay, please hurry."

He was worried; she didn't sound like herself. Just before getting out, he opened the glove box and removed the revolver Rey had stolen from the cabin. He stuffed the handgun in his hoodie's pocket before closing the door. Anthony knew something was wrong; he could tell by the tone in her voice. With trepidation, he took a deep breath and entered his building. His slashed leg left a dribbling blood trail in his wake.

As he shuffled down the hall, he detected a rancid, earthy scent. He began to perspire with fear and stuffed his hand inside his pocket. With his heart racing, he clutched the cold handle of the gun as he opened his door. He entered to see a slender charcoal-haired Lycan. The beast glared at him with vengeful yellow eyes. He recognized the creature; it was the same being that had been tied to the stake in Dr. Geani's grainy film. The Lycan had its claws wrapped around Sidney's neck. Anthony frantically withdrew the gun and shakingly aimed at the hostage-taking beast.

"Let her go!" He shook with fear.

Sidney's eyes dilated in horror as she struggled to free herself from the monster's claws. The Lycan was something more powerful and ancient than Anthony could have ever fathomed. He knew he had to shoot, or his love's throat would be ripped open. He nodded for her to duck. Sidney made eye contact with him and suddenly ripped away. Anthony squeezed the trigger.

A loud bang sounded; he peered through the gun smoke in devastation as Sidney's chest exploded in a bloody gush before she dropped to the floor. He was beside himself with grief as he watched her fall. He let off another shot, but the Lycan was too fast. The agile beast darted for him, dodging the blast. The Ultima wrapped its claws around his neck

262

and sliced his throat.

Anthony dropped the smoking gun as warm blood trickled over his neck. He gargled before collapsing. He writhed on the floor, reaching for the pale hand of his slain love, knowing this was the end. He now wished he had died in the helicopter crash as he watched Sidney, fading with labored gasps, studying her features one last time.

"I'm sorry... Please...don't die... Please," he desperately gurgled, clenching his slashed throat. The Lycan's taloned foot stomped between them. Its protracted claws scraped the hardwood floor.

Anthony watched Sidney's withering eyes as the beast trudged over their collected pools of blood. He was barely able to stay conscious. He turned his head and observed the Lycan's paw effortlessly shape-shift into a human foot. His eyes grew heavy, and his body went cold. As he struggled for breath, he heard Luna's voice.

"Hello, yes, there are gunshots coming from apartment 7-E. Please send someone quick!"

It was then that he realized: Luna was the Ultima that had bitten him in those backwoods and dragged him through the forest. She was the Lycan that had turned him and was, ultimately, the cause of his destruction. He took one last fleeting glimpse at Sidney before blacking out.

Anthony's mind descended into darkness; his existence was in a perpetual state of abyssal purgatory. He only knew he was conscious by the mechanical beeping radiating from the ventilator beside him. Time and space ceased to exist. His conscious and subconscious were in a constant state of limbo, and although his senses were still intact, he was unable to move. His eyes remained closed in his vegetative state. He could discern that he was in some kind of hospital as he heard the clacking of high heels. He smelled a rancid, earthy scent as the door creaked open. He felt a cold, slender hand touch his arm and immediately thought of Sidney.

"All this could've been avoided if you would've just slept with me. But no, you wanted to do things the hard way," Luna's bewitching voice whispered in his ear.

You fucking bitch! His heart raced with vengeful anger. He was helpless; all he could do was lay there and listen.

"I know you can hear me. What's the matter? Wolf got your tongue?" Tears of rage welled under his closed eyelids, but there was nothing he could do.

"Oh, don't worry, your girlfriend is doing just fine. The paramedics did a great job on her, and I heard the life growing inside her belly. Your offspring will make a nice new addition to our pack. You can't stop evolution, and soon we will have one bloodline. What? Did you think all this was all about you? I should be thanking you, really. I mean, all I had to do was sit back and watch while you boys ripped yourselves apart. I didn't even have to kill anyone!" She let out a howling cackle.

"You really should be thanking me though. I saved your life twice. Once when my halfwit brother tried to eat you in those backwoods—can't believe I had to drag your heavy ass out of that thicket—and again when I carried you home after Kane knocked you off the roof. I did all that, and you still won't even go out for a fucking drink with me!" she shrieked while withdrawing her hand.

She paced the room. Anthony heard the relentless racket of her heels against the tile. His vengeful thoughts burned with a fiery wrath as he helplessly listened to her discord.

"Too bad about my brother, but that's what he gets for killing his own. Well, what's done is done. No use in crying over spilled blood." She hunched over his bedside.

"It's a good thing you signed that board member contract. Because of that, your medical needs and the needs of your significant other will be completely covered by MGE, which I am now the CEO of, given the fact that all the other board members are dead thanks to you and my idiot brother. You see, Anthony, we can keep you in this comatose state for centuries. Remember, Lycans can live for thousands of years, and you have a long life to live. But should you manage to wake from your coma, you will be facing attempted murder charges for your part in shooting Sidney. I guess you could say you have a dark future ahead of you." She bent down and kissed his forehead before stabbing him with a needle in the bend of his arm.

She withdrew the syringe; a tiny droplet of blood formed over the small puncture as Anthony heard her leave. He laid there, powerless in his vegetative state, wishing for death as the drugs coursed through his veins. He contemplated all that he had lost before his consciousness fell into darkness.

Made in the USA
Middletown, DE
21 January 2024

48215944R00148